ELYSIAN I

By

SARAH BURCHETT-COOK

A GOLDEN STORYLINE BOOKS PUBLICATION

This book was first published by Golden Storyline Books

PART ONE

CHAPTER ONE - VISIT

Benji only half heard Professor Long droning on – the previous night's blackout, and subsequent recurring nightmare, still fresh in his thoughts. A trickle of sweat worked its way down the side of his face, as the pounding of hooves and the raging battlefield, replayed in glorious technicolour in his mind. He could almost smell the blood-soaked soil.

He sat next to the aisle at the back of the lecture theatre ready to make a quick getaway when the bell rang. As Benji wiped his face with his sleeve, the Prof's voice filtered through again.

"There are three possible reasons why you're doing this module. In order of probability these are: one – your parents decided for you; two – you have 'issues' of your own and you're looking for answers; and three – you're actually interested in psychology. Well, there may be a fourth, but we don't need to go into that right now. Most of you think you're a three, but ones and twos are far more probable. Have a think about where you really sit on this. Analyse your reasons for being here…"

The Prof's voice faded into the distance once more. Benji's phone was in his lap and he was ordering a pizza when everything went quiet. The only sound a little snigger somewhere nearby. Benji snapped to and glanced up, all eyes were turned on him, except his girlfriend, Kim's, of course.

She had her elbow on the writing tablet and her head in her hand, her long ebony hair obscuring the side of her perfect face. Benji cringed; he was in for some grief.

"Well Mr Jarrett?" came the voice from the podium.

Benji gazed at Long. "Um er four sir. I'm a four."

The Prof looked long and hard at his quarry. "Mmm. See me after class Mr Jarrett."

Benji ran his fingers through his mop of golden hair and looked behind him at the door. Could he make a run for it? Probably not. The rest of the lesson passed by in a blur. The bell sounded. He glanced at the nearby door again as everyone began to move in his direction.

"Mr Jarrett." Long wasn't about to miss his opportunity to give him some stick. He headed down the wide steps.

As he passed Kim she raised her eyebrows at him but said nothing. She'd be waiting outside for him.

"So Mr Jarrett, what exactly is your number four?"

"Er well sir, um, I'm kind of interested in the mythology and folklore." Benji became more animated. "It's in the module brief."

"I see. You realise that section is covered in only two lectures? The two sessions focus on how mysticism has played a role in developing the human psyche, and how that has extended into the arts. You plan to do a whole module just for this? I ask, because you clearly have very little interest in the rest of what I have to say."

Benji studied the portly teacher more closely. He wasn't actually smiling, but there was a sly twinkle in the old man's eye. It encouraged Benji to engage him a little further. "Sir, you've written five books on the subject. I've read them all, cover to cover. It's fascinating. If there had been a module just on this topic, I'd have done that instead."

Long was quiet for a few moments as he studied Benji's face. "So what – are you expecting me to produce a fae or a kelpie or something on the podium here for those lectures?"

Benji's heart skipped a beat. Kim was going to go mad at him. He frowned at his own random thought. Why would she go mad at him? He shrugged. Now he could look anywhere except at Long. He knew he had to say something – anything. "Can I go Sir? I need to get ready for my next class." Long's eyes bored into him, but the old man just nodded his assent and Benji bolted for the door, his long, skinny legs carrying him quickly up the steps and away.

The doors banged open and Benji burst through, a little breathless. Kim had been talking to a couple of other girls, but they left when they saw him coming. He melted at the sight of her as she turned her full attention on him. Even now, after all this time, he could hardly believe this amazing girl chose to be with him. Flicking her hair over her shoulder Kim said, "I saved the seat next to me for you. I thought perhaps, for once, I could keep you from embarrassing yourself. A forlorn hope it seems. What did Long say to you anyway?"

Benji's breathing slowed to normal. "He wanted to know why I'm doing this module. He asked if I was expecting him to bring a fae or a kelpie to class."

Kim's eyes widened. "What? What did you say?"

"I panicked. Don't know why." He shrugged. "I just had to get away so I told him I needed to get to my next class."

She pulled him to one side, out of earshot of the passing students. "Tell me the whole conversation. Word for word."

*****

Slowly the room came into focus. Damn, another blackout. The first thing Benji noticed was the empty space on the wall where Kim had taken down the 'girly' calendar – again, a pity, he particularly liked Miss October. The throbbing in his head became more pronounced as he swung his legs round and tried to sit. He gave up, curled back up in a ball, pulling the pillow across his face. It didn't help, and in a momentary flash of irritation the pillow went flying across the room knocking Kim's cittern over with a distinct sigh of the strings. "Oh shit!" He looked around as if she might suddenly manifest in the tiny bedroom. Almost as if thinking of her had conjured her up, her voice came through from the next room. Staggering over to the window as the fog slowly cleared from his mind, Benji picked up the cittern and stood it back into its normal position against the wall, grateful for its thick case.

Kim's words filtered through to him as he walked over to the door.

"We can't leave this too much longer mother. I can't keep doing this to him." A pause.

She must be on the phone – to her mother? She's never mentioned her before. It then occurred to Benji that maybe he should have asked Kim about her family. Why hadn't he? And what was she doing to him – if she was talking about him that is?

"When?" Another pause. "Someone needs to make the assessment soon. If Dom can't make it himself, and no surprises there, then perhaps you could come." Her voice softened. "It would be good to see you mother, and anyway, Dom values your opinions."

Benji waited to hear what else she might say, but Kim said no more. Curiosity burned inside of him as he opened the door. "Who were you talking to?"

Kim swivelled, quickly hiding something behind her back. "My cittern better not be damaged. Are you feeling better?"

Benji remembered the headache as the pounding reasserted itself. "What happened? I don't remember getting drunk."

"Well, it really doesn't take much does it? Don't you recall? It was your idea to go to The Corn Exchange."

He didn't remember going there, not at all, and this wasn't the first time he'd completely blanked out a session at the club. "You seem to be ok," he accused.

Kim ignored his comment and went to get her cittern. She started to play a soothing melody as she once more she changed the subject. "By the way, my mother's coming for a visit next week."

All the urgency had left her voice now. He kept his own voice on an even keel too, but tested the water none the less. "Oh, that'll be nice for you. Do you want me to make myself scarce?"

Kim stopped playing, a flash of shock showed momentarily in her eyes, and then it was gone. "No. No of course not. She'd love to meet you. We should go to lunch, how about the Bridge Café?"

4

CHAPTER TWO - TEST

Sitting at the corner table of the Bridge Café, Benji's skin almost prickled at the tension between the three of them. It was a busy lunchtime, the general chatter in the room and the piped classical music barely covered the sound of clanking dishes coming from the kitchen. Benji could hardly keep from staring at Luci Maine. She didn't look old enough to be Kim's mother, an older sister maybe, but mother! She had the same ebony hair Kim had, and the same green eyes with gold flecks. Her skin was flawless, but unlike Kim who put comfort first, her demeanour and dress were very business-like.

"So, you're the gangly youth that's stolen my daughter's heart."

Benji caught the warning look Kim flashed at her mother. He thought he'd better say something. "Have you come far Mrs Maine? Did you drive up, or fly into Edinburgh?"

"Actually I took the train."

Benji wriggled in his chair. He ought to try to keep on the right side of Kim's mother, but there was something a little disturbing about her. He couldn't quite put his finger on what that was, but he was certain she hadn't blinked since she sat down. This was going to be a difficult lunch date.

It was an overcast day, yet a beam of sunlight shone through the window behind Mrs Maine's back. It made her hair gleam. Benji tilted his head but couldn't quite see the break in the clouds that must have been there, odd. He glanced Kim's way. The brightness surrounded her too. Doubly odd. A tiny, yet distant smile broke on her mother's otherwise stern, no not stern, sorrowful face.

At last the waiter came over with the menus. It broke the tension that had crept over their little gathering. He perused the lunch options, but when he looked up he found Kim's mother staring at him instead of at her own menu. "D...do you know what you're having?" he asked. "The paninis here are great, or if you go for the jacket potato, they bake their own in the oven, they're not nuked in the microwave."

Both the women turned their noses up when Benji ordered the coronation chicken panini. Kim and Luci went for vegetarian options.

"What did you think of the station?" Benji knew he was making inane small-talk, but Luci Maine's silent scrutiny was messing with his nerves.

"What?"

"Edinburgh station. It's quite an impressive building don't you think?"

"I suppose so. I didn't have much time to look."

An awkward silence.

"You really take after your mother Kim."

Another awkward silence. Kim fidgeted, darting her eyes between him and her mother. Why? She was normally so composed.

"Are you planning on staying in Edinburgh for long Mrs Maine?"

Luci stared at Benji for a moment, then sighed and dumped her serviette on top of her unfinished salad. She ignored Benji's question and looked at Kim. "Enough of this mindless small talk. Let's get this over with."

"Mother!"

Benji, smiling politely, looked from Kim to Luci and back to Kim again. "What? Get what over with? What are you talking about?"

"Let's go back to the flat. We need to talk," said Kim.

*****

6

Benji slowly roused to consciousness. Not again! He didn't remember walking back to the flat after that awkward lunch with Kim's mother. In fact he couldn't remember anything after starting his lunch. His regular blackouts after a night out worried him. Kim always had to fill in the blanks. This time it was different. They'd just gone out to lunch, and he didn't think he'd even had a drink – in fact he was certain he hadn't. He'd never had a blackout during the daytime before. He must be getting worse. He should see a doctor. He frowned. Kim always played his blackouts down, insisting he didn't need to see anyone about them. Benji sat up on the bed. As usual his head was thumping, but it didn't stop him going to the door to listen in to the urgent, whispered conversation going on in the next room.

"...are you sure?" It was Kim's voice.

Her mother answered. "There's no doubt about it. It's the strongest reading I've seen in centuries."

Benji frowned, centuries?

"Shhh, keep your voice down."

"Oh, don't worry, I gave him enough amnotin to keep him out for hours yet."

"Don't count on it. I've been having to up the dose as he comes out of it more quickly each time. It's getting harder and harder to keep the truth from him. His innate clan memories reassert themselves that much sooner after every dose. I'm pumping with amnotin at least once a week now."

"We need to move quickly then, before they become permanently suppressed and he's of no use to us. I'll get back and talk to Dom about making preparations."

Benji's heart was thumping. His mind swirled and he fought down the queasiness in his stomach. His legs turned to jelly and he turned, slid down the door to the floor and wrapped his arms around his knees.

Kim had been drugging him.

Kim...had...been...drugging...him. What the hell! He'd trusted her. He loved her. Desperation warred with the hurt of betrayal, but for what purpose? Something nefarious – but what could they possibly want to do to him? The front door closed. His eyes widened, they mustn't know he'd heard them. Scrambling back to the bed, he pretended to be asleep. Kim came in. Benji squeezed his eyelids tighter.

"Been awake long?" Kim asked then.

Dammit. "Er no, I just woke up when I heard the door shut. I have a headache. I just want to sleep it off. Leave me alone." He rolled over to face the wall.

"Ok hun. I'm just going to get a few bits from the shop, can I get you anything?"

"I'm good thanks." He pulled the blanket over his head.

The front door closed and Benji sprang up. He pulled a spare sweatshirt, some socks and a pair of jockey's into his rucksack, grabbed his toothbrush, toothpaste and a bar of soap from the bathroom, donned his coat and trainers and quickly left. Where to go, he wasn't sure. He only knew he had to get away from his crazy girlfriend and her weird mother. Whatever game they had in mind for him, he wasn't going to play.

CHAPTER THREE – ESCAPE

With more than a little trepidation, Kim phoned her mother to tell her Benji had slipped her grasp.

"You were supposed to be watching him. This isn't like you Kimjora. You have clearly developed feelings for this boy, goodness only knows why, but it's affected your objectivity. Your mission is compromised, I'll send in a team to help you find and recover him."

"No Mother. I have a few ideas where he might have gone. Let me see if I can find him first. You gave him quite a big dose of amnotin – it should be at least a week before he starts seeing anything. Even then he won't understand what's happening."

"Alright. You have one week. If you haven't found him and brought him in by then, I'm taking this case out of your hands. Dom is furious. I've had to do some fast-talking to keep you in the field as it is. He wanted you back home to face the Court."

Kim breathed in sharply as relief flooded through her. "Thank you Mother. I won't let you down."

"Kim, our auras slipped for a while in that café? You know he could see that, right?"

Kim nodded, even though her mother couldn't see her. "I know. It wasn't the first time he's seen it, but the amnotin takes the memory away each time."

"Benji, please pick up. I know what you heard sounds weird, but it's not what it seems. Just come back to the flat and I'll explain everything. Trust me." Kim's sixth call to Benji had gone straight to answerphone, just like the last three. He must have switched the damn thing off after her second call, but she kept trying anyway. He wouldn't be at a friend's house. Benji didn't have any friends, she'd made sure of that. She dropped her phone into her bag and headed over to the uni. When she got to the uni library she went straight to the desk. "Hi Ruth. Has Benji been in today?"

"Sorry Kim, no I haven't seen him," she rolled her eyes, "perhaps he's got lost somewhere."

Kim frowned. She didn't much like Ruth's sarcastic tone. Maybe she'd done too good a job at isolating him. "If you see him, ask him to call me would you?"

"Sure."

Where else? Pizza Hut? The Corn Exchange? The public library? Burger King? Kim tried everywhere she could think of that Benji might be hanging out, then traipsed slowly back to the flat they shared. Kim paced the living room floor. It was the morning of the fourth day she was at a loss as to where he might be. She cursed and thumped the wall with her fist, wincing at the discomfort of grazed knuckles. Her mother was right, she'd taken her eye off the ball, and her current project had slipped her grasp. Only three more days before it got taken out of her hands, and Dom would recall her and confine her to quarters.

Reluctantly she made a controversial decision, cringing as she thought of how her mother and Dom would react. From the privacy of the flat, Kim slung her rucksack over her shoulder, took a deep breath and phased home to Elysia. The shift cost her. In human form she was so weak. She turned full circle. She could see for miles across the grassy plain. The mountains were a grey blur on the horizon. No one was about. Kim sat down on a rock and swallowed some of her precious restorative. The blue-green juice of the hawbleberry was thick and bitter with age. Squinting at the taste she made a note-to-self; she needed to get some fresh as soon as possible. Sitting with her head in her hands, the sweat tickled

10

as it dripped down her back. Her hair stuck to her forehead, but slowly Kim recovered her strength.

Sprites could be difficult to deal with. Most of them rarely left the mountains, but they were the best trackers. She just needed to convince Arbani that her quest was just, and she needed one of his subjects as a matter of urgency to find Benji. She didn't relish that particular conversation, but it was necessary.

*****

When Benji left the flat he roamed the streets at random. His thoughts were in turmoil and he felt so alone. He never actually went anywhere in Edinburgh without Kim. The phone rang. It was her. He ignored it. For the first time he wondered at himself for becoming so reliant on her. They studied the same modules at uni. They went to the same places to socialise and to eat – even though she was vegetarian, and he was out and out carnivore. They had friends… but actually they were her friends. Somehow everyone just tolerated him as he came as part of the package with the ever-popular Kim. What happened to him? As a kid he used to play football, go swimming, belong to clubs, he had lots of friends before Kim came along. The phone rang, Kim again. He switched it off, and then he cursed himself. He'd left the charger at the flat. Well he wasn't going back for it. Kim was the only one who rang him during the day, and his mum only rang on Saturdays.

Wandering aimlessly around Edinburgh, Benji started going over everything that had happened since Kim breezed into his life. He'd been going through puberty. He had a rough time of it. He shot up over eight inches in no time at all, and had suffered major growing pains. His skin had looked like the surface of the moon, and as for the weird dreams!

Benji needed coffee so went into Costa and ordered a caramel latte. She wouldn't look for him there, as it wasn't one of their haunts. He sat at the back of the coffee house for nearly two hours pondering those dreams. Dark dreams, of battles with strange creatures out of myth, of riding horses, but not quite horses, they were just too…sentient…yes, in his dreams he talked to his horse – and it talked back! He

11

pictured the battleground. Flower-filled meadows ruined, trampled and red with the blood of his foes. There were human-like creatures emerging from the sea, and yet more strange folk with crazy hair heading down the slopes to engage in battle. Weird. The more he thought about his dreams the more vivid the memories of them became. With the back of his hand, he wiped away the sweat beading on his forehead even as he fought down the rising panic brought on by the memories of these dark, disturbing dreams.

Then Kim had come into his life. She eased his pain. She didn't care about his boyish acne. He'd never questioned her presence. She helped him through all of that growing up stuff, and then she coached him during his A levels – she was so clever and knowledgeable. She never met Mum though. Mum was some kind of corporate executive so wasn't home much. Kim only ever went to his house when he was alone, something that had never struck him as odd until now. After that they got into Edinburgh uni together, to do the same course, and even the exact same modules. Benji shook his head slowly. All this time she's been watching me, making me dependent on her…drugging me! How could I have been so blind?

He didn't hear what the woman standing by the table said. He looked blankly at her, the impatience showed in the tilt of her head. "Sir? Excuse me, but we're closing now. Can I take your mug?"

"Oh. Yes. Sorry." Benji got up and left. But now he knew exactly whom he needed to talk to. He'd better get his skates on, or the Prof would have left for the day.

"Professor Long, have you got a minute?" Benji called. The Prof was just getting into his car, a newish sporty-looking Merc. In Benji's head, the Prof and the car didn't fit together. He pictured him driving an old-style Jag, or one of the older Rover models.

"Benjamin Jarrett? What are you doing here at this time of day?" he looked past Benji, then said, "what no Kim Maine? I thought you two were joined at the hip."

"Well, actually that's part of what I want to talk to you about."

12

"Humph! You're barking up the wrong tree there. I'm the last person to give advice on the affairs of the heart to a young lad like you." He was chuckling and had that glint in his eye again that somehow just made him so much more approachable.

"You don't understand. I don't think Kim is… quite what she seems."

This caught Long's attention. "Oh? What makes you say that?"

"Well, I met her mother, she looks the same age, as Kim that is, and she's shiny. I think Kim's shiny too, I just didn't notice before, I've been having weird dreams, Kim says it's nothing, but I think it's something, she's been drugging me, her mother drugged me too, I've run away…"

"Whoa, stop. You're rambling Jarrett…" he changed tack and softened his voice a little, "…Benjamin. Calm down. Drugged?"

"I heard them talking. They drugged me, and Kim said she's been giving me…whatever it is she's been giving me…once or twice a week, and that if she keeps doing it I'll be no use to them, I had to get away, whatever they've got planned for me, it can't be good."

The Prof's eyes widened, and he stared at Benji. "Get in lad. I think you'd better come with me to my house. We'll get to the bottom of this."

CHAPTER FOUR – KAYLEN

It took Kim the rest of the day to hike into the Kaylen Mountains, the home of the mountain sprites. She cursed under her breath. With only two more days to locate Benji before her mother sent in an extraction team, she still had to convince Arbani to assign her a tracker. It was a risk, and she wished she'd made her mind up to do it sooner.

"What brings you to Kaylen, traveller?" asked the young sprite at the gate.

Kim had no time for the social niceties of court. "I would speak with Arbani."

He raised one fluffy eyebrow. "That's Lord Arbani to you. And what business would a…whatever you are, have with our illustrious Lord?"

Kim gazed at the gatekeeper. Her human body may not be as magnificent as her natural kelpie form, but she still found it more aesthetically pleasing than that of a sprite – diminutive, though somewhat rounded and lumpy. Their dry, silvery-white hair stuck out in all directions and made them look a bit cranky. She had to admit, their hair could look quite stunning when they emanated their rosy auras, though it paled in comparison to the golden auras of the kelpies. She lifted her chin and allowed a little of her aura to shine through. "Oh drop it. Since when did a kelpie need to justify their presence to a servant?"

The sprite's eyes widened. "I apologise. We have not been visited by many of your kind since… well, since your unfortunate…" he struggled to find a description for the transformation that had afflicted the kelpies.

"Well?"

"Please enter. I'll send word to Lord Arbani. Er, who shall I say is calling on him?"

"I am Kimjora, daughter of Lucivarsh."

The sprite bowed and scuttled off.

Kim paced the entrance hall as she waited.

"Kimjora! You are most welcome. Arbani will be along shortly. How is Lucivarsh?" Dailabi, the sprite lady, and Arbani's wife, was adorned in a crimson, floor-length dress trimmed with silver thread and rubies.

Kim took the sprite lady in a polite embrace. "It's been a long time Dailabi. I've missed you. My mother is well thank you."

"Tell me, how goes the search?"

"That's why I'm here. We think we've found someone with enough of the right fae markers in their blood at last, but well," Kim winced, "I've kind of lost him."

"Lost?"

"I picked him up, as normal, when he reached puberty. I've cultured him in the usual manner. At first I thought he was just another waste of time with so little fae blood as to have no power at all, but after a while he displayed more and more inclination to the old ways. I'm only giving him tiny doses of amnotin, of course, but I've had to re-dose so much more regularly. I think he might be the one."

"Yes dear, but LOST?"

"I've been living with him, in all senses…"

Dailabi's eyes widened at the admission.

"…I know, but sometimes it's the only way to gain their trust. It's hardly the first time I've had to go so far. Anyway, I've grown quite fond of him," her cheeks felt suddenly hot, "and I guess I lost a bit of perspective."

Dailabi paled. "The boy's fae, at least in part! Don't forget what they did to your people. And you still haven't explained about him being lost."

15

"Benji has no idea. He's more human than fae in so many ways, and such a gentle soul. It seems more likely his ancestry goes back to the days of the light fae clans, when they still had magic. Don't forget, not all of the fae were in agreement after the war."

"Lost?"

Kim sighed. "He overheard me talking with my mother. I went out briefly when I thought he was sleeping and he slipped away. He's on the run."

Dailabi shook her head. "And now you need a tracker to find him. Why not just send in an extraction team?"

"I don't want him hurt or frightened."

"Yes, you certainly have lost perspective. You need to supress those feelings Kimjora. Think what it will mean to your people."

"I understand this, but I believe I can convince him to work with us voluntarily. I just need to bring him to Elysia and explain everything."

Dailabi tilted her head to one side. "Are you certain of this?"

"I'm sure."

"Come. You can meet with Arbani in the dining hall. We'll get some food and drink down him, then I think he'll be more receptive to your request."

Kim smiled. "You've always been a good friend to the kelpies."

"Absolutely not."

At Arbani's outraged expression, Kim barely managed to resist taking a step back.

"You want one of my trackers to go to the human world? Don't you think one of our people might just stand out somewhat? What if she gets caught? How will she explain herself?"

"'She' Arbani? It sounds to me as if you've already selected someone for this mission. Pynora perhaps?" Dailabi said, exchanging a triumphant look with Kim.

Kim chimed in. "Arbani, humans come in all shapes and sizes, and many colour their hair too. Pynora would be perfect, and I'll make sure she doesn't stand out. We can phase straight back into the flat I've been living in with

Benji; I created a portal there. I have some loose clothing that should fit her ok. Besides, we have less than two full days now to find him before my mother sends in a team. Whether we succeed or not Pynora will be back by sunset the day after tomorrow."

Arbani narrowed his eyes. "Does Lucivarsh know that you've come to us for help?"

"Well, er, no, I haven't got around to discussing it with her yet." Kim winced and looked sidelong at Arbani.

He burst out laughing. "If this is successful, the kelpies will owe me."

Kim winced again. She was definitely not looking forward to her next conversation with her mother.

CHAPTER FIVE - SEARCH

Kim rummaged through her drawers and found a green American-style football shirt with a number 12 on it. It was meaningless to her. She never understood competitive sport – it just seemed like the civilisation of war to her, and having fought in a real war, it was an anathema to her. She'd broken Benji of that particular nasty habit straight away. Trousers were more difficult. In the end she settled on a pair of Benji's long shorts. These almost reached Pynora's ankles anyway. Her own reed and hide shoes would have to do, and a baseball cap completed the ensemble.

Pynora stood in front of the mirror, her expression nonplussed as she picked at the strange attire, "I look ridiculous."

"Well, I can't argue against that. But it's all for the greater good, and it won't be for long."

"Humph."

"So how does this work? I find something that smells of Benji and you follow the scent?"

Pynora swung round and bared her teeth at Kim. "What do you think I am, a blasted broosher-hound or something?"

Kim cringed. "I'm sorry, I didn't want to be rude. I just don't understand how you do this."

"Mmm. Well actually, something with his smell would be useful, for when we get close that is. First things first. Are you sure he hasn't left the city?"

18

"Not completely. His mother lives a long way south of here. She's his only living relative. If he's headed down there we won't find him in time anyway. But knowing him, it's more likely he's somewhere in Edinburgh still."

"We need to get up high. If he has any fae aura at all, I should be able to see where he has been in the last couple of days."

Kim's eyes widened. "Really? I can barely see his aura, even when the amnotin has completely worn off."

Pynora gave her a sharp look. "You've allowed it to wear off? It's too risky Kimjora. You know he has no control over his aura. Damn it, it's unlikely he knows he even has an aura."

"It's a risk I know, but if I let it wear off completely, I can talk about Elysia and the war to him. He thinks I'm making most of it up, but it gives me an insight into his inherited memory. He forgets the conversations once I've dosed him again. Anyway, how is it you can see the aura eminence so long after the subject has gone?"

"There's always a residual trace. Sprite eyes are significantly more efficient and any other being that I know of. What do you think makes us such good trackers? When I'm at home I can see a web of rosy tracks all over the city even when my people aren't emanating, and other auras too if we have visitors."

"So how is it the sprite at the gate didn't know I was a kelpie until I emanated? Should he not have been able to see my gold aura, even when I've quietened it down?"

Pynora shrugged. "It's an ability that develops with age. Atloni isn't all that old. Now, can we go and get this done?"

*****

There was a gathering at a stately home on the edge of Northumberland National Park – the English side of the border with Scotland close to the east coast. A helicopter landed on the pad, and an array of fast cars swept up the driveway. Clan leader Osun had called the meeting He watched his guests arrive with a mix of anticipation of what was to come, and disgust at how openly ostentatious they were. Greeting his guests in person, he directed them to the reception room where his staff had laid out food and drink

19

before he dismissed them for the day. In all twenty-two full blood dark fae men and women had responded to the summons. Possibly all that was left of their clan, no one was sure. They were a glittering, wealthy collection of successful entrepreneurs and business people in the human world, and all highly self-important. None of them, however, wanted to be the one that didn't show when called to an extraordinary meeting at 'The House'.

"What's this all about Osun? I have an important meeting later this week. I'd planned to be on my way to Montreal by now," said one.

"You've dragged me away from a shoot in Scotland. This had better be important," said another.

"Well we were on our yacht off Sicily. It's lovely there this time of year. We're keen to get back as soon as possible," said yet another.

"Silence!" Osun demanded. "Let's not forget who we are and why we're stuck in the human world. Why our people have to keep our identities hidden when we are the ones that should be running things."

"Oh come on Osun, we're hardly destitute," said one of the female guests, "our natural superiority over the humans has presented us with numerous opportunities, with land and riches. I for one don't feel 'stuck', as you put it, at all."

"You are missing the point. Yes, we've worked hard to acquire the things we have, but we still have to remain clandestine. And who are to blame? The damned kelpies, that's who. Well I had word from one of my contacts in Elysia. Kimjora has hired a sprite tracker. They're in Edinburgh even as we speak searching out one of our mixed blood descendants. The implications of this are clear. If the kelpies are allowed to transition back to their natural form, they'll quickly learn of our existence. They'll hunt us down and kill us all. Our numbers are too small to resist."

Alarm swept through the room, and soon people were shouting as arguments broke out.

Osun watched, at once amused at how easily these elite lost their composure, but also concerned they'd lost all concept of the dangers they all faced should their identities be compromised. He gave it some time to let the information settle into the psyche of the fae in the room, then he raised his hands. "Please, please everyone, calm down."

One of the fae called over to him. "What do you suggest we do?"

"It's simple. We have to get to this 'pretender' before Kimjora does. We have to kill him or her."

"But what about the tracker sprite. As soon as we get anywhere near, she'll see our auras. It'll be more than just the kelpies we have to worry about then."

"We have to find and kill the sprite too. And we have to do this quickly. I have a plan."

*****

Breaking and entering came easily to Kim. As a warrior and an agent of her people she was trained in multiple skills from spying to evading security systems to unarmed combat. So getting herself and Pynora into Edinburgh Castle in the middle of the night was a cinch. They squatted on the roof of the New Barracks, having already been to the top of the Hospital building, walked around the Half Moon Battery and attempted a daring climb up the roof of the Royal Palace.

Pynora had surveyed the city from all directions. "I'm sorry Kimjora. I'm still only getting the faintest of traces. Nothing is less than three or even four days old. Your boy seems to have wandered about a lot, but then he must have left the city."

Kim's heart sank. She knew she could totally trust Pynora's skills and instincts. "Thanks for trying my friend. Come on let's get back to the flat, I'll do us some food. Then you can get back into your own clothes and phase home."

Kim and Pynora scrambled back down from the roof and headed away from the castle. They took back the lanes, the sprite's disguise may work from a distance, but close up she could never pass for human.

Suddenly Pynora stopped in her tracks. Her head was turned up as she scanned all around.

"What is it? Have you caught a sense of Benji?" asked Kim.

"No. I don't know." Pynora was frowning. "There's something. A new track. Something fresh, and strong."

"You don't think it's Benji?"

21

"No. There's a darkness…something sucking at the light, it's…" Suddenly she looked up at Kim, her eyes wide with terror and she was breathing hard.

"What? What is it?...Pynora…What?" Kim she spun round, looking this way and that for the threat. Dropping into a low combat posture, she slid her two knives from their arm sheaths into her hands.

"Dark Fae!"

"What?"

"Dark Fae, four of them I think."

Kim pushed Pynora back against the wall anticipating the attack. She still couldn't see anyone else. "How? It can't be! There are none of them left!"

"That's where you're wrong…Kelpie," the new voice spat.

"Show yourselves, cowards." Kim's warrior training came to the fore as she crouched low, settling into her stance.

"Huh! How the mighty fall. Look at you. Skulking around the back streets of a human city…with a sprite!"

Four tall figures manifested out of the dark but she could only see one of them clearly.

Kim's heart was thumping as she glared at the speaker, but she kept her voice steady. "So Brok, where have you been holing up all these years?"

"You remember me. I'm flattered…Oh! No I'm not."

Another voice. "Stop toying with her Brok. Lets get this over with."

"Now now Leeta, there's no reason to abandon civility. We have after all integrated into the upper echelons of human society." With a nonchalant lift of his eyebrows, Brok laughed.

The other two fae closed in, and a third voice entered the game. "Hello Kimjora."

Recognition flooded through Kim, and was almost her undoing, as she momentarily relaxed her stance in shock. "Darsh?"

"It's agreeable to see you again. It's a shame it has to be under these circumstances."

CHAPTER SIX - HIDING

Professor Long lived in a charming bungalow in the countryside about fifteen miles southwest of Edinburgh. Benji nosed about a bit. He looked out the window, perused the bookshelf, and picked up and studied family photos from the sideboard while the Prof made tea.

Long looked over Benji's shoulder. "My wife Marcie. I lost her nearly four back. And that's my daughter Penny. She emigrated to Australia fifteen years ago with her husband and my two grandsons, and I've never seen my granddaughter there. I plan to visit them when I retire."

Benji put the photo back down and sat on one of the two floral armchairs to the side of the unlit fireplace. Professor Long sat opposite him after putting a tray of tea and biscuits on the coffee table between them. The grandmother clock on the mantelpiece ticked the time away as an old brown and white terrier cross, wandered in from the kitchen following her nose to the plate of biscuits. Long broke a digestive in half, gave one piece to the dog and shovelled the other half into his mouth. "This is Tina. She's thirteen and sleeps most of the time. She still likes her walk, and there's nothing wrong with her appetite. If you give her a bit of biscuit, you'll be her friend for life."

Benji followed Long's suit and fed Tina half a biscuit. After that she got closer to Benji, then sat and looked pleadingly at him with sad rheumy eyes.

"So Benjamin. Why don't you start at the beginning?"

Benji described how he'd first met Kim at secondary school in Surrey. "She was just so...different..."

Long tilted his head in question.

"Oh, I don't know. She wasn't like the other girls in class. Don't get me wrong, they were great, well most of them. They were my friends. We all got along. But when Kim came along, I just seemed to stop seeing everyone else... it's hard to explain. She became my life. I stopped going to football practice because it ate into the time I could be spending with her. My friends didn't understand, they tried to get me to stop seeing her. It made me so angry." Benji gritted his teeth and clenched his fists, then glanced at the Prof's raised eyebrows and relaxed. "Slowly everyone else just drifted out of my life. But I didn't care...I can't believe it now. It's like I was under some kind of love spell, and now I've snapped out of it." He pursed his lips. "What must everyone think of me?"

"Calm down Benjamin. Just be grateful you have broken the spell, because that is likely what it was."

"What? Professor Long, you don't actually believe that do you?"

"Indeed I do. And I think you do too, even if the rational side of your mind rejects such thoughts. Carry on with your story."

Benji's heart skipped a beat. That the Professor Long believed... he frowned, believed what exactly? That there was magic in the world? Part of him wanted to run again, escape the madness his life had suddenly become. Was the Prof a bit cracked? But no. Strange things had been happening to him, and perhaps Long was just the person to help him.

He continued. "When the time came to apply to uni, Kim and I decided to apply to Edinburgh as our first choice. I'd already read all your books, and I'd decided I wanted to come here years ago. Kim wanted to study psychology too. It was great. At least I thought it was at the time. Maybe she's not even interested in psychology, she just wanted to be with

24

me." Benji frowned then. "Why me? There's nothing special about me."

"We'll talk about that in a moment. Tell me the rest."

"Well, it was the same story once we got to Edinburgh. We just did everything together…" Benji felt the heat rise in his face. Long just nodded, acknowledging what 'everything' meant. "…we got a flat together. It was great. Kim would play her cittern and we…"

"Wait. She plays the cittern?"

"Yes. It's very soothing. Not the sort of music I used to listen too, but it's all I want to hear now."

Long nodded. He was wearing one of those infuriating 'knowing' looks, but he indicated to continue.

"It was then I started to have these blackouts."

"Blackouts?"

"Yes. It had only ever happened during evenings out – before this last time. We'd go out for food. Or to a bar, Usually the Corn Exchange, but sometimes, well quite often really, the next thing I'd know, I'd be waking up in bed with a thumping headache. Sometimes I didn't even remember going out I the first place. I wanted to see a doctor, but Kim assured me it was nothing to worry about, that's weird isn't it? I just believed her when she said it was ok. Why? It's not normal to have blackouts!"

"You said that it was just in the evening 'before the last time'. Something changed?"

"Yes. Last week, just as I was coming round from one of my blackouts I heard Kim on the phone to her mother. She'd never mentioned her family before. She was saying that 'she couldn't leave it much longer' and that 'she couldn't keep doing it to me'. Well I assume she was talking about me. Oh yeah, I meant to say, Kim got very agitated about our conversation. You know when you joked about bringing a fae or a kelpie to the lecture. She made me recite what was said word for word."

Long's eyes narrowed. Was he going to throw him out in a minute for talking such nonsense? Well, 'in for a penny in for a pound' as his mum always says.

He continued. "Well, the last time was Saturday when I met Kim's mum. Honestly, she didn't look any older than Kim. But she was so weird."

"What do you mean by 'weird'?"

"Just her manner really. Oh and her hair seemed to light up."

"Lucivarsh!" Long spat.

"Sorry?"

"Never mind. Just tell me the rest."

The twinkle in Long's eye had been replaced with… what? Anger? Determination? Benji couldn't sit still as he watched the old man cogitate. Kim would scold him… No! There was no more Kim controlling his life.

Well, he'd gone this far with his story he may as well finish. "So anyway, Kim's mother got irritated, not sure why, and Kim said we should go back to the flat and talk. Next thing I knew I was coming round from yet another blackout. It was the first time it had happened during the day. I heard them talking. Her mother said it was the strongest reading she'd seen in centuries – centuries! How crazy is that? They'd given me something called amnotin, have you heard of that?…" he rambled on without waiting for an answer, "…and something about innate clan memories and keeping the truth from me. It was then I realised Kim had been drugging me all this time. And lying to me. Her mother left then, and I pretended to be asleep. When Kim went out, I made a run for it and came to find you."

"You did the right thing coming to find me," said Long.

"You seem to know what's going on. Can you tell me please, because my whole life had just turned upside-down and I have no idea why?"

"There is a lot I need to explain to you. But first I must emphasise that you are in terrible danger. You will be safe here, at least for a while. You must not leave this house unless it is with me. Do you understand?"

"Yes… No… I don't understand any of this. Why am I in danger?"

"I will tell you everything. I promise. But first I need to go out for a while. I'll bring provisions back with me, then we'll talk after dinner. Ok?"

Provisions? Who calls grocery shopping 'provisions'? "Ok."

After Long went out Benji ran the strange turn of events that had afflicted his life over in his mind. "'I will tell you everything. I promise". Hadn't Kim said the exact same thing?' Could he trust Professor Long? Could he trust anyone? He was just a nobody. Why should he be in any danger? Perhaps he should get out of here, go to Mum's house. He yawned…

Benji woke to the sound of the front door closing. He tipped Tina off his lap, and stood up. She grumbled at the disturbance. "I got mince for dinner, thought I'd make a shepherd's pie, is that alright for you?" Called Long as he bundled through to the kitchen.

"Er yeah. Fine." Benji cursed himself for falling asleep when he should have skedaddled. Well, he may as well hear out the Prof's explanation. Then he could decide whether or not to stay. "Want any help?"

"If you could just chop the onions for me. They make my tired old eyes watery and sore."

It was nearly 10pm. Benji's belly was full as he and Professor Long went into the living room and sat in the armchairs once again. Tina curled up on Long's lap and was soon gently snoring. Long smiled at her. "She's old, like me."

Benji looked at Tina. He smiled briefly then looked expectantly at Long.

CHAPTER SEVEN - ATTACK

Kim was stunned into inaction. "Oh my god Darsh. You were dead. I know you were dead."

"And so you left me to rot in that bloody field. If Brok hadn't found me and carried me home my bones would be rotting there still."

Kim scanned her up and down drinking in the sight of her old friend's very 'alive' body. "I'm so sorry. But you had no pulse, you weren't breathing. How can this be?"

"We were a team Kimjora. Even if you thought me dead you should have carried me home."

Kim shook her head in denial. Her soldier's poise abandoned from the shock of seeing her battle partner for the first time in centuries. "You're right, I shouldn't have left you there, but the battle was hotting up and the dark clans were over-running us. It was a desperate time." She gentled her voice. "You have no idea how I mourned you Darsh."

"Well, I'm touched I'm sure."

The sarcasm in Darsh's words stung. "Why are you here, with these." Kim indicated the other fae with a wave of her hand.

"Kimjora," Pylora cried. It snapped Kim back to the moment.

"Enough of this banter. We have a job to do Darsh. Let's get it over with," said Bord, the forth fae. He moved into the lamplight. A short-sword flashed in his hand.

Kim felt a weight on her foot as she repositioned herself back into battle stance. A dark pool formed around Pynora's head and her lifeless eyes stared back up at her. "Nooo." Kim leapt high with a whinnying battle cry. Her two knives flashed as she landed on one knee on the other side of the narrow lane. With no time to take a breath, she was up, turned around and back in battle stance before Brok and Darsh had time to see their comrades fall.

"I see you haven't lost your edge after all these years Kimjora," said Darsh.

"Don't do this Darsh. After all we went through together." Kim screwed her eyes up as she looked closely at her old partner. "I see your aura my friend. It's dark, but it doesn't suck out the light like theirs." She indicated Brok and the two fallen fae with one small movement of her head. "Come back to the light. You know there are still light fae in Elysia? Come with me to see them. I know they can help you."

Brok moved suddenly. Kim wasn't quick enough. She screamed as burning flared across her shoulder and down her arm. The knife in her left hand dropped to the floor as her fingers sprung open. Her own blood poured onto the ground – she was in trouble. She raised the other knife and prepared for Brok's follow-up attack, but she was severely weakened. Fae knives were tainted with poison from the crushed leaves of the chowmat tree. She could already feel its effects coursing through her body. She would not survive this attack. Kim's knees buckled and the last thing she saw before losing consciousness was Brok's ugly smirk looming over her.

Bright sunlight penetrated Kim's closed eyelids as she finally came round. She wished she hadn't. The agony from the slash to her left arm was almost more than she could bear. She whimpered as she swung her legs round, forcing herself into a standing position. Her eyes watered from the pain, but the soldier in her knew she needed to assess her situation and look for any further danger. It was disorientating to find herself in a large, comfortable living room, on a massive leather sofa beside a huge fireplace. She wished it were alight as the cold air seeped through her. Though her arm felt like a lump of lead, it had been tended and was bound in a tight bandage. The poison had left her with a throbbing headache, but she was alive. She should be dead. Feeling for her knives, she took comfort in finding them safely in their sheaths. 'How can any of this be?'

"So you're finally back in the land of the living. It was touch and go for a while."

Kim swung round. Darsh stood in the doorway with a glass in each hand.

"Whiskey?"

Kim nodded and sat back down on the sofa. "I don't understand. You came to kill me. What happened?"

Darsh sat down beside her. "I remained light fae. It's taken a great deal of effort to emanate a dark aura. When you said my aura wasn't dark like the others, I realised I'd let it slip a bit, probably because of seeing you. Brok had already written you off after he'd needled you with the chowmat, so he turned on me. I had to kill him to maintain my cover. His kill will be put down to you, but it hardly matters at the moment. I told Osun that Brok had got a cut in, so they'll think you're dead by now. You're safe for the time being."

"Osun? Damn him. He was the one who started all this in the first place, him and that fae witch, what was her name? Orla? Orma? Humph, something like that." Kim felt her arm with her right hand. "How did you get the poison out? I thought I was a gonner for sure."

"The dark fae are volatile, their arguments often come to blows, so they keep a breeding stock of fik leeches."

A shiver of revulsion ran down Kim's spine. "Is it out?"

"Now don't pull that face. It's what saved your life. I had to leave it in until I was sure all the poison was gone. Here." Darsh sat down beside Kim and unravelled the dressing. Taking some tiny tweezers from a breast pocket, she extracted the, now fat, little fik leech. Its stench immediately pervaded the whole room, so she popped it into a jar and sealed it. "I'll run you a bath. You stink almost as bad as our little friend here. I've pulled out some clothes that should fit... sort of."

"Darsh, we need to talk. There's a lot at stake here. I need to go and see Arbani too, to tell him about Pylora."

30

"I'm sorry about the sprite. I just couldn't envision a scenario where I could save her too, not against three armed fae."

"After all this time, for the dark fae to reveal themselves now, means they're aware we've found a potential human/fae descendant – one that may have enough magic to restore us. He is in terrible danger."

"Osun sent Drima after this 'Benji'. Lucivarsh also sent out an extraction team. But it's alright, he is safe."

"How can he possibly be safe?" Kim went to get up, but staggered.

"Sit down. You're a long way from recovered. The boy is under the protection of a wizard."

"What? Who? You know they don't want us to regain our natural form too don't you? They see us as part of the problem. They think we were responsible for the clan wars. It's ridiculous."

"I know. I know. One thing at a time. The Wizard of Mount Laskala is looking after the boy. He's been posing as a university professor for years. He'll keep him safe while we decide what to do," said Darsh.

The penny dropped. "Long!"

"Yes, that's him."

"Damn it, I should have realised, and then told my mother about him. He writes mythology books but actually, he's been writing our history all these years." Kim slammed her fist on the coffee table and almost knocked her whiskey glass over. "If I'd have read his books I'd have known. How could I have been so sloppy? I've been studying in his classes this term."

"It's not like you Kimjora. Are you smitten with this boy? Is that why you've been so slack in your duties?"

Kim felt a bit sheepish. "Oh, I don't know what it is about him. I've been keeping his mind under, just like all the others, but he's different. Special."

"Oh dear! This can only complicate things. Your objectivity is compromised."

"Mmm. Dailabi made the same accusation. You will help me won't you Darsh?"

31

"Mmm. Well let me see. I've saved your life, lied about your fate to Osun, killed the fae that saved my life when you left me on the battlefield – I haven't forgiven you for that you know – and now you want more?"

"I'm sorry. I shouldn't ask any more of you."

Darsh's stern expression cracked into a lopsided grin. "Of course I'll help you. We're partners remember." She paused a moment, and her face became serious again. "It's so good to be with you again my friend. Don't think I'm not still pissed with you mind!"

The two women hugged tentatively for the first time in nearly six hundred years, and a stray tear roll down Kim's cheek.

"Now, I need to report back to Osun. He mustn't suspect. What I don't understand is why the wizard didn't suspect you. He must have been able to see your aura."

"No. Wizards are powerful, but they have to invoke their power. They are so strong they have to keep it supressed until needed. When they do invoke, their own purple auras are so bright, even humans can see them."

"Funny how I never knew that. Interesting."

"Speaking of auras, it's good to see your silver light again. You're so beautiful."

"Aw shucks."

"Shucks?"

"I know, I've been watching too much old American TV. I need to go, I'll be back in a few hours. Have your bath, spray this room for me, it still stinks of fik leech. Get something to eat, there's plenty in the fridge, and for goodness sake relax. When I get back we'll make plans, ok?"

"Ok."

CHAPTER EIGHT - REVELATION

"Tell me, what drew you to my books in the first place?" Professor Long asked.

Benji shrugged. "I've just always liked..." he stopped short and frowned as a forgotten memory resurfaced. "No wait. I remember. I was in Waterstones in Guildford, in the Sci-Fi and Fantasy section. I guess I was about ten or eleven at the time, but I'd kinda outgrown the kids' books. I remember I was looking for some Robin Hobb stuff, I'd read the Liveships series right through start to finish twice on the trot and wanted some more. Mum always let me have whatever books I wanted, my bedroom already had two bookshelves full to bursting..."

Long moved his hand in a circle to encourage Benji to move on and get to the point.

"... Yes sorry. Anyway this guy was standing next to me. He said 'try this one son'. I took the book and flicked through the pages. When I looked up the man was gone – just gone! I didn't even notice him leaving. Anyway, the image of the kelpie in the centre pages just got me, you know? 'Creatures in Our Souls by Jonas Long'. That was it. After that I read everything you wrote."

"What did this man look like?"

"I don't really remember much. He was tall, his hat obscured his face, and he had a raincoat on. He looked a bit 'Dick Barton' if you know what I mean."

"Mmm. Well, young Benjamin. You haven't read everything I've written. Only everything I've published. There's a difference. I'll let you have another piece of my work to read while you're here. But read it quickly, I don't want it leaving the house." Long handed Benji a manuscript. No pictures. The title had been hand written on the front as if he hadn't decided what to call it until after he printed it. 'Clan Wars – A Shift to Darkness'.

"So, are you going to tell me what this is all about? Why am I in danger?"

"Before that, I want you to read page twelve of this manuscript. I'm just going to pop Tina out for ten minutes. We'll talk then."

Benji flipped the pages, held together with just a treasury tag in the top corner, and found page twelve. He began to read:

Once there was an alliance between kelpies and fae as, alongside the smaller light clans, they fought the dark forces. The war spread widely, and spanned the borders between The Dark Realm, Elysia and the human's world. Slowly the light clans moved toward victory, having suffered many losses, but as everything began to change the kelpies and the fae did not see eye to eye on how the new world should look. The smaller clans – the wood nymphs with their bright green auras, mountain sprites with their rose auras and merfolk with their ice-blue auras, faded quietly back to their homes not wishing to involve themselves in further conflict, having already lost so many of their people. Many of the fae, however, believing themselves superior, expected humans to worship them and they took many as lovers. The kelpies were horse-like beings with shape-shifting abilities that allowed them to take human form. They were of three main species. The Mira Kelpies, who reside in the sea, the Lochanar that live in lochs and rivers and the Prenya Kelpies of the plains. In mythology, the Prenya are rarely mentioned, though they are far more numerous than the Mira or the Lochanar. They believed, like the smaller light clans, they should step back, and leave the humans be – after all they had their own world to rebuild. But the fae faction were determined to rule. When the Prenya kelpies tried to force them to retreat to Elysia with the rest of the light clans, those fae, now turned to the dark, hatched a plan. Their queen, Orma, used previously hidden magic to force them into their human form, unable to shift back. Stuck now within their human bodies, the Prenya were weakened, their gold auras barely visible even to their own kind, but they were determined to make the fae restore their shape-shifting abilities. They developed a drug that made the fae forget who they were. They were playing for time. They planned to coerce the fae into helping them by 're-educating' those that were more malleable. Over time, however, the fae blood became diluted as they integrated into human society, no longer aware of their heritage – the kelpie's plan had backfired. But kelpies could sense the silver auras of those with fae blood and one after another they befriended and tested anyone that may have inherited fae magic powers. They believed the genes that gave them such magic lived on and could be enhanced until someone somewhere could restore them. Then they would remove or destroy all fae that would not leave the human realm.

Benji jumped up off the chair and threw the manuscript down onto the table in disgust, almost as if it would burn him. One moment he was reading mythology written by one of his favourite authors, the next... "I've been sleeping with a horse!"

Tina trotted back into the living room, frisky from the chill night air. Long was right behind her. "Well, not really. In their human form they are fully human. Well physically at least."

Benji instinctively backed away from Long. "No. No no no. This is crazy. You can't believe this is real! How can... but... wait a minute, how would you know all this stuff anyway? It's just mythology...folklore. You've been writing this stuff for so long, now you're starting to believe it." He stood still now, his sensible rationale finally settling comfortably back in his mind.

"Benjamin. What ever you choose to believe, that fact remains that Kim and her mother drugged you. That Kim has been lying to you since she met you. That she has plans that you know are nefarious, as she wouldn't reveal anything about them. At the very least, believe the danger you are in. But no one will come looking here. Tell me something, how old is Kim?"

Taken aback by such an apparently random question, Benji frowned. "What? I don't know, my age I suppose."

"And you were, what, thirteen? fourteen? when you met her, and you're about nineteen now? How much have you changed in that time? You were a boy and now you're a man. What about Kim? How much has she changed in that time? Was she just a young girl back then?"

Benji brow creased again as he thought back. 'She hasn't changed a bit. In all that time, she hasn't changed!' Wide-eyed he gaped at the Prof.

Long didn't wait for him to answer. He just nodded and said, "I thought as much. Her magic, her cittern music, oh and her pheromone too, by the way, has clouded your mind for so long, and in so many ways."

"Pheromone?"

"Kelpies produce it in a gland behind their ear. It…pacifies the weak-minded. Sorry! Anyway, it's late. I suggest we get some sleep, we can talk more tomorrow."

*****

Benji slowly awoke from a dreamless sleep with the sun beaming gentle warmth down onto his face through the window. His eyes were closed, but rosy light penetrated his eyelids. He reached blindly for Kim, but only found a side table with a mug of tea as he snatched his hand back from the unexpected heat. He peeled his eyes open taking in the unfamiliar bedroom. The events of the last few days came flooding back and he sighed. How he missed waking to that beautiful face on the pillow next to him, and the warm sensuous body sidling up close to his. He sat up and picked up the mug. He wasn't normally fond of tea, but there was something comforting about wrapping his hands around the hot mug as he perused his surroundings. A dark-wood wardrobe stood against the wall with carved designs running down the door panels. The dressing table with its ornate mirror and a yellow frilly-cushioned stool caught the morning light. A chest of drawers sat under the window with a china

36

vase of silk flowers standing on an embroidered runner. A print with an overly fussy gold-coloured frame was on the wall opposite the bed. The picture some famous pre-Raphaelite that Benji couldn't recall the name of – some woman floating in a pond. He shrugged and decided it must be the Prof's daughter's old room. Something nagged at him. He sipped at his tea, and gradually sounds filtered through to his morning-fuzzed head. Benji heard voices then. Long's and a woman's. The circumstances were similar enough to coming around in his flat to hear Kim and her mother plotting against him that he decided suspicion was what had been nagging away at him. He quietly pulled on his clothes and tried to creep out of his room and along hall, but the creaky old floorboards gave him away.

The talking paused briefly, then Long called out. "Ah! Awake at last. We're in the kitchen Benjamin."

Benji took a breath, counted to three in his mind, put on his best nonchalant expression and breezed into the kitchen. Tina was in her basket. She lifted her head and pounded her tail when she saw him, making him smile. He then took in the rest of the scene. Long and the newcomer, a woman at least as old as the Prof, sat at the seventies-style formica table drinking tea from mugs like the now empty one in his hand. A box of cornflakes, a carton of semi-skimmed milk, sugar, bread, butter and marmalade were in the middle of the table. Cereal bowls, plates and cutlery were laid out ready for breakfast.

"Sit yourself down lad. This is my sister Jean."

"Nice to meet you Benjamin. Jonas has been telling me all about you."

To Benji that seemed unlikely all things considered. He nodded in acknowledgement, but didn't say anything. This woman clearly wasn't the Prof's sister. She was black and the Prof was as white as white can be. He found it almost funny that having breakfast with a couple of old people in an ordinary kitchen in an ordinary bungalow in the Scottish countryside could seem such a surreal experience.

"Something amusing?"

As usual, Benji's face had given him away, but then Kim always told him he 'wore his heart on his sleeve'. He poured

37

some cornflakes into a bowl and grabbed the milk carton. Well, he may as well say it now. "Er no, it's just, well, you can't really be brother and sister can you?"

Jean chuckled and turned toward him, her gold-flecked, green eyes shone bright like opalescent jewels. Benji startled back a moment at the sight. "Being family isn't always about parentage or genetics young Benjamin."

"Sorry, I didn't mean to seem rude."

"Not at all. Toast?"

"Please."

"We will protect you from any danger young Benjamin. I will stay here while Jonas goes to work. I suspect you have many questions. I will try to explain as best I can."

Benji's eyes widened. He didn't want to stay here with this woman. There was something unsettling about her, especially those weird eyes. "I...have classes today," he protested rather weakly.

"I'm afraid your university career is on hold until we can eliminate the danger," said Long.

"Eliminate? What do you mean? You're not going to harm Kim!"

"Listen lad," said the Prof, "she's not the girl you fell in love with. I'm sorry, it's a sad thing for you, but she's your enemy. Her name is Kimjora, she's a kelpie with an agenda; an agenda that you may not survive. Oh, and she's nearly seven hundred years old by the way. She is a warrior of her people and an agent. She has 'worked' many young lads just like you over the centuries, then discarded them when they've turned out not to be suited to the kelpie's purpose. What makes you special isn't that she has feelings for you; it's only that you seem to be stronger than most with the fae blood. The kelpies will want to exploit that. We don't know exactly what procedures they use, but they will certainly change you beyond all recognition. They will want you to give them their shape-shifting abilities back. But in the end, if you can't do that for them, where do you think that leaves you?"

"Leave the lad be, Jonas. You're scaring him. You'd best get going or you'll be late. I'll look after our boy here."

38

Long made up a packed lunch and drove off while Jean cleared the table and washed the dishes.

Benji didn't know what to believe. Were these people crazy? Could any of this be real? Kim had always looked after him, helped him with his studies, lived with him…made love to him, been good to him…apart from the whole drugging business of course. He didn't want any harm to come to her. Long was alright he supposed, if a bit odd. But this Jean woman – what's with those eyes? She was scary. He had to get away from her, find Kim and warn her. He couldn't ever trust her again of course, but he couldn't let anyone hurt her either. "Er. I could use some fresh air. I'm going for a walk."

"I don't think so. Sit down, I'll make some coffee."

"Thanks, I'll have it when I get back. I won't be long." He headed for the door. But the door slammed shut. He turned and stared at Jean.

"Must be the wind. Now sit down young man."

"But…"

"Sit."

He sat.

"You have to understand. All my brothers and sisters are… like guardians. The clan wars should never have intruded on your world. The history books don't tell of this. It's been screened out of the human psyche. But the clans are still out there. They still come to the human world, and there is still darkness. We keep the peace. We prevent any possibility of folk from Elysia or The Dark Realm interfering with the affairs of humans. If the fae had not been so belligerent and tried to rule the human world, if they hadn't been so…randy, and bred with humans so rampantly, if the kelpies weren't bent on taking their revenge here, we would not have this burden."

"When you say all your brother and sisters, how many are we talking about?"

"Oh, only eighty-three of us around the globe. But there is a concentration of us here in Scotland as this was the focus of most of the fighting during the wars."

Benji's head was full of strange and random thoughts. Was he actually as descendent of some horny fae? What did

39

that say about Mum? He needed some time to think. Could he somehow he get away from Jean? That door didn't slam because of the wind. There wasn't any. It was a warm, sunny autumn morning. So did she do that? What was she?

Tina got up then and went to the door.

He got up to let her out. When he opened the back door, he saw his opportunity and bolted. He didn't have his coat, his rucksack or his phone. He just ran.

Long was beside himself with anger. "What do you mean – Gone?"

"He went to let the dog out and hare-tailed it out of here. It was so fast I didn't have time to put anything in place to stop him."

"Damn it Jean. You were supposed to keep him here."

Jean just shrugged.

CHAPTER NINE – RUNNING

Benji looked around him frowning. He hadn't paid a huge amount of attention to the journey from Edinburgh to the Prof's home, so he had no idea which way to go when he ran away from the Prof's scary sister. He just picked a direction at random and ran. He couldn't run for long, he headed across country, and had to negotiate fences, hedges, a short stretch of woodland, until finally he found a narrow lane leading to the village of West Linton. From here he got a bus back to Edinburgh. He had to find Kim. He couldn't ring as his phone was in his backpack at the Prof's house. Long said his life was in danger, but actually Kim was the one in peril. Despite everything she'd done to him, he had to save her. When he got off the bus he headed straight home hoping she'd be there. Then they could talk.

As Benji rounded the corner, he spotted a big black limo with a uniformed driver at the wheel. The entrance door to the small block of flats stood open. Something wasn't right. What if they'd found Kim? What if they'd killed her? Did the Prof really have that much influence that he could send people like this to do his dirty work?

Secreting himself in a doorway about fifty feet away, he watched. Eventually two smartly dressed men came out of the building, got in the car and left. Benji ran to the door and up the stairs, wondering if he'd find Kim dead. He broke out in a cold sweat at the thought. He stopped at his flat door. What would he find?

Slowly he turned the key. His heart thumped wildly, his breathing rapid. Taking a few deep breaths, he stepped inside. "Kkkim?" he croaked, then more clearly, "Kim. Are you here?" No answer. Treading slowing, and peering through to the kitchen, then the bathroom, he braced himself for a moment in front of the bedroom door, then gently pushed it open. The breath Benji hadn't realised he'd been holding released in a huge sigh. She wasn't there. Thank goodness. Flopping down on the edge of the bed he put his head in his hands. What should he do now?

Benji wasn't sure how long he sat there trying to weigh up his options, but he came up with nothing except to sit tight and hope she came home.

He made a mug of coffee and a sandwich. There was only cheese and salad. Kim was vegetarian and she refused to buy ham or cold chicken or anything for sandwiches. If he wanted that sort of thing, she told him, he'd have to buy it himself. Usually that was too much bother for him, so a cheese sandwich it was. He fired up his laptop while he was eating getting butter from his fingers all over the lid. He made a cursory attempt at wiping it off with his sleeve. Kim would get cross with him for doing that. But then she'd forfeited any right to influence his behaviour when she betrayed his trust in her. A quick look at the news indicated there was nothing out of the ordinary. His whole world had been turned upside down, but somehow life just carried on as normal. There was one new message waiting. It was four days old:

Benji hun, I hope you get this. I know everything seems weird, but you must call me, I promise I'll tell you everything. I know I should have done so before, but you'll understand why when I explain it all to you. If I don't find you first, there will be people looking for you. Don't stay in the flat, it's the first place they'll look. If you don't want to ring me, I'll be at the Corn Exchange every evening at seven o'clock. You can find me there. I know you don't trust me, but it's a public place, and when you hear what I have to say, I know things will be ok again. Love you. Kim XXX

Benji closed the laptop. Were those men looking for Kim or for him? He dug out his old sports bag and stuffed a few clothes and a spare pair of trainers in it. Put the laptop in its case and pushed that in too, and remembered to take the charger with him. Grabbing a can of Coke out of the fridge, he headed out again. He needed to find somewhere to hang out until seven o'clock. It was just over three hours away. He headed towards Princes Street. It would be busy and he could just disappear into the crowd. As he walked he became conscious of footsteps. He dared to look behind him. There was no one obvious. There were people everywhere. He was just being paranoid. He wandered into Primark and made a show of looking at the clothes, whilst surreptitiously looking around to see if anyone was watching him. There were, two people, a man and a woman. Store detectives. He cursed himself for being so obvious and left the shop. There was a MacDonald's just up the road, so he went and sat there with a Big Mac and a latte, nursing the cup for as long as he could, all the time looking around. The logical part of his brain knew he was over-reacting, but it seemed to him that everyone was looking at him, and the room was closing in on him.

Benji checked his watch for the umpteenth time. It was still only five twenty five. The shops would be shutting for the day. 'Where to go for the last hour and a half.' He wandered out of MacDonald's and headed to the church on the corner. They're safe places to be. Right?

He'd never been one for going to church, and he dearly hoped some priest wouldn't approach him to see if he needed to 'talk'. It's what always happens in films when a fugitive takes refuge in a church. What would he say? 'Edinburgh's full of magical beings all out to find ordinary old me.' He chuckled as he pictured the scene in his head. Nobody approached him. He didn't really want them to, but at the same time a little bit of him was disappointed.

Finally, six forty-five. Benji left the church and headed for the Corn Exchange. They knew him and Kim in there. It was a comfortable place to be.

"Hello Benji, beer? No Kim tonight?"

Benji wanted a beer, but thought better of it. He needed a clear head. "Just a coke please. I'm meeting her here." The barman capped a bottle of coke and put it in front of Benji along with a small dish of Bombay Mix. "I've been…away. Has Kim waited for long for me the last few evenings?"

"Kim? No. Haven't seen her mate."

Benji's world came crashing down. He stared at the barman. "Are you sure?"

"Sorry. I've worked all week, she's not been in." The barman shrugged and wandered off to serve another customer.

What would he do now? She said she'd be here every night. Had they got to her? How could he get in touch? What was her number? It was programmed into his phone so he hadn't needed to remember it. He couldn't go back to the flat. That left him only one option. He had to go back to the Prof's house when the old man wasn't there, break in somehow and get his phone – and hope the scary woman wasn't still there. The phone charger was still at the flat. He'd have to go there too to get it. Damn, why didn't he think of that when he'd picked up the computer charger? So the plan was: get the charger from the flat, and his sleeping bag. Get the bus back to West Linton. Spend the night in the woods between West Linton and the Prof's house, then break in after the old man had gone off to work. He'll have to charge the phone up while he's there, and call Kim. Benji smiled. It was a good plan.

44

CHAPTER TEN – OSUN

"This is serious Osun. There are only twenty of us left now," said Drima.

"Indeed. Brok, Leeta and Bord are a great loss. They, however, were up against a formidable adversary. At least Darsh managed to escape, and we know now that Kimjora and the sprite are dead. But what of you Drima? How is it that you couldn't take out one clueless human boy?"

"He is hidden Osun. The only possible explanation is that the wizards have him."

Osun pondered that idea for a moment, scratching the side of his head with his forefinger. "Mmm. Yes, that is a possibility. They have no love for the kelpies, or at least no desire to see them return to their true form. If they do have the boy, that would work for us. We need to be certain though. Contact Rola, she's friendly with the Lomari River Wizard. What is it the bloody wizard calls herself? Jean? See if she can find anything out."

Drima gave a curt bow. "Yes Osun."

Osun scowled at Drima's clear lack of respect, but she, like him was one of only a handful of dark fae left with any magic. All the full-blood offspring they'd ever produced were born light fae and had to be killed at birth. Still, they kept trying. Olia was carrying his child, in the next week or two it would be born. He was ever hopeful of begetting a dark fae child to raise in his own image. Darsh argued every time against killing the children, saying they may turn dark later. She'd convinced him to allow her own son to live, and look what happened there! The light fae felt his presence in the world and somehow spirited him away to Elysia. He wasn't about to let that happen again. That was nearly fifty years ago, and Darsh had never been able to conceive since. Pity.

"One other thing before you go Drima, find out if word's got back to Arbani about the sprite tracker's death."

"Yes Osun."

*****

Darsh sipped her Earl Grey in the Cherry Tree Tea Room. The wizard Long was hanging his jacket on a hook by the entrance. He came and sat opposite her and indicated to the waitress that he was ready to order straight away.

"A pot of Orange Pekoe and a toasted teacake please."

The waitress nodded in response and went to place the order.

"So Darsh, after all this time with almost no contact, this is the second time we've met in a week. These are strange times indeed. Do you have Kimjora tucked away?"

"She's at my house, but she can't stay there. If any of the dark fae come over, they'll sense her presence. She's badly injured, and will take some time to heal, but now that you have the boy, she's happy to keep a low profile for a while. It's important the dark fae don't find out she's alive for a while. As soon as they become aware she didn't die they'll know I saved her and my cover is blown."

"The longer we can hold that off the better. But there's a complication…" Professor Long stopped talking while the waitress delivered his order. "…the stupid boy took fright and ran off. Jean's trying to locate him to take him back to my house, but as I'm sure you're aware, Lucivarsh has a team looking for him. It's only a matter of time before Osun gets wind that he's out and about too. He'll have that vicious Drima after him again."

A moment's irritation crossed Darsh's face. "How could you have lost control of him? Oh well never mind that. If Kimjora finds out, she'll want to get him back too."

"Can you keep it from her?"

46

"Best not. If she finds out I knew, then I'll lose her trust again. It's tentative enough as it is. Besides, she seems to be fond of the boy for some reason. She wants to be the one to take him to the kelpies so she can keep him safe. I may be able to persuade her to bring him back to you until things have calmed down. She won't like it, but she knows she's in no condition to protect him at the moment."

"It's not like her to develop feelings for her little projects. But then Benjamin is a nice enough lad, and she's been cultivating him for quite a while. They've been in my psychology class this term. Of course I didn't know who they were until last week, but they do seem to have quite a connection. I can hardly believe she was right under my nose and I didn't recognise her. Anyway, I agree with you. Go home and tell her he's on the run, and to find him and bring him to me. It'll give him a fighting chance at least."

Darsh nodded. Swallowed the last of her tea and left, leaving Long to pay the bill.

*****

"I bet Jonas was pleased with you. Ha Ha – Professor Jonas Long! I wonder how the humans would react if they found out what he is."

Jean didn't much like Rola's sarcastic tone, or her smug grin. "Babysitting some human brat wasn't exactly my idea in the first place. I'd have just disposed of him, the whole problem would have just gone away then, but the Council of Wizards has deemed such actions as 'outside our remit.' We're here to observe and to counter any action by the clans, light or dark, that interferes in human affairs." She reeled off this last like a mantra.

"But you've never agreed with that have you?"

"We are the most powerful creatures ever to have existed. In our heyday all bowed to our knowledge and to our rule. It is the natural order of things. I would restore our power, in all worlds, but I am over-ruled, and now I find myself out looking for an unprepossessing human boy just to protect him from you, when I'd just as happily give him up to you. It's so damn frustrating!"

Rola's grin stayed in place and a chuckle escaped her lips. "Don't give me that 'natural order of things' nonsense

47

Jean. It was the wizard's laxity of control that set off the clan wars in the first place."

"Mmm. Well we can certainly learn from that," Jean conceded, "but to say we're not exactly using our skills to the best of their potential would be an understatement."

The lime, plane and chestnut trees were shedding their leaves in Edinburgh's London Road Park as the autumn progressed. The two women had walked its length as they talked. They had now reached the far end. "I need to get back and report to Osun. Drima should be able to track the boy down easily enough now."

"If I don't find him first that is. I still have to obey Jonas, at least for the time being, whether I like it or not."

CHAPTER ELEVEN – CONVERGENCE

Benji stood in a doorway opposite the entrance to his flat with his loose hood up, obscuring his face. He waited for twenty minutes or so to see if there was anyone watching the doorway, or indeed coming and going from the building. He saw nothing suspicious. Finally he headed across the road, let himself in and went up the stairs to his own doorway. As he turned the key he heard a floorboard creaking inside. He froze. Slowly he pulled the key back out, trying his best not to make a sound. His hand was shaking so much he dropped the key as it slid from the lock. What was probably just a tiny sound seemed to blast through Benji's head as the key hit the bare floor. A shiver ran down his spine and perspiration beaded his forehead as he dipped down to recover the miscreant key. As he stood back up the door opened and he took an involuntary step back.

"Benji! Thank goodness. I've been looking everywhere for you." She pulled him inside and shut the door. "Listen, we can't stay here, everyone's looking for you."

"Kim? What happened to you, you look terrible?"

"We have to go. Right now."

"No. I'm not budging until you tell me what's going on. And why you've been drugging me. And why so many people are looking for me. And why Professor Long knows so much more than anyone else. And why there's a scary woman at his house that he calls his sister. And why your

49

mother looks the same age as you, and wants to drug me too. And why…why you look like you've gone ten rounds with Mike Tyson."

Kim bit her lip and gave Benji a sympathetic look. Reaching out to touch his face, she ran a finger gently down his cheek. "I promise I'll explain everything. But you have to understand that you're in terrible danger. We need to get you to safety first. Then we'll talk."

"We'll talk now." Benji planted his feet, folded his arms and lifted his head in defiance.

She grabbed hold of his arm, pulling him back toward the door. "The longer we stand here arguing about it the closer your enemies are."

"Until last week I didn't have any enemies. I was happy doing my degree and living with my beautiful girlfriend."

Kim's panicked expression softened. "I'm so sorry hun. But that doesn't change the fact that we need to get out of here. Now."

The sound of several pairs of feet coming up the stairs made Kim hiss and Benji's eyes widen.

"Damn. They're here." Kim pulled Benji further into the room and started to drag the sofa front of it. But she flagged under her injuries, and Benji finished the job, finally picking up on the urgency of the moment. Rushing to the bedroom and over to the window, Kim yanked it open and stepped out onto the tiny balcony, grabbing her cittern as she went. Benji frowned at that. Of all the things they might take with them, she thought of that!

There was a call from the hallway outside the front door. "Kimjora."

"Damn. Mother came with them?" she whispered. "This is not good. Benji, do you think you can make it to the ground without actually falling and hurting yourself?"

Benji nodded, sidled past Kim, climbed over the railing and took hold of the drainpipe. Shimmying down, he was almost at the bottom when it came away from the wall. Pain lanced through his whole body as he landed unceremoniously on the ground with a bump and a sharp intake of breath. He looked up to the balcony as Kim was climbing the railing. "How are you going to get down?"

50

Kim looked at him. Her expression an odd mix of determination and sorrow. She jumped, and landed in an easy, dignified crouch on the ground next to him. Benji stared at her, then back up to the balcony, then back to her once more. "How...how did you...what..?"

"Never mind that now. It won't take them long to figure out what happened. I have a car just around the corner. Quickly."

"Car? You don't have a car. You can't drive!"

"Wrong, I can drive, but it's not my car."

A silver Maserati sprung to life just ahead as Kim pressed the button on the remote she'd taken out of her pocket. But just as Benji thought they were home and dry, a woman appeared, stepping out, almost casually, from a nearby side street, and planted herself in front of the car.

Benji looked from the newcomer to Kim and back again, confusion and fear turning his legs to jelly.

"Drima!"

"Kimjora. What a pleasure to see you. It seems Darsh wasn't entirely candid with us after all. I've often had my suspicions about her, but Osun wouldn't listen to me. You know what he's like."

"Stay behind me." Kim hissed at Benji. Then her voice changed to match her opponent's tone. "Well Drima. It's been a long time, and you know, I'd love to stop and chat, but I have somewhere else to be."

"That's fine with me. Just leave the puny human and you're free to go."

"Not happening Drima. Now get out of my way."

Drima tipped her head to one side as she looked Kim up and down. "You're in no fit state to fight me Kimjora. I'll just kill you and take the boy anyway. You may as well save yourself the trouble."

"You're not touching a hair on my daughter's head, bitch." Lucivarsh and a team of three tall men in dark suits appeared from round the corner.

Drima's head snapped up. She didn't look quite so confident now, Benji noticed. He'd been following the bizarre conversation and had already worked out that Kim, even if she wasn't so bashed about, would be no match for

51

this Drima woman. She was big and muscular next to Kim's average height, and slim frame. But it didn't matter now. Whatever Kim's mother had in mind for him, at least she wouldn't let anything happen to Kim, not with that bunch of heavy's in tow. Benji quietly sloped backwards away from the unfolding events, and slowly eased his way along a wall. As he got further and further away the sound of raised voices receded. At one point he thought he heard Kim's voice calling to him. He stopped walking and turned, but there was nothing to see. They must have dispersed, but would probably still be looking for him. He needed to hide somewhere. He turned back and his heart skipped a beat.

"Well young man, you've been sending us all on a merry dance haven't you?" Jean put her hand on Benji's shoulder and steered him into the passenger seat of her yellow mini. He knew he should resist, run the other way, but he didn't. He was caught up in sight of those strange eyes and he just did as she told him.

*****

"Benjamin I'm so pleased you're alright. You gave us quite a fright running off like that."

Benji sat at the kitchen table with Professor Long. Tina had been very excited to see him back, and curled up by his feet. After all he'd been through, he was now back at the Prof's house drinking tea and eating biscuits again. Jean had dropped him off there and left. He sighed in relief as she left. Still he felt like a bit like a prisoner.

"Won't they just all come over here?"

"No. There's a shield surrounding the house. No one can sense where you are whilst you stay in here. That's why I told you to stay put. But the young never listen." Long sighed.

"Why are all these people after me Professor? I don't understand."

"Did you finish reading the manuscript I lent you?"

"No, sorry."

"Mmm well. There's someone arriving soon. Then we'll tell you everything."

'Where have I heard that before?'

A little while later, a car pulled up and two doors opened and shut. Benji went to the window. The first woman was tall

52

and striking, her long, wavy chestnut hair with silver streaks bounced with her confident walk. She moved slightly to the side then and Benji blanched as he saw who the other woman was. Kim's betrayal of him was complete.

CHAPTER TWELVE – EXPLANATIONS

Benji went to the door and watched Kim and her stunning companion approach. Kim's regret was apparent in her expression. But that didn't detract from her actions. Their eyes met.

"Benji…"

"Don't. Just don't." Benji went back to the kitchen and the two women followed.

"Kimjora. Darsh," acknowledged Long.

"Huh! To think I was listening to lectures on psychology – from a wizard. What a joke," spat Kim.

"Not at all. Observation of humanity is one of our key roles in these modern times. But I haven't asked you here to bandy insults with you. This boy…" he waved a hand at Benji, "…needs to know what this is all about. It seems only fair that he gets this from all viewpoints. Mine, as a wizard, committed to keeping clan affairs out of the human realm; yours, Kimjora, as a kelpie, equally committed to regaining your true form; and yours…" he looked at Darsh, "…as a fae, light, but having lived with the dark fae, a mother and an agent of the wizard council."

Kim turned and stared at Darsh. "You've been working with the wizards? Wait. Mother?"

Darsh was about to speak, but Long interrupted her. "You two can catch up later. Right now I think we need to give Benjamin all the information, from all viewpoints, then it is up to him what he wants to do about it."

Benji sat on a stool in the corner of the kitchen still nursing the tea mug he'd drained ten minutes earlier. He'd been looking from one face to another whilst they were talking. Right now, Long seemed the most reasonable, so he moved over to the kitchen table and sat beside him. He looked again at Kim. This woman he'd shared so much with. That he'd loved with every fibre of his being and given so much up for. But who'd been drugging him, and lying to him ever since they'd met, and who now wanted…what? Just looking at her caused a lump in his throat and made him feel utterly wretched. But he had to know. "What is it exactly that you want from me Kim? After all we've been through together can't you at least tell me that?"

"Benji. You understand that I am a kelpie?" Benji nodded. "You must surely realise by now that you are not fully human. You have fae blood. Probably only about one sixteenth, I'm not sure, but the fae genes you have are dominant."

"I think it's best we start at the beginning Kimjora," suggested Long. "Shall I take up the story?"

Kim nodded curtly.

"On other…planes of existence, shall we say, there live many races of people. We call them clans. Some light some dark. For thousands of years we lived peaceably enough, there was plenty of land for all. The dark clans were murderous, wicked people, but all the while they kept themselves to themselves, and stayed mostly in the Dark Realm, nobody troubled them. However, rumours of them mixing with humans and producing half-blood offspring abounded, though this was never proven. Anyway, over time these dark clans became greedy for more and they started to make inroads into areas occupied by the light clans. Many of the light clans are small in number. The dryads for instance. Each dryad clan occupies a single forest, and some only have a few hundred people."

"Don't forget to mention the wizard's role in all this," said Kim.

55

Long pursed his lips. "Indeed. The wizards are not clan – we are brethren, selected by The Ein…"

"The Ein?" asked Benji.

Kim interjected. "Huh! It's supposed to be some all-powerful earth magic. A bit like 'The Force' in Star Wars. Such nonsense!"

Long dismissed her comment with a sharp hand-wave before continuing. "…we… presided, shall we say, over all the clans. It was up to us to keep the dark clans at bay, maintain the peace in our lands, and to advise, settle disputes and so on. But I'm ashamed to say, we were so caught up in how important we were, we lost perspective, and we lost control. Finally the light clans took it upon themselves to band together and fight the dark clans that had come across The Boundary between the worlds. As well as the kelpies and the fae, there were, sprites, dryads, merfolk, and so on. There are numerous others all around the world. A bloody war ensued, it lasted many years, but in the end the light clans prevailed and the dark clans were killed or exiled back to the Dark Realm."

"Apart from the dark fae?" Benji asked.

"Oh no. Back then there were no dark fae. The fae worked in partnership with the Prenya kelpies, and they were the two most numerous clans. Kimjora and Darsh here were a pair, and fought together during the clan wars."

Benji gazed at Kim as he slowly adjusted to her alternative identity.

Long went on. "What you have to understand is that, in the minds of the clans, the human world was all part of their existence, they didn't see it as separate at all. Many of the people would cross into the human world, either just for a visit, but some lived a high proportion of their lives here, especially the fae. Striking as they are, they actually look pretty much human. They involved themselves in politics and the business world – you'd be surprised just how many famous people throughout human history are actually fae! Most other clans look nothing like humans, so when they visited the human world, they elicited a whole raft of stories, myths and legends." He shook his head. "But I digress. Anyway, the fae believed that as they were so successful in

56

their lives in the human world, that this meant they were superior. They believed it was their role to dominate humans." Long stopped a moment and licked his lips.

"Pop the kettle on Darsh, my throat's getting a bit dry," he said.

Darsh moved to comply.

"The kelpies, though in many ways considering themselves superior too, disagreed with the fae. They said we should not make ourselves known to the humans. The wizards were in agreement with this, and for a while kelpies and wizards worked together to try to convince the fae to back down. Kelpies and fae had a major falling out and no longer partnered one another. It was a terrible schism that should never have happened."

"But the 'balance of life' had been disrupted with the loss of so many of the dark clan folk, and The Ein will not stand for that. A proportion of the fae became dark. Their shining silver auras darkened to near black and they began to absorb light instead of emanating it. It was a sorry business for sure but this process somehow made them even stronger. A small number of fae, less than five per-cent in fact, possess magical talent. As the kelpies were now their greatest adversaries, they did a spell casting that forced the kelpies into their human form, and prevented them from returning to their natural state."

"Why? What did they have to gain by that?"

"Well Benjamin. The kelpies are strong and powerful. Even in human form they're strong, but in their natural form they are formidable indeed. The fae are powerless against them. The kelpies are determined to do two things. Stop the fae from taking over the human world, and to get their shape-shifting abilities back."

"You said the kelpies and wizards worked together."

"To stop the fae? Yes. But we also don't want the kelpies to regain what they've lost. There can only be one outcome to that. Another war. The dark fae that are left are all in the human world now, so another war would be fought right here. The wizards are determined to prevent this from happening."

Darsh spoke up then. "You do realise there are only nineteen of them left – as far as we know. It would hardly be a war. They would just take out those that remain and that would be an end to it."

Kim looked gratefully at Darsh. "Exactly."

"It's not as simple as that. Let me finish explaining to the boy." Both women nodded. Benji's face contorted to a grimace, he was getting irritated at being constantly described as 'the boy'.

"Well the kelpies, of course, always had the ability to shape-shift into human form, and when they spent time in the human world they tended toward the sciences. So they developed a drug that made the fae forget who they were. One after another they located all the fae and part-fae, light and dark that lived in the human world, and gave them a huge dose of their new drug. Mostly the fae just go about their lives completely oblivious to their own origins. They marry and have children, so now there are tens of thousands, maybe hundreds of thousands probably, we don't know for sure, of people with at least some fae blood. Anyway, it turned out that the kelpies didn't get them all. A small group of pure blood dark fae with all their memories intact, and with a serious axe to grind, formed a hub. They still breed with humans, and with each other, determined to increase their dark fae numbers. They too have moved into the world of science, and it looks like they may well find the means to reverse the kelpies' drug. They're getting close to it."

Kim's eyes widened at this revelation. "How do you know this?"

"As I mentioned before, Darsh works as an operative for the wizard council. Or at least she did. Her cover is now blown unfortunately. It'll be much harder to monitor the dark fae now."

Benji shifted uncomfortably on his stool. "Ok, thanks for the history lesson, but I still don't understand what any of this has to do with me."

Long waved a hand at Kim, and she took up the story. "Some of the descendants of the more magical dark fae, not the pure bloods, they kill them straight away apparently..." she looked briefly at Darsh, "...well some seem to have a

58

kind of residual, inherited clan memory. Not many, but those that do, start having weird dreams and flashes of memory when they reach puberty. Just as you did Benji," she said affectionately. "We can locate people like this when one of our people see their faint auras. Then an operative goes in, that would be me in your case, and spends time observing to see how it develops. We use a very mild dose of the same suppressant drug, called amnotin, is about eighty times weaker, to keep the subject oblivious. It's not an attack, Benji, it stops you from going mad. What with all those inherited memories entering your mind, and no idea where they come from. Can you imagine what that would be like if it's not suppressed? Anyway, we've been looking for someone strong enough in fae magical genes that can learn our ways, that we can teach, and that maybe, they can do a spell-casting that will restore our shape-shifting abilities. But first those genes have to be activated. You are the strongest any of us have found so far. We believe you could be the one to do this for us."

Benji looked from Kim to Long and back to Kim whilst Darsh remembered the kettle and got up to make tea. "Ok so I get why the dark fae want me out of the picture, but why is your mother chasing me down?"

Kim looked a bit contrite. "My mother wants to force you to help us. Honestly, it's always been how we planned to do this if we found the right candidate, to ensure we get what we need. But I'm determined that if you do this for us, it'll be voluntary. I do love you Benji. I want you to do this for me, because you want to. You're not just going to be a lab rat for my mother. Also there may be some risks associated with stimulating the fae genes that carry magic. We don't really know for sure."

Benji nodded and looked back to the Prof. "And you. Explain your role in this and why exactly you want to put a stop to it."

"As I said earlier. The fae are close to reversing the effects of the drug. They want to awaken the memories of all the fae in the world. I'm not sure how they plan to implement that yet, but I believe they are close to a solution. If they succeed in their plans, who knows how many of them will be dark? And if the kelpies are restored as well, a vast global battle between the two clans could easily ensue right here and it will devastate the human world. The wizards are determined to keep that from happening."

"You are a fool wizard. The quicker we restore our shape-shifting talent, the quicker we can rid the world of the dark fae. They won't be able to reverse the effects of our drug if they're all dead."

"As I said, we understand they're further along in their plans than we originally believed. It may already be too late."

"All the more reason to restore us. The humans won't stand a chance against them. We are the only ones that can fight them. Benji, hun, I want you to really think about this. I know you'll make the right decision and offer to help us."

"Benji, think what would happen if there's all an out clan war in this world," said Long.

Darsh said nothing.

CHAPTER THIRTEEN – FACTS

Benji suddenly felt as though he were the one in charge. He was holding all the cards. Everyone wanted him to do their bidding, but he would be the one to make the final decision. He was lying on the bed in the Prof's daughter's old room, where he'd slept just a couple of nights – and a lifetime ago. The clock on the wall ticked the moments by with mournful monotony. He hadn't really noticed it before, but it seemed so loud to him now. He'd locked the door to keep Kim out. He knew she be there, working on him, otherwise. But he needed to think things through on his own. The Prof seemed to understand that. Perhaps he was his best ally after all. But he's a wizard. How crazy is that? He picked up the manuscript the Prof had lent him before and started to read, this time from the beginning:

They say there's 'no smoke without fire'. It's a good analogy as human stories are replete with examples of mythical beings. Why? Because all the peoples of Elysia have travelled to the human world. They've been seen by, and they've interacted with humans, and now they've all found their places in mythology across the whole of the human world, even the elusive merfolk.

Legend has it that Elysia, also known as The Elysian Fields, was a place of beauty in the underworld created by the Greek Gods. Homer referred to Elysia in his writings, but it is believed the clans pre-dated him in the naming of this world by many millennia. The clan histories also allude to stories of the Norse and Roman Gods, the shamanic peoples from the African and South American Continents, Elders of aboriginal peoples, Chinese animal gods and the spirit guides of the First Nation Peoples of North America, Canada and across to the Northern wastes of the great Asian Continent, to name but a few. Indeed during my travels in Elysia, I have never met any clan or tribe without their own mythology describing how our world came to be…

Benji looked up from the pages, wide-eyed, thinking it wasn't any wonder this manuscript has not, and could not be published.

There was a tap on the door. "Benji, I need to talk to you."

"Go away Kim. I'm thinking."

"Come on hun, we need to have this out. I know you think I've let you down, but you have to understand. My people are at risk, and now so is everyone else, both on my world and yours."

"I said GO AWAY. I'm thinking."

"Benji!"

"The sooner you leave the boy alone to think things through and come to a conclusion, the sooner we can start to plan our next move."

Benji identified Darsh's deep, rich tones. He then heard them sniping at each other, getting quieter as they moved away from the door. "Good." He picked the manuscript up again, and flicked a few pages along. All that talk about mythological origins of Elysia wasn't going to help him make any kind of decision. He flipped further along again, then yet more, as the narrative waffled on and on. Then he came to a section about the wizards. Ok getting somewhere now…

…there were always exactly one hundred wizards. Of whom ten were 'called' by The Ein to be on the wizard's council. Each had their regions to oversee, and subjects to whom they provided guidance and counsel. The position of the wizards was never in question until their arrogance at their own omnipotence allowed the dark clans to wrest power from them and begin their march across Elysia. Sadly seventeen wizards were lost in the clan wars, and the universe has not deemed is necessary to replace them. Are the wizards destined to die out after all? Has their rule become that compromised? Is this the punishment for allowing the events that led to war? Finally a closed meeting of the wizard's council sort to answer these questions - and one more important question that troubled their minds. How is that, having destroyed the dark clans, did an element of the fae change to such a degree that they become dark? Had the war upset the natural balance and order of things? Were light and dark two sides of a balance of power that was meant to remain intact? If so, do we have the right to interfere with the dark fae's existence? In the end the council concluded that the wizards take on a new role - to live in the human world, where all the dark fae now exist, and to ensure that none of their machinations, or indeed those of the light clans, who would destroy them, interferes with human existence. The wizard's new role was that of guardians…

Benji put the manuscript back down. What was he to make of this? Clearly the wizards wanted to keep all the strife from Elysia out of his world. Getting behind that philosophy had to be the right choice. He picked up the book once more and flicked through until he came to the chapter about kelpies…

…the kelpies are without doubt the most magnificent of all the species in Elysia and one of the most numerous. However, human mythology only records them in Scotland, Wales and the Isle of Man, and describes them as vicious aquatic creatures that lure children to a watery death. Mythology, as always, has a way of distorting the facts. In reality only three true kelpie clans exist, though many sub-species are prevalent across the globe. Of the true kelpies, only the Mira and the Lochanar are aquatic and they most closely fit the description prescribed in legend. I will not elaborate about them now as they largely kept to themselves and only a few of them got involved in the clan wars. The other clan, the Prenya, are of the grassland plains and hill country. Historically they formed a close alliance with the fae that became more predominant during the clan wars. At this time they formed partnerships as the fae rode their Prenya partner into battle; formidable teams indeed, they were mainly responsible for putting down the dark clans.

All the kelpie clans have the capacity to shape-shift into human form, but whilst the Mira and Lochanar may have used this ability in the past to their own ends, the Prenya typically opted to change form in order to go unnoticed when in the human world. Their talent for luring humans and bending them to their will has not, however, depleted one iota following the fae spell-cast that rendered them incapable of changing back to their natural form, and now, with the help of a pheromone exuded from a gland behind their ear, they use this tactic to enthral pubescent humans, when the need arises in their search for part-fae with the potential for magic…

Not for the first time, Benji threw the manuscript down. This time it hit the floor. He looked at his hands then, as if they may be tainted from touching something evil. Then he looked at the bedroom door. She was out there. This beautiful woman he'd fallen in love with. Or had he? Was that what this was? Was he under her thrall? Had she used her pheromone on him? Only a week ago they were two young university students living – and loving - together in a flat in Edinburgh. It was normal. They did normal things. Went to classes, had coffee or beers out with friends, shopped for food, did laundry, watched tv. Now? Now she was an ancient mythological creature with an agenda. She was on the hunt, and he was her quarry. His favourite professor was a wizard, and there was some kind of underworld cold war going on – and somehow he, of all people, was in the thick of it. He didn't have any magic. He'd know right? What happens when she works that out, will she kill him? No. Even now she claims to care for him. Surely after all they'd been through together she did have true feelings for him. He pictured her smile, her sensuous lips brushing his own, her naked body pressed against him, the fun, the laughter. She played her

64

cittern for him, those beautiful tunes. And what if she is a kelpie. The Prof said in his manuscript that they were magnificent. If there's any way he can help them, maybe he should.

Benji could hear talking in the kitchen as he unlocked the door and headed down the hall to join the others. Kim, Darsh and the Prof sat drinking tea. They stopped and looked at him as he entered. His sense of the theatrical kept him silent as he casually poured himself a cup, stirred in the milk and sugar, pulled up a chair and grabbed a biscuit from the plate on the table. He smiled down at Tina as she sat looking up at him expectantly, her expression not unlike that of the human-like creatures around the table. It made him chuckle as he broke a piece off and passed it to her.

"Something funny young man?"

Benji looked at the Prof, then briefly at Darsh, and then turned his attention to Kim. He looked into her stunning dark brown eyes as she gazed back at him. Yes there was definitely something there. Something just for him. Finally he spoke. "I've been reading the Prof's manuscript. It says what you used to be, you know, in your natural form. It's incredible to me, way out of my comfort zone, but I want to hear your side of this story Kim, only you have to promise me that you tell it without this…mojo…thing you have over me. Then I want to talk to the fae…" he waved a hand toward Darsh, "…but not your bestie here. I want to talk to some of the others. Maybe even the dark fae…"

Kim interrupted. "Benji No! They'll kill you for sure, you can't…"

"I know I'll need some kind of protection, perhaps Darsh here can arrange for me to meet just one of them, in some kind of controlled environment." Darsh gave a sharp nod.

"Benji, hun it…"

"I have a decision to make, and I want all the facts."

The Prof piped up then. "That's not unreasonable. I'm sure it can be arranged. I do have to point out that Lucivarsh won't be inclined to stand for any of this. If she gets hold of you, she will force you into compliance. Also most of the light fae are in Elysia. Those that are in the human world

65

have lives here and don't even know what they are. It would be more prudent to talk to the light fae in Elysia."

"Then that's where we'll go. To Elysia," said Benji.

PART TWO

CHAPTER FOURTEEN – ELYSIA

Benji lay, pretending to be asleep as he listened in to the conversation between Kim and Darsh.

"If your mother gets wind of you being here with the boy, without going straight to her, she's going to have a major hissy-fit." Darsh had decided to go along to 'keep them out of trouble'.

"How will she know? I'm not going to tell her." Kim was sat on a large, flat rock with her head in her hands recovering from the shift and cursing herself for not replenishing her supplies of hawbleberry juice. Her cittern was propped beside her.

Darsh seemed unaffected, but then she was in her natural form – fae weren't shape-shifters.

Benji was laid out on the grass, eyes closed and barely conscious, but listening in to their conversation.

Darsh indicated Benji with a tip of her head. "What's with him?"

Kim said. "It's never taken much to floor him. Even a couple of beers and it's like he's been on a bender."

"I don't get it Kimjora, what do you see in him? He's just another human, and hardly the most spectacular specimen at that."

"Do you know, I've been trying to work it out for myself. He's reasonably bright, but not brainy. He's ok to look at, but not handsome. He likes a joke, but isn't that

68

funny himself. He's very average in bed. In fact he's very average in every way I can think of. Nevertheless, there's something about him I can't put my finger on. I just really like him. A lot."

Despite the brain fog, Benji felt at once indignant that Kim found him so 'average', but also slightly gratified that she actually did admit to having genuine feelings for him after all.

Darsh shook her head, frowning. "Some of your other projects have been much more comely."

"How would you know?"

"I've been watching from afar."

Benji opened one eye and saw that Kim was frowning at the implications of that. He too was pissed that she'd apparently been spying on them.

"Why didn't you talk to me before?"

"I was under instructions not to blow my cover – in any way."

"The wizards? Why would you do what they tell you?"

Darsh twisted her mouth to one side and gave her answer serious thought before speaking. "You see this is the problem Kim. If the kelpies weren't so antagonistic to the wizards they might be more agreeable about helping you getting your shape-shifting abilities back."

"Huh! I doubt that. Arrogant tossers!"

Darsh just shook her head again in exasperation.

Benji groaned.

"Hey hun. You feeling better?"

Benji sat up, squinting at the bright light, and peered around him. The landscape was lush and green, the trees full of singing birds, a small brook nearby tinkled as the water splashed over a series of small rock falls, and brightly coloured butterflies flitted about in the sunshine. "Am I dead? No I can't be. If I was in heaven I wouldn't have a thumping headache."

"Here. I only gave you a tiny sip of restorative as I didn't know how it might affect you. A little more should help clear your head. We need to get moving now." Kim waved the bottle under Benji's nose.

He sniffed it, and was about to refuse, but after that look from Kim, he snatched the bottle out of her hand and swallowed a mouthful. "It's disgusting."

"I know. It's an old batch, I need to make some more. It's actually quite nice when it's fresh. It works quicker too. Come on." Kim looked across to Darsh. "We'll need to go through Kaylen. I guess it would be a good time to go and see Arbani and Dailabi and tell them about Pylora. We'll have to keep your role in the attack from them. They won't understand."

Benji frowned once again at the strange names and events and peeved at being kept out of the loop. Kim seemed in no hurry to explain.

The three travellers headed across the meadows in the direction of the Kaylen Mountains, to the haunting sound of eagles calling from high up in the peaks. The walk to Arbani's court was a full day, but they were starting out late in the afternoon so they would need an overnight stop. They didn't encounter anyone else as they walked, and the going was easy, but finally, shortly after they started to climb in the rocky foothills, they came to a wayfarers hut just as the light was fading. The temperature dropped as the sun went down so Kim lit the fire that was already laid by the previous occupant, and put the kettle on, while Darsh unpacked buttered bread rolls, cheese and apples from her pack.

After they'd eaten, Kim played some gentle songs on her cittern. Benji loved to hear her play, but now he wondered if it was all part of the brainwashing trip she'd put him on. Still, there were worse ways to spend an evening. Suddenly he fervently wished Darsh wasn't there. Just for now it would be nice if it were just him and Kim once again.

Darsh somehow picked up on his thoughts, leaned in and spoke quietly to him. "It'll never be the same you know. Between you and Kimjora I mean."

Benji just scowled back at her.

She smiled in return, one of those annoying, knowing smiles.

Later, as they were all settled in their sleeping bags on the floor of the hut, there was a creaking sound as several pairs of feet collected on the deck outside. Benji opened his eyes wondering what the noise was. Kim and Darsh were already on their feet with knives in their hands, poised like coiled springs.

"What's going on?"

Kim put a finger to her lips to silence him.

A little more floorboard creaking, then suddenly the door flew open. Two crazy-looking characters, in royal blue uniforms, and carrying spears, came in first and took up positions to either side of the door. Then another of their kind strode in. This one seemed to be in charge. His mass of wild, silvery-white hair made him appear just a little comical to Benji's eyes. The creature took in the scene as Kim and Darsh relaxed their stance just a little though they still held their knives. Then his gaze fell on Benji. "So, this is the boy at the heart of all the fuss is it?"

"My Lord Arbani, you did not need to make this journey. We were on our way to court to see you."

Arbani turned toward Kim. "When I agreed to allow Pylora to travel to the human world with you Kimjora, it was with the understanding that you would protect her from harm."

She flinched. "It's true. I failed her and I failed you. I can't tell you how sorry I am."

Benji had no idea who this Pylora was, or how Kim could have protected her against anyone, she was just a girl. 'Well, okay, more than just a girl, but she's only one small...person.' "What's going on?"

Arbani didn't even deign to look at Benji, he just pointed a finger in his direction and boomed, "SILENCE."

'Who is this pig-ignorant troll to speak to him that way, and why is Kim calling him 'Lord'?' He opened his mouth to speak again, but Kim passed him a brief warning look and he kept his peace.

Kim said, "Lord, you need to understand what's going on..."

"You'll have the opportunity to present your case at court Kimjora." Then he turned to his guards. "Take them," he said as he strode back out the door where six more warriors waited, along with two barely tamed, fearsome

71

looking beasts. Benji peered at the creatures. They looked a bit like giant hyenas, though their coats were shaggy and pale-coloured. One pushed its head through the door, pulling on a chain that only partially restrained it. Saliva dripped from the huge canines. Benji could smell its foul breath from across the room. He shuddered as the beast caught his eye.

Darsh had taken up the stance again ready to fight, but Kim shook her head. "No Darsh. Put the knife away. I'll get this all straightened out." Kim went to sheath her own knives, but one of the guards went to take them from her. She bristled, biting her lip but then relented. Darsh held tight to her weapon, narrowing her eyes as a guard approached. He stepped back involuntarily at the sight of this muscular fae, and she grinned at the effect she had on him. After another warning look from Kim she reluctantly spun her knife and passed it, handle forward, for him to take. The guards bound their hands behind their backs and the party moved out in the dead of night.

A bright orange sunrise lit the final part of the journey to Arbani's court. The two handlers, with what Benji now knew were called broosher-hounds, were leading the way. The going was tough, the terrain getting rougher as they climbed the trail up the side of the mountain. It was not easy to negotiate with their hands tied. Benji watched as Kim seemed to recognise the smirking young gate guard as they passed by. She stared at him menacingly, but didn't speak.

A sprite woman came to the entrance hall to greet them. "Arbani, is this really necessary?" she indicated the bindings. Then her gaze fell on Benji. "This is him I take it?"

"A fae and a kelpie, even one in human-form, is a formidable pairing, and I've no wish to lose any more of my people for the sake of being a little cautious. And yes this is the one." Arbani looked Benji up and down shaking his head.

"If you were in any danger from us, sprite…" Darsh spat, "we would not have handed over our weapons so lightly."

"Darsh!" Kim admonished. Then she bowed to the woman. "My Lady Dailabi. I am so sorry for the loss of Pylora. We were attacked by dark fae."

Dailabi took a sharp intake of breath, but Arbani didn't sound convinced. "Nonsense. There are no dark fae left."

"Oh but there are. I didn't know about them either, though the wizards apparently did. They decided not to inform us. I would never have asked for a tracker had I known there were dark fae out there looking for Benji." A brief glance passed between Kim and Darsh.

Arbani and Dailabi both turned toward Benji then, but Dailabi continued to speak. "Your mother came to see us Kimjora. She was not pleased that you hired a sprite tracker without permission. She also said you would be travelling across our mountains to reach the fae clans, and asked that we detain you here with us until she arrives and can take this one…" she indicated Benji, "…into custody."

"Dailabi, no, please. You must…"

Arbani was red in the face with fury. "We must? Who are you to tell us what we must do. You lost one of our own, and we don't even have her body to cremate. You do not dictate to us." He turned. "Guards, take Kimjora and the human to guest rooms. Lock them in and put guards on the doors. Take the murderer to the dungeon and clap her in irons."

Benji had been watching this 'Lord Arbani'. Despite his words, he didn't seem a bit surprised to learn that the dark fae existed. Darsh did not go quietly and Benji could see the regret and worry in Kim's eyes.

As they were led to their rooms, Kim explained. "Putting Darsh in irons is harsh. Fae react badly to iron, it will weaken her and blister her skin wherever it touches. The main thing now is to devise a way of escaping. We then have to rescue Darsh, and we need to do all this before my mother arrives." Benji's heart sank. 'How could they possibly achieve any of that?'

Benji paced in his room. He had watched all the events of the last couple of days with grim fascination. It was all just too wild, like a scene out of Lord of the Rings. Sprites were holding him captive in fairyland! How nuts was that? Perhaps he'd wake up in a minute and be in his flat in Edinburgh, and Kim would just be his Kim again. Also, Saturday had come and gone, and he hadn't talked to his mum. They always talked once a week, whether she was at home or off on one of her highfalutin business trips, they still had their little chat about how their week went. She'd be worried. What would she do? Call the uni? Call the police? If he ever got out of this mess, where would he say he'd been? 'Well Mum, it's like this, Hobgoblins are trying to kill me. Kim's a horse that looks like a human, and she cast a spell on me. She was just taking me to the elves when a bunch of sprites threw us in the brig. Oh, and my uni teacher's a wizard by the way.' Yeah that'd work!

CHAPTER FIFTEEN – BREAKOUT

Kim was pacing too. The room she was in was high up in the building. The window opened okay and was just about big enough to squeeze through, but it was a sheer drop to the rocks below, too high for even her to jump, and the walls were smooth, so there was no way to get any purchase there. She considered trying to fight her way out when the guard at the door brought her meal. That would probably work if she only had herself to think about, but the whole court would be alerted almost immediately. She wouldn't get the chance to get Benji out of his room, especially as she had to find him first, and she definitely wouldn't be able to rescue Darsh from the dungeon. The messenger will have reached her mother by now so they only had a day, or maybe a day and a half to get away.

A stroke of luck. Following a shift change, the sprite that brought her meal that night was little more than a boy. Her special wiles might just work on one so young, though she'd never used it on any non-human before, so it was a risk. She surreptitiously rubbed the little gland behind her ear, released a small amount of her pheromone.

"What have we got tonight?" Kim asked, looking into the boy's eyes instead of at the tray.

The sprite took a step back, eyes wide. The plate rattled on the metal of the tray as his hands shook. "Um. Some sort of stew I think. It smells alright."

Kim edged up to him and lifted the lid. Steam rose from the dish beneath, and she took a deep sniff. "Mmm! Scrumptious." Raising her face their eyes met briefly. The boy looked about all around him, anywhere but at her. He was quite helpless standing there holding the tray of food, she could easily overcome him, but that wouldn't do her any good at the moment. "What's your name?"

"My name?"

"Yes your name, you have a name I presume."

"Y... yes. Tobi."

Kim dropped her voice to a deeper, sexier pitch. "Tobi? What a nice name. Do you want to sit with me while I eat, Tobi? We could share it, there's quite a lot here."

"N...no ma'am, I had my dinner already. B...but thanks."

"Well sit with me anyway. It would be nice to have someone to talk to, especially such a handsome young sprite as you. So many of the soldiers are such old, warty, grouchy miseries. Here sit. Tell me about yourself Tobi. How long have you been at court?"

Tobi sat on one end of the bed, stiff as a board, perching on the edge. "Er well, only since last summer, I'm still in training."

Kim took the tray from him and put it on the little bedside table; then she shifted along the bed to sit close to the boy. Her pheromone was beginning to take effect. She smiled. This would never have worked on one of the older sprites. A contented smile washed over Tobi's face, and his body posture eased. Kim touched the back of her ear with her forefinger, picking up a concentrated drop of pheromone. Then she gently rubbed her finger along Tobi's bottom lip. He was hers. Tobi sighed in contentment.

Kim talked to him for a little while, telling him how interesting he was, and how handsome, then she said, "You look so tired, they must be overworking you. Why don't you just rest your head for a while." She gently pulled his head down to her shoulder. Tobi's eyelids grew heavy and finally closed. Slowly she eased him down onto the bed, and grinned to see his blissful, sleepy smile as she drew his small knife from its sheath.

Kim had no idea where Benji was, but he probably wasn't far as surely the guest quarters would all be in the same area. All she had to do was find another room with a guard on it. She crept silently through the maze-like hallways. Once she had to duck into an open doorway when she heard footsteps coming her way. Hear heart skipped a beat. But no one was alerted to her escape yet, so they weren't looking for her. Two soldiers, chatting about their impending visit to the tavern, wandered past her position. She let out a breath she hadn't realised she'd been holding, and wiped a little sweat from her brow.

Finally she spotted a guard outside a locked room. It wasn't one of the guards that had brought her and Benji up to the guest rooms, so she took a chance that he wouldn't know who she was. Casually and blatantly Kim walked toward the guard smiling. "Good evening," she said.

"Ma'am." The guard nodded. There was no surprise or suspicion on his face.

"Who have you got in there then?"

"Huh! I don't know, some boy. Don't know what clan mind. He looks too much of a weakling to be fae, and too ugly to be kelpie. Don't know what he is."

Kim stifled a laugh. That a sprite, of all creatures, could think of Benji as ugly struck her as hilarious, but it was something to pack away and bring out later. Her pheromones were still emanating around her. Though she didn't think they'd have much effect on this, much older, sprite, but perhaps there'd be a little capacity for suggestion. "Can I take a look? Perhaps I'll recognise it."

The guard rubbed his chin, frowning. "Aw, I don't know ma'am. I'm not supposed to let anyone in."

He was fidgeting in a very un-soldier-like manner. Clearly he was wavering. 'This is almost too easy'. "What harm could it do? I'll just take a quick peek, you'll be right beside me to protect me if it gets aggressive."

"Ha! Aggressive? That one. No. He's no warrior."

"Well then, all the easier. Come on."

For reasons Kim knew the guard would never understand, he took the key off his belt and opened up. Benji was sat on the bed with his knees drawn up to his chin. He looked up. "Kim! Are they releasing us?"

"Oh hell!" said Kim as the guard snapped to. Benji was nothing of not consistently uncool! She shoved the door closed, and before the guard had time to react, she affected a two-footed flying kick to his chest landing on her feet after a somersault follow-through. He hit the ground with a groan. As he tried to get up, she hit him across the head with the chamber pot, splattering urine everywhere in the process.

Benji looked at Kim in amazement. "What have you done? You haven't killed him have you?"

"No. He'll just wake up with a headache." She sniffed and screwed up her face. "And a burning desire to do his laundry."

Benji was incredulous. "You're making a joke of this?"

Kim just shrugged, led him out of the room and locked the guard inside. "Now Benji, we need to rescue Darsh. I need you to keep close to me while we get down to the dungeon and find her. But if I end up having to fight, you need to back up against a wall, or better still get out of sight if possible."

"You. Fight?"

Kim threw her arms in the air. "For goodness sake. Haven't you been paying attention? I'm a warrior; it's what I do! No time to talk now. Come on, and keep as quiet as you can." Kim led Benji along the hallways until she found some narrow steps leading downwards at the end of a passage. That they were narrow, and not central, probably meant they led to staff quarters or the kitchens or something. She certainly didn't want to blunder into the Great Hall, or Arbani's private quarters. As they headed along the corridor, they heard people approaching. Kim held a finger to her mouth and pushed Benji behind a wide pillar. His eyes were wide with fear. After the footsteps passed, she laid a quick, reassuring kiss on his cheek and squeezed his arm. The startled look eased from his eyes and they moved on. There were a couple more times when they needed to hide to avoid soldiers, courtiers or staff that were moving around the court. But it was clear their escape hadn't been found out as yet.

The dungeon wasn't that hard to find, they just kept going down and down until they felt the chill of the very heart of the mountain. The light was poor, with just a sparse collection of lamps partially illuminating roughly hacked-out chambers. The solid rock walls were streaked near-white where mineral-rich water had been dripping to the slippery floors for centuries. Stalactites and stalagmites, formed over thousands of years, dominated the edges of the caverns. It was noisy too, with the sound of falling hammers. There was some kind of forge nearby. Kim could see the orange glow emanating from the direction of the falling hammers. She steered Benji in the opposite direction. Finally they started to hear other sounds, voices, crying out, beseeching in utter despair. The smell of urine, faeces, unwashed bodies and rotten food assaulted her senses. She could see the distress on Benji's face. All this was so very far removed from anything he could possibly have ever encountered. Gently she touched his arm in encouragement, but he jumped as if bitten. "Come on hun. Darsh must be nearby." He turned a grim face toward her and nodded.

Kim looked inside a number of cells, but they were either occupied by sorry-looking sprites, or they were empty. Finally they came to a wide chamber. Darsh was the only one chained to the wall. No one else seemed to be about. She had to stop Benji from rushing in headlong. Her suspicious nature made her cautious, and had kept her alive on many occasions. The side of the cavern was in almost complete darkness, so Kim indicated to Benji to stay where he was while she sidled along the wall. Still no one came. 'Strange!' She reached the barely conscious Darsh and used the point of the sharp little knife she'd extracted from the guard, currently resting in her 'guest room', to pick the lock and release her friend. Darsh slumped to the floor, and Kim beckoned Benji to come over and help. Darsh could barely stand. Her wrists were blistered, her face swollen, and her lower lip was bleeding. She'd taken a beating. Kim was furious with Arbani. There hadn't been any kind of hearing. This treatment was unacceptable even by sprite standards. He would pay for this.

"Benji, help me lift her. Try to be careful, I have a feeling they wouldn't have stopped at a cut lip." Benji slid his arm across Darsh's back and tried to lift. She cried out in pain. Kim hissed. "Broken ribs." Slowly the two of them got her up and moving, and they headed for the sloping passage that led back up to where they'd seen the forge.

"Your reputation is well deserved I see," said Arbani from the bottom of the steps that should have led to their freedom.

CHAPTER SIXTEEN – WAITING

"Arbani. Torture? I thought you were better than this," spat Kim. Benji had never seen this side of her. Suddenly any doubts he'd harboured about her warrior status went out the window. With her tight, slightly torn clothes, grubby skin, yet shiny from sweat and the menacing look in her eyes, she appeared terrifying – and oh so smoking hot!

"Ah! You misunderstand the situation. The prisoner broke free of her guard, and it took four of them to subdue her. Believe me, they are in no better shape. I have to say, even impaired by the iron, this fae creature was most impressive."

Arbani's light, conversational tone just served to wind Kim up even further. "How dare you even think to pin another Elysian to a wall like this without a proper trial?"

The easy-going manner immediately dropped, and Arbani raised his chin and stood tall. "This is my realm kelpie. I dare all I want in this place. You are in no position to get snippy with me. I've a mind to put all three of you in irons…"

"You wouldn't dare. My mother…"

"Your mother will be here within the hour. I suggest you save your indignation for her. Oh, and Kimjora, after she takes you away from here…don't come back. Not ever. Guards, lock them in a cell."

"Arbani, you…" but he was gone.

Darsh curled up in a ball on the pallet in the cell and didn't move, while Benji and Kim sat next to each other the floor, propped up against the wall, knees pulled up to their chests.

"I thought sprites were of the light clans," commented Benji frowning.

Kim looked surprised. "They are."

"But... all this..." he waved his arm about, "...beatings? Locking people up in a cell? All seems pretty dark to me."

Kim frowned as she tried to find an explanation. "Would you say humans were light or dark?"

"I don't know. Some and some I guess."

"And yet somehow all the same?"

"Hadn't really given it much thought I s'pose."

Kim sighed and rubbed her chin. "Let me put it another way. People have dark sides to them, yet they are largely good. They help each other, and yet they go to war. Some humans are killers, but most just want to go about their lives...what I'm trying to say is that 'light' isn't always good. Sprites are good people that sometimes do bad things. I guess that applies to most folk. There would have to be a fundamental change in who they are for them to go dark on us."

"Like the dark fae?"

"Yes. The dark fae sap energy from the living world around them – from The Ein. They've lost any conscience they once had. If you think of it in human terms, they have no souls."

Benji shivered at the thought. "So are all the fae in Elysia light, or are there dark fae here too?"

"No. They can't live here and go unnoticed. Anyway, if anyone of the clan folk tried to completely supress their aura here, they'd stand out like a sore thumb. You must have noticed this by now, even though the auras are faint, of course, except when someone's in a heightened state of stress or happiness – or any emotion really." Benji nodded, Kim continued. "If the dark fae were here, they would be pulling light and energy from all around. Everyone would just home in on them."

Benji was quiet for a while, but the burning question that had been tugging away at him needed to be asked. "Kim, what's going to happen to me when your mother takes me away?"

Kim looked deep into Benji's eyes. "I won't let anyone harm you hun. I promise."

"But what are they going to actually do to me?"

Kim frowned as she struggled to find an explanation. "I don't really know. Kelpies have become scientists over the centuries. I think it's some kind of gene therapy to stimulate the fae DNA into action. Honestly, I've never asked how it works. I'm not sure they know themselves, we've been such a long time searching for the right person."

"But why me? I'm just an ordinary bloke – a human."

"Oh you have fae in you, believe me. You are descended from one of the fae that had magic. It's very rare. None of the light fae that we've ever been able to locate in the human world have any magic, not any more that is…" she hesitated before continuing, "…we think that all the fae with magic became dark, though we can't be certain."

A shiver pulsed through Benji's body. "So you think I'm descended from a dark fae? And…and you want to stimulate that trait in me?"

"Once, all the fae were light. Those with magic were light. There's no reason to assume you won't be light when they… do whatever it is they're going to do."

"And no reason to assume I will be either!"

"Benji, hun, you're a good guy. A really good guy. I don't believe there's any dark in you at all."

A shout went up outside at the approach of travellers. Benji gave Kim a worried look knowing the time had come. Kim's mother had arrived. Kim gently squeezed his arm. Darsh stirred and tried to sit up. Kim went to her side and helped her into a sitting position. She sounded exhausted. "Lucivarsh?"

"Yes," replied Kim.

Footsteps came down the hallway. Kim stood and took up position beside Benji as they both faced the door. A gentle thud, and a rattle of keys and the door swung open.

CHAPTER SEVENTEEN – RESCUE

Darsh managed to push herself up from the bed and shuffle over to join Kim and Benji facing the door. They stood in line awaiting whatever plans Lucivarsh had in mind for them. One figure strode in.

"Professor Long?" Benji was incredulous. The Prof looked so different dressed in a full-length purple robe tied at the waist with a wide, ornate leather belt. As he pushed back the large hood, his rich purple aura spilled into the room encompassing all four of them. A cold wave passed through him. His head spun and he could barely breathe. Time seemed to stand still. He couldn't see the others. He couldn't see anything. Panicking, he reached for Kim, but instead of her warm arm his hand met something solid, rough and cold. He struggled to remain conscious, determined not be rendered helpless, as so often seemed to happen to him. A sharp pains shot through his hand as it scraped down the hard surface. Then he was on his knees. The purple haze slowly dissipated.

He was kneeling outside on a rock ledge. There was a freezing wind howling eerily through the peaks. He looked at the snow, it's purity marred by the red smear where his hand was bleeding from contact with the sharp rock. Standing up Benji looked around. He was alone, his body shaking uncontrollably from the cold. Moving over to the edge of a precipice, his head swam as he caught momentary glimpses through the swirling whiteout from the top of the mountain. "Shit," he said out loud.

"Benji? Is that you?"

Benji, followed the sound around a corner of the ridge, but couldn't see anything as the blizzard blew up around him. "Darsh? Are you ok?" He found her huddled between two large boulders barely keeping out of the tempest. Darsh was weak. Somehow he had to find better shelter for them both.

Darsh's voice was barely more than a choked whisper. "Where are Kim and the wizard?"

"I don't know. I'm going to have a look around, see if I can find somewhere out of this wind, then I'll try to find them."

Darsh nodded.

A short distance away Benji found an overhang. It wasn't ideal, but it was in the lee of the wind. He went back to get Darsh. She had slid further to the ground and her eyes were shut. Once again panic pulsed through his body. He put his fingers to her neck, but they were too numb to feel anything. Her eyes flicked open making Benji jump. He breathed a sigh of relief. Helping Darsh to her feet, he grabbed her arm and slung it across his shoulder. He practically had to drag her to the overhang, and gently helped her to the ground on a spot that was protected, at least a little, from the swirling snow being whipped up by the relentless wind. This was probably a worse fate than he had previously been facing before he was unceremoniously rescued.

Benji took one more look at Darsh, she nodded, and he headed back out into the fray. After half an hour or so, he headed back the way he'd come. He'd seen nothing, it was a total whiteout. The best they could do was to huddle together for what little warmth that might provide, and hope the others found them before they died in this bleak place.

Slowly Kim's echoing voice penetrated through the booming wind. "BENJeeeeeee."

Benji prised open encrusted eyelids. "Kim?"

"Can you stand?"

Benji made several attempts to stand. Stiff and freezing he turned over and got onto his hands and knees. Taking a few deep breaths, he walked his hands along the wall of the overhung rock until he gained sufficient purchase to push himself up. Kim gave him a bit of a boost from behind, but, numb as he was, he only realised he'd had help when her hands dropped away. 'Darsh!' He looked down to where he'd last seen her. She was gone.

"It's alright. The wizard thinks we made it in time. He's jumped her to a healer in the Vaskra Forest. As soon as she gets really pissed off at being tended to by the dryads, we'll know she's on the mend! The wizard will be back for us soon."

Benji sighed his relief.

"You saved her life you know, and she'll never forget that."

Benji wasn't sure he wanted Darsh to think she was in any way indebted to him. Right now though, he was so cold, he couldn't concentrate on anything else, at least not until Kim leaned in and kissed him on the lips. 'How was she so warm?' Slowly his muscles eased and his face and hands began to ache as a little body heat found its way into his extremities.

Benji jumped as, out of nowhere, the Prof appeared. He didn't say a word, he just swamped the three of them amidst his purple aura. Benji succumbed to exhaustion and sank into darkness.

*****

Bird song and the sound of rushing water drew Benji up from the depths into consciousness. At first he didn't open his eyes, he just wanted to quietly enjoy the warmth of the sun on the side of his face. Vaguely he wondered why only one side of his face was getting the sunshine. Finally he opened his eyes and attempted to move. He was swinging. Someone had let him sleep it off in a hammock slung between two trees. The sun was now low in the sky, so the tree canopy no longer shaded his position. He clambered awkwardly out and fell to the ground. He quickly scanned the immediate space to see if anyone had seen his undignified exit from the hammock, but there was no one in sight. He went looking for Kim and the Prof.

The sunlit glade nestled at the base of an escarpment. A waterfall tumbled down from its crest into a river that was lined with oak and willow trees, and to one side gave way to a small cluster of round, whitewashed huts. He walked over to one of them approaching a mature, thin woman who was sweeping the surrounding deck with a besom broom.

"Er, excuse me. Madam. Hello."

She continued sweeping. He got a little closer.

"Um, hello. Could you tell me where I might find Kim and Professor Long…um…I mean the wizard?"

The woman stopped sweeping and looked at him. Her penetrating eyes examined Benji up and down and she pointed to another hut on the far side of the track that led away from the settlement toward a great forest. She went back to her sweeping.

Benji followed her direction, as he did so he called back to her. "Thank you."

"Ah, you're awake Benjamin." The Prof was sitting in a comfortable chair with his feet up on a big leather pouffe, drinking from a goblet. He still had his purple robe on. The hood was down, only now he wasn't emanating that startling, bright aura, or at least, Benji thought, not much of it. There was still a slightly purplish shimmer around his head.

He frowned with effort as he tried to focus on it.

"Ah! I see you're beginning to recognise auras. Tell me can you see Kimjora's at all? It's really quite magnificent when full, though somewhat diminished when she's in her human form."

Benji turned and saw Kim stretched out on big, well-stuffed, green sofa. Her goblet sat empty on a small table beside her. He cocked his head to one side as he looked at her. Was there a light around her, or was that just the golden evening sunlight coming in through the window? Or maybe just brain-fog after everything he'd been through. He decided not to commit himself to answering that just at the moment. His stomach grumbled. "Is there anything to eat? I'm starving."

Kim answered. "There's food laid out on the kitchen table. Be a love and bring me one of those little apple pies would you hun?"

Benji went into the kitchen and found some chicken pieces, bread and butter and boiled eggs. Piling his plate with some of each, though avoiding the watercress salad, he grabbed a pie for Kim and went back into the main room.

Kim sat up and swung her legs round to give him a sitting space as he handed over the pie.

She looked at him closely. "How are you feeling now?"

"Better. How did we get here, and what was all that excursion up to the mountain peak all about?"

Long answered. "We wizards have certain… talents, though I have to say that transporting you all out of Arbani's court and up to the peak of Mount Kamia was no mean feat, even for me, but it was necessary, you know, line of sight? It took me a while to recoup before I could home in on where you and Darsh landed. Then, of course, I had to transport her to the dryads in Vaskra Forest, before coming back for you two and bringing you here."

"And where is here?"

"We are in the Hamlet of Daeburn, close to the edge of the Cheylor Forest. Lovely isn't it? One of my favourite places in Elysia."

"So why did you rescue us?"

"As I've explained before, it is the role of wizards to oversee and maintain balance. I will not have Lucivarsh snatching you away to satisfy her own ends. You wanted to talk to the fae, and so you shall. They are about eight days walking in that direction…" he pointed in the general direction of the forest, "…but if we can secure some ponies in the next village we can shorten that by several days. We leave first thing in the morning."

Benji started to wonder if all this was such a good idea.

CHAPTER EIGHTEEN – JOURNEY

The three travellers left the hamlet of Daeburn early the next morning on foot. Within half an hour they were following a track through a dense forest of huge broad-leaved trees. Benji gazed at the portly old Prof, wondering if he was up to a lengthy journey like this. He cocked his head to one side as he watched him from behind. Long's pace seemed odd somehow. It was like his feet weren't quite touching the ground, and at each step, he seemed to glide just a little further than the stride he should have taken him. It was fascinating. Benji was so distracted that he tripped over a protruding root and ended up flat on his face.

Kim sighed. "For goodness sake, can't you even walk in a straight line without getting yourself into trouble?" She stopped and helped him to his feet.

"Have you seen how he walks?" said Benji pointing to the Prof.

"He's a wizard," Kim answered as if that explained everything. "Come on, let's catch up."

"Wait. Something that's been bugging me. His aura is a deep purple. Does that make him dark fae?"

Kim stopped in her tracks. She looked positively scandalised. "Of course not. He's a wizard!"

"So you keep saying, as if I'm supposed to know what that entails."

"Wizards are neutral. Haven't we been saying that over and over? They can't be light or dark. They are the very embodiment of balance and neutrality. They always look at all sides of any argument. Quite annoying actually when you know your cause is just."

Benji smiled at the way Kim had taken that opportunity to press her own case. They started walking again, but he continued with his questions. "So does everyone in Elysia have an aura?"

"Of course, well everyone apart from the humans that is, very few humans emanate auras, not unless they have a little Elysian somewhere in their background."

"Humans? Someone said before there were humans here."

"Yes, many humans live in Elysia, especial over in the eastern coastal areas."

"How did they get here?"

Kim shrugged. "It varies I suppose. Some were brought as workers by fae landowners. Others have been here for generations. They chose to come when some Elysian or another revealed themselves to them. Many, as I've said, have at least a bit of Elysian in them, and probably just found their own way here."

Benji scratched his head, frowning. "And wizards are the only ones that are neutral. Everyone else is light or dark, but all the dark clans have been driven out. Is that right?"

"Well almost. The dragons are neutral too. They have deep red auras. There are also some obscure light-dark hybrids that live in some of the more remote regions."

Benji grabbed Kim's arm and forced another stop. "Dragons? You're kidding!"

Kim gazed at him for a moment. "So you've accepted the existence of kelpies, fae, sprites, wizards and so on, taking them in your stride with hardly a blink of an eye. But you don't find dragons believable?"

"Surely they're just a myth."

"In the human world, we are all just a myth. What's the difference?"

"Well. You know. DRAGONS! Talking, breathing fire, collecting gold and jewels."

Kim brushed his hand away and snorted. "Don't be ridiculous. If they breathed fire they'd burn themselves. Myths and legends have a way of exaggerating. Their saliva is acidic and toxic, so if they spit at you, it would certainly burn and probably kill you. We think the Komodo Dragon is actually a descendent of some of the eastern dragons. They can kind of talk, but it's more like a series of distinct sounds that have meaning. It takes a while to learn their 'language', if you can describe it as that. I guess it's a bit like the complex whistles and calls of dolphins, but they certainly haven't evolved voice boxes. As for collecting, well there's some truth in that. They seem to like shiny things, somewhat like a jackdaw I suppose."

"Are they dangerous?"

"I guess so. It's rare they come into contact with other Elysians. Sometimes you can see them flying high up in the mountains apparently, though I've never seen one. The wizards are the only ones who visit them. Professor Long there is actually The Wizard of Mount Laskala. That's the highest peak in the Crusians, so he's probably spent time with the dragons. Why don't you ask him?"

An inexplicable rush of excitement washed through Benji at the thought of communing with dragons. "I will." Right now, though, the Prof was bent on keeping his own counsel. Benji was aware when it was the right and the wrong time to trouble him with questions.

After about three hours they came to a large clearing in the forest where a substantial village stood.

"This is Oakwood Glade," said Long.

Some of the buildings were similar to the huts in Daeburn, others were larger, multi-roomed houses made of timber. There was also a smithy, a stable, a water mill beside a river, a bakery, a series of shops and an inn, and sheep grazed in another clearing on the outskirts of the village. Benji and Kim followed the Prof into the inn where he ordered coffee and cake for all of them.

"Coffee? Do they grow coffee in Elysia?"

The innkeeper, a jolly woman with a huge amount of ginger hair piled on top of her head, overheard him. "Of course not young man," she replied, "every once in a while I

91

jump across to the human world and go to Tesco's." Benji stared at the woman. At the mention of something as mundane as a supermarket, reality, his reality, once again filtered through into his psyche. He thought about his mum. She must be going frantic by now. She's probably got the police searching for him. He drank his coffee and ate a slice of carrot cake, worry gnawing at him.

Kim tuned in to his distress. "What is it hun?"

"Oh, I was just thinking about my mum."

She gave his arm a sympathetic squeeze.

"You two go and get provisions for three days travel. I'll go and sort out borrowing some ponies." With that Long was out the door.

"Why can't he just zap us to where we're going, you know with his purple haze thing?" asked Benji.

"Huh! If only. It's emergency use only – wizards code or something. All that power, and the only thing limiting what they do is themselves. It's always seemed daft to me."

"Probably as well. What was it Baron Acton said? 'Power corrupts and absolute power corrupts absolutely.'"

"Well, I would consider their 'absolute' inability to be corrupted is one of their main faults. But that's just me I suppose."

Benji wasn't sure if she was joking or not.

Long led three sturdy ponies into the village square where Benji and Kim were waiting for him. After distributing the supplies into the saddlebags, Kim leapt onto the back of a chestnut mare. Long climbed onto his black gelding, whilst Benji stood looking helplessly at the grey mare he was expected to ride for the next three days.

"Never ridden before Benjamin?"

"No Sir."

"You'll get the hang of it. Come on, up you get."

Benji put one foot in the stirrup, swung his other leg over the back of the pony, and half slid down the other side.

The pony had clearly detected her burden wasn't going to be the one in charge of their partnership, and she whinnied and back-stepped a few paces.

"Stand still," Benji demanded.

92

Kim was going red in the face in an attempt to supress her mirth.

He gave her an annoyed look, and finally managed to slide himself into the proper position, quickly putting his other foot into the stirrup before the mare had a chance to offload him. He glanced up to find a number of villagers watching, either in amusement. Benji scowled and kicked his heel into the pony's flank. "Gee up."

The pony huffed in disgust, but didn't move.

That was it. Kim finally let her laughter fly, as tears rolled down her cheeks. "Gee up? Really? What are you four?"

Benji was still scowling.

Long shook his head. "Enough of this. Come on, we need to get some miles behind us before nightfall." He took off at a modest trot, with Kim right behind him. Benji's bounced along in the saddle as his mount followed the other ponies, and they re-entered the forest.

The rough road through the forest seemed never-ending to Benji. A few times he drifted into a half-doze once they'd slowed to walking pace, but each time was rudely awakened by thin, leafy branches that stretched across the road. He'd been brutally attacked by biting insects. His bum, back and legs were sore and he was feeling grumpier by the minute.

In contrast the Prof and Kim seemed to be having a marvellous time. Chatting, laughing, pointing out birds and insects along the way.

He scowled. 'How could they be so cheerful?'

As the sky darkened, Long picked up the pace. "We still have a few miles to the next wayfarers hut," he called back to Benji. As if things couldn't have got worse, the faster trot made him bob around even more on the pony's back.

Kim neatly turned her mount, came back and took up a position alongside Benji. "I'm going to have to give you a quick crash course in rising to the trot before we set out tomorrow. That must be very uncomfortable."

"Huh! It certainly is. I never knew it was possible to be numb and in pain at the same time."

Kim looked at him in surprise. "I meant it must be very uncomfortable for this poor pony having you bobbing around on her back like that."

Finally they arrived at the hut, and Benji all but fell out of the saddle onto the ground. All he wanted to do was to go and find a nice comfy bed.

Kim was having none of that. "We need to rub the ponies down, put their blankets over them for the night and make sure they have plenty of food and water. Only then do we attend to our own needs. I'll do mine and the wizard's, you just concentrate on yours. She'll work better with you tomorrow if you look after her well tonight. Oh, and Benji, talk to her."

Benji watched Kim for a few minutes, taking her lead, then started on his mare. He wasn't sure what to say to her, but decided it wouldn't really matter, as she wouldn't understand anyway. He just started talking. "So horse. You and me in the forest. Who'd have thought eh? You wouldn't like it where I come from. Busy streets, full of cars and busses, noise, hundreds of people, all rushing about…" He glanced at Kim and watched her grooming technique. He tried to mimic her brisk, yet gentle brushes. She was talking to her mare in quiet tones, he couldn't hear what she was saying, so he went back to his own one-way conversation, "…we've got a couple more days together. Well actually probably more as we have to come back too of course…I'm sorry if my clumsy riding hurts you. It is my first time you know…" Kim had finished and moved on to the gelding. "…are we good? Only we've got a whole day at it tomorrow." Almost as if the pony had understood his words, she whinnied and nodded her head up and down. He stood back and stared at her. Normally he'd have put that down to coincidence, but things were different here. He looked over to Kim. "Did you see that? I asked her a question and she nodded."

"Benji, hun, it's just a horse." He felt like saying 'well so are you' but he thought better of it.

94

CHAPTER NINETEEN – MISSING

It was the second night and Kim was enjoying the journey through the forest. The wizard, who she first knew as Professor Long, turned out to be quite entertaining company, full of amusing anecdotes. He also had a profound knowledge of the plants and invertebrates that occupied the wood. She'd never had much truck with wizards before. For one thing, they seemed bent on stopping the kelpies from regaining their true form. Perhaps out here in the wilds, he'd be a little more relaxed and candid about that. She determined she would bring it up after sleepyhead Benji had gone off to bed.

That night, as they sat with a jug of beer in front of the small fire in the hearth, she raised the subject. "So wizard, tell me. Why are the wizards really so determined to stop us from regaining our natural form?"

Long looked at her for a few moments, clearly trying to make his mind up about something. Finally he spoke. "Firstly my true name is Longmarrino…"

Kim's eyes widened and she took a sharp intake of breath. To be given a wizard's true name was an honour beyond imagining, and an indication of trust. This was most unexpected.

"…please, continue to call me Long, it has a degree of accuracy, doesn't entirely give me away to those that do not deserve to know my name, and actually, I'm used to it. I've been a university professor and an author for a very long time under that name. To answer your question, I would love to see the kelpies restored to full glory. I miss seeing the great herds of your people on the Plains of Garemon. You of all people, Kimjora, deserve that. But you have to understand about the great balance of life. Think about it. What happened when the light clans wiped out most of the dark clans?" he didn't wait for her to answer, "immediately new dark clans, well, one new dark clan arose. The balance is still only partially restored. You won't want to hear this, but we believe more clans may yet go dark, and if the last of the dark fae are killed by the kelpies after your strength and power is restored, then who will be next? Many of the kelpies have become powerful over time, even in human form. There's a new hierarchy in the kelpie clans as certain…elements grab more and more power. It is the opinion of the wizard council that these are the people that will go dark next in order to restore the balance of nature."

Kim stared at Long. A whole range of emotions passed through her in turn. Incredulity, anger, fear, denial, and finally realisation as his meaning hit home. "My mother. You're talking about my mother!"

"She would have taken Benjamin and used him against his will to gain her own ends. She had no thought for the morality of that and no consideration for the consequences. Kimjora, she is already half way there. Can you imagine if she and her cohort became dark AND regained their power? They would immediately begin to spread their darkness through Elysia, and no one would be able to stop them, not even the wizards. This is one side of an argument that Benjamin needs to be told if he is to have a balanced view in order to make his decision."

Kim was more than a little cross. In many ways she wanted to deny the wizard's words, but at the same time, could what he was saying be possible? "Fine," she snapped, "I'll go and get him and we'll discuss it with him."

"What do mean, gone?"

Kim was frantic. "I thought he was asleep in the bedroom, but he's not there. I've looked all around the cabin and the stable. I called out, but got no answer. He's just gone!"

"Dammit. We're on the borders of Wood Nymph country now. Whatever would possess him to go wandering off? You did warn him about the Wood Nymphs?"

"Well no. There didn't seem much point when we're keeping company with a wizard. I guess I'd have mentioned them on the road tomorrow."

"Kimjora, your feelings for this human boy has addled your mind. You're a kelpie warrior first and foremost. 'Caution Above All' is one of the kelpie mantras is it not?"

She felt a little embarrassed. The wizard was right - she had lost perspective. "Well, it's no good crying over spilt milk, we have to find him before those bloody nymphs start playing with him."

"Oh, they won't do him any real harm, they're mischievous rather than dangerous. The issue here is that Lucivarsh will be on his trail, and she'll be able track him more easily now he's outside of my protective shield. We'll never find him in these woods in the dark, we'll head out at first light."

CHAPTER TWENTY – CAPTIVE

Benji was pinned to the ground in a small clearing. Many thin, woven, green fibre ropes held him in place, and there were at least twenty or so small people standing around staring joyfully at him, and perhaps another dozen sitting on a nearby low branch. There were numerous lamps on the ground and in the trees lighting up the little glade. He tried to move, but found he was held fast. He felt like Gulliver in Lilliput, and pictured the image that matched his current predicament from Swift's Gulliver's Travels. It was one of the first books he'd ever read. He started laughing manically as the absurdity of his situation. His captors jumped back in surprise. These people, however, weren't miniscule like the Lilliputians, they were, at a guess, between a foot and a half to two feet tall, all very lithe-looking and as far as he could tell from his limited viewpoint, all female.

"What do you want from me?" he demanded. Some of the small folk leapt back again as if shocked to hear him speak. A couple of others looked meaningfully at each other, grinned, then came closer and poked him with sticks. "Hey! Stop that." They all started laughing. Slowly they gained confidence, and soon he was surrounded by these creatures, all poking, laughing and even climbing on him. Many were drinking from wooden goblets, and some even seemed intoxicated. He tried shouting at them, cajoling them, reasoning with them, but they just laughed all the more. His only comfort was the lightening sky. Morning. Kim and the Prof will be out looking for him. "They'll be a wizard and a kelpie along soon, looking for me." At that, many of his captors looked frightened, putting their hands to their mouths, or throwing up their arms. Benji couldn't help but find these people comical, but he'd clearly got through to them. "They won't be happy with you…people," he warned. For a moment they were quiet, then they started chatting amongst themselves. Then some shrugged and they all resumed their previous tormenting behaviour.

"Well well well. What do we have here?"

Benji managed to shuffle a little to one side and turn his head just enough to see the source of the new voice. Lucivarsh! 'Oh hell!' a shiver of cold helplessness journey swiftly through his whole body.

"Perhaps I should thank the Wood Nymphs. They've certainly made things easier for me."

Wood Nymphs. So that's what they were. Benji looked around, they'd all melted into the forest. Still pinned to the ground and helpless, his predicament had definitely taken yet another a turn for the worse. Lucivarsh stood above him, holding her horses' rein and smiling down at him, but with no real amusement apparent in her eyes. There were six other, still mounted, grinning people in the clearing. No five. One other saddle was empty, he guessed that was for him.

"Well, you've certainly sent me on a merry dance young Benjamin. But now you're coming with me." She indicated to one of the other kelpies. "Cut his bindings and get him mounted. Quickly, before that meddlesome wizard shows up."

"Too late Lucivarsh, this meddlesome wizard is already here." Long and Kim climbed down from their saddles and strode into the clearing.

Lucivarsh didn't look at the wizard. Her gaze fell on Kim and she slowly shook her head. "That a daughter of mine would betray her people."

"I am not the betrayer Mother. You are. I found and identified this boy. It was never the way of our people to force others against their will. We are not of the dark clans. Look at what you have become."

99

"He is just one human boy, and not the first whose life you've ruined I might add. He could be the one to restore our full glory. Do you think I want him harmed?"

"I think he has to make his own decision based on all the facts. I'm confident he'll make the right one."

"Kimjora, we've waited centuries for the right person to come along. We can't risk losing this opportunity."

"I'm sorry Mother. It has to be done this way."

Benji listened to the conversation, fascinated by the interaction between Kim and her mother, and still a little disturbed that his girlfriend was centuries old. He knew before then of course, but actually hearing her mother say it out loud really brought the fact crashing down on him.

Long spoke then. "Lucivarsh. I don't know why you have pursued this boy. You are fully aware that he is now under my protection. We are taking him to Rimor City. There he will learn everything he needs to know before he decides if he will help you or not."

"Oh, and you won't influence that decision at all of course," her voice dripping venom.

"You are fully aware that the wizards are neutral."

"So if, as you say, this boy should hear all sides, when does he get to hear mine?"

"He will get the kelpie view point from Kimjora."

"Huh! The betrayer."

"I happen to know that she is highly motivated. She too wishes to have her shape-shifting abilities restored. Now. I'm done with this conversation. Go home Lucivarsh. I will brook no further argument from you."

With one last look at her daughter, Lucivarsh mounted and led her team away.

"Hellooo," said Benji. "Is someone going to untie me?"

Kim got out her knife and cut through the bindings, but at the same time addressed Long. "She won't go home. You know that, right? She'll follow at a distance and take up any opportunity to reacquire Benji."

"I know. We need to keep him close from now on. Now Benjamin. Tell us what happened."

Benji couldn't hide his embarrassment. "I couldn't sleep. I heard you two talking, though I couldn't make out what you were saying. It was just a fuzz of voices and it kept me awake. I didn't want to disturb you, so I went out the window. I just wanted to get some air. At first it seemed so quiet in the forest. Then the cicadas started calling. It reminded me of holidays in Asia with my mum when I was a kid, kind of comforting really. I just started wandering toward the sound, but the call changed. It was more like music…" a knowing look passed between Kim and the Prof, "…I just couldn't help finding out where it was coming from. The closer I got the more beautiful the music. Then I felt a sharp prick on my neck…" he lifted his hand to the spot as he remembered that detail, "…and the next thing I knew I woke up tied to the ground surrounded by those annoying nymphs. Of course I didn't know what they were at the time." He looked at Kim then. "It seems that musical enchantment and rendering people unconscious is common practice for Elysians."

Kim winced. "I'm never going to live that down am I? The binding the nymphs used to tie you down is made from the aerial roots of the Jintor Tree. It's indigenous to this forest. I used the same tough roots to make the strings for my cittern, and the body of the cittern is made from the wood of the tree, it's what gives it that rich reddish-brown colour. Anything made from Jintor wood is very rare. No one cuts the trees down, only when one falls in a storm, or is struck by lightening is the wood available to use. Even then there's a great deal of demand for it, so it's hard to get hold of."

Benji looked at the gear stowed on Kim's pony, only just realising the instrument wasn't there. "Your cittern?"

"It's still in Arbani's court. Somehow I need to retrieve it, but I'm banished from that land now."

Benji looked at her sympathetically, He knew how much it meant to her. He turned to face Long. "Perhaps the Prof can get it for you?"

"Mmm! Well, I'm not exactly flavour of the month with the sprite lord either you know. Right now we have more important things to think about. Come on. I would like to get to Winsomebrook before nightfall. There we can swap these ponies for some larger mounts. Tomorrow we ride for Rimor."

CHAPTER TWENTY-ONE – RIMOR

Benji normally he liked being amongst trees, but his recent experience with the wood nymphs left him yearning for wide open spaces. Following his chat with the mare, that he'd decide to name Snowy, and his quick crash course in riding from Kim, his time on horseback went a little more smoothly. He still ached like hell.

"She probably already has a name you know," Kim told him.

"Well it wouldn't have hurt if the Prof had bothered to find out what their names actually are."

"I think I had more important things on my mind at the time," came Long's voice from up ahead. Kim smiled at Benji. Despite everything he now knew about her, and her motivations for entering into his life, that electrifying smile still melted him. He grinned back.

They trotted comfortably into Winsomebrook with the sun still fairly high in the sky. Benji was feeling a little more positive now the trees had given way to rolling hills, low bushes and tumbling streams. The aroma of roasting meats coming from a building close by a large longhouse made his mouth water, but he knew he had to tend to Snowy before he could satisfy his own hunger and thirst.

"You kids get us some rooms at the inn once you're done at the stables. I'm going to get the latest 'news off the presses' so to speak from Jumor."

"Jumor?"

"Village head man." Kim was frowning.

"What's up?"

"Well firstly, I'm hardly a kid. I'm only a few years short of seven hundred by now I think. Not that that really matters. But I know what Jumor's like. Never stops talking, he's a terrible gossip. What he has to say will be coloured by his own opinions, and washed down with copious amounts of ale. Likely we won't see the wizard until morning, and he'll be grumpy with a hangover by then."

Benji gazed at Kim. He still hadn't got past the revelation of her age, and was a bit surprised that she wasn't too sure exactly what it was herself. "You look about twenty." A memory of their sexual antics flashed through his mind. He knew she'd been around a while, but... 'no wonder she finds me so average in bed - all the experience she must have had.' How could he compete with seven hundred years worth of lovers? Almost as if she'd heard his thoughts, she grinned and winked at him.

As Kim had predicted, Long looked like hell the next morning. Benji tried to reconcile the university Prof he'd known with the bleary-eyed, unshaven, dishevelled man slumped in the saddle of his new black mount.

Kim wanted to know if his binge had been worthwhile. "So did you get anything of value from Jumor?"

Long didn't speak for a while. Finally he turned red-rimmed eyes on her. "We'll discuss it over lunch. I'm mulling things over at the moment."

"Huh!" Kim's expression was lofty. She was clearly not convinced by that excuse to be left alone.

They found a nice spot by a stream to stop for lunch. There were convenient large flat boulders there, where Kim could lay out the cold meats, bread and cheese they'd procured before leaving Winsomebrook, and they used stream water to boil for the coffee Long had stashed in his saddlebag.

"Well?" Kim asked as she perched on the edge of a rock nursing her coffee mug and eating her cheese roll.

Long sighed, his eyes weren't quite so red now, but they did look rheumy. The drinking had taken its toll on the old

103

wizard. "You know what Jumor's like. I got a tirade of nonsense about who's sleeping with whom, and how much wealth this or that person has made at the trade markets. But I got a few snippets of information that may be of value. The fae know about the dark fae in the human world. It's rumoured that they knew all along and kept quiet about it; I'll be asking Zebrella about that when I see her. Anyway, they apparently believe if they can convince the dark fae to come home to Elysia, they can turn them back to the light."

"From the way Darsh was talking, the dark fae don't want to be light again. They're seduced by the power of their dark ways, and the prosperity it brings them in the human world."

"Well, it seems you're right about that. They've sent two envoys to the human world in order to discuss the possibility, and neither have ever returned. I've sent a message to Jeanetta – that's Jean to you Benji – and she's going to look into it," Long said, nodding in Benji's direction.

Benji shuddered at the thought of the scary female wizard, but then he frowned. "Wait a minute. A message? How did you send a message?"

Long looked a little smug. "We wizards have our ways."

Kim rolled her eyes. "Anything else?"

"Yes. It seems that Carylinia is back in Elysia. She's apparently been to see Zebrella in Rimor a few times, and has taken up residence again in her manse, Castle Fairburn, on the Plains of Garemon."

A sharp intake of breath from Kim caught Benji's attention. "Who's Carylinia and what's the big deal with her?"

Kim answered him. "She's a light fae witch. Very powerful. The kelpies as well as the fae have been looking for her ever since the clan wars. It was rumoured she'd died in battle as no one has seen her since, but we were never certain as her body wasn't found. We've searched high and low in both Elysia and the human world. We think she may be the only pure blood light fae that still has powerful magic, and that maybe she can restore us to our natural form, so if she's alive..."

104

Long looked at Kim sidelong then continued. "If it's true, and don't forget we only have Jumor's word on this at the moment, then Lucivarsh can't have heard about it, otherwise why would she be chasing Benji down?"

Benji frowned, feeling he wasn't being included in the conversation, and it was about him after all. "Hello! I'm here by the way."

Long gave Benji an irritated glance, but Kim gently touched his arm. "Don't you see what this means hun? If it's true, and Carylinia is back, you're off the hook. The sooner we get to Rimor and talk to Zebrella the better."

Benji felt some relief at the thought, but there was also a part of him that enjoyed being needed, and important. It was a good feeling. Could he just go back to his normal life after everything that had happened?

The three travellers trotted through Rimor's north city gate as the sun was tipping toward the horizon in a blaze of red and orange. They dismounted in the cobbled courtyard of a castle, no less, and grabbed their bags as three grooms led their mounts away to the stables. Benji grinned, he couldn't help but feel as though he'd just stepped into the film set of some medieval epic.

"What are you grinning at?"

Benji turned to look at Kim. "Well, it's a bit 'Connecticut Yankee in King Arthur's Court' isn't it? You know kind of medieval."

Kim scowled at him. "Firstly Arthur lived in the Dark Ages, not Medieval times – he really existed by the way, though not as the legends portray at all – and secondly, this land, Elysia, is my home. We're not primitives you know, we just take the best of modern times and modern technology, whilst keeping with the best of traditional life."

"What are you talking about, there's nothing of modern life in Elysia at all, not from what I've seen of it anyway."

Kim flashed him a wicked grin. "If you get to enjoy the pleasures of the inside of my mother's lab, you may wish there wasn't!"

Benji choked on that.

"Are you two coming, or are you standing there bickering all day?" Long was already half way up the rather grand steps that led into the main building.

Looking up, Benji could see it was a fortified house, about as close to being a medieval castle as possible but just without the crenelated towers. But this was no ruin, or tourist attraction, this was full-on occupied "Wow!"

There were two fae guards on the door. They stepped forward crossing their ceremonial spears in front of the wizard. Long spoke to them for a moment, though Benji couldn't hear what he was saying, then the guards stood back and admitted them to a huge entrance hall.

A young girl in an elaborately laced cream-coloured tunic and dark trews approached them. "Zebrella is in the main hall at the moment with the Lady Carylinia. She asked that you take a seat and she will send for you shortly. Can I offer you refreshments?"

Long scowled at being kept waiting. "Starmia nectar for me please." He looked at the others.

"For us too."

Benji looked at Kim. What, she thought he couldn't order his own drink now? Still, he may as well try it. So he nodded at the girl when she looked askance at him. She went off to get their drinks. They sat in an orderly row on a bench along the wall, with Kim in the middle. The girl came back with three wooden goblets, elaborately carved with images of leaves, flowers and butterflies. The pale yellow liquid inside was the most delicious thing Benji had ever tasted, kind of sharp, yet sweet, lemony and mildly spicy. His gastric juices went into overdrive as he sipped his nectar.

"Good isn't it? The drink of the gods they call it."

"I knew nectar was the drink of the gods, but I've not heard it called starmia nectar before."

Kim shrugged. "It's the fae name for it. It's made from the fruits of the starmia tree which only grows in this part of Elysia."

They must have sat there for the best part of an hour before they were summoned. They headed into the main hall where Zebrella stood smiling at them in greeting. They each

106

politely acknowledged their host's greeting, then all eyes turned to the tall woman standing nearby, her face in the shadow of the drapes. All they could see was the elaborate pale blue, full-length dress she wore, that seemed to emanate its own light. Then she took a step forward, and the full glory of this striking woman could clearly be seen.

Benji's jaw dropped in stunned amazement at the sight. He felt his knees turn to jelly, and he struggled to stay upright. "Mum?"

PART THREE

CHAPTER TWENTY-TWO – REUNION

Benji was vaguely aware of Kim and the Prof turning to stare at him. But his eyes were only for his mum. He always knew she was an attractive woman for her age, but he struggled to reconcile the radiant apparition before him with the woman who raised him; who tended him when he was poorly; who drove him to school in her four by four Vauxhall; who sat with him on the sofa, sharing the footstool while they watched a film on tv and scoffed popcorn, and who phoned him every Saturday – until three weeks ago when he'd disappeared from his world.

"Well this is a turn up for the books!"

Benji snapped out of his silent amazement at Long's words and turned to look at the Prof. "You didn't know? Really?"

Long looked genuinely shocked at the accusation, and Benji quickly revised his initial thoughts that the Prof had been manipulating him from the start.

"Honestly Benjamin, I had no idea, but it does make some sense. After all, why you? You seemed so…ordinary. No offence."

"None taken." Slowly, almost reluctantly, Benji turned to Kim. If she didn't seem equally shocked, then her betrayal would be complete. But her face gave nothing away. As she studied his mum, her eyebrows were knitted and her head tipped to one side. He had no idea what was passing through her mind right then.

"I would like to speak with my son in private." The voice was at once familiar and strangely commanding.

Zebrella ushered everyone from the hall leaving Benji and Carylinia alone.

Kim had gently squeezed his arm in her usual way as she passed.

When the huge doors clicked shut, Benji suddenly found himself wrapped up in his mum's embrace. She took his face between her hands and looked deep into his eyes. Her tears welled – a sight he could never have imagined, yet now she was just Mum again, and his own cheeks dampen.

"I'd hoped to spare you all of this. Stupid of me. I should have known the damn kelpies would home in on you. Huh! Your Kim. Your study buddy and girlfriend. She made you so happy, and all along she was the infamous warrior Kimjora. Why didn't I see it before? No wonder she kept out of my way, only coming to the house when I was off on business, never around when I came to see you." She shook her head and pursed her lips.

"You think she knew?"

"It stands to reason, why else would she have done such a good job of avoiding me? Son, I know you love her, but she is not the Kim you fell for. She is her mother's daughter, and she has an agenda. The kelpies want to manipulate you and turn you into a lab rat for their experiments."

Benji pulled away slightly. His mum needed to understand. "No Mum. She does really care for me. I heard her telling Darsh when she thought I was unconscious."

Alarm swept his mum's face, her voice become urgent. "Darsh! She is dark fae. If Kimjora is in cahoots with that one then it's even worse than I thought. I need to keep you safe, we will stay here in Rimor City."

"Mum, listen to me. Darsh is not dark fae. She was undercover and working for the wizards all along."

"No, it's you that doesn't understand Benji. She's undercover alright, working for Osun…" His mum looked to the ceiling as her hand went to her chin. She started pacing, the frown looked so wrong on her normally composed face.

110

"...The kelpies hate the dark fae. They believed they'd wiped them out." She looked back at him. "It may be that Kimjora doesn't realise, and she's being manipulated too...and the wizards! But to what end?" She came and stood back in front of him. "Son, you must trust no one. I will get to the bottom of this. Is Darsh here?"

"No. The sprite lord tortured her and the Prof took her to the dryads for healing."

"What! We need to get her away from the dryads. They are a gentle folk. Mmm. Torture? That doesn't sound like Arbani, it may be that he's cleverer than he seems. And who is the 'Prof'?"

"The wizard I came here with. He was my psychology lecturer at uni. Professor Long. The Wizard of Mount Laskala apparently."

Carylinia frowned. "Was he indeed? I can see I need to have words with him too, it can't be coincidence that he just happened to be a lecturer at the very university you were attending, or that you ended up studying his modules. I assume Kimjora had a hand in that too."

Benji stared at his mum. He was beset with doubts. Was everything he'd ever known, or thought he'd known, about everyone he knew just an elaborate ruse?

*****

Kim paced up and down the reception room, repeatedly looking back toward the doors to the Great Hall. "What can they be talking about in there for so long?"

"Kimjora, sit down. You're wearing out the flagstones. Surely after everything that's happened to the boy you don't expect them to have a quick chat and done?" said Long.

Kim sat on the edge of the bench. "She'll turn him against me. There's no love lost between her and my mother."

"Give Benjamin some credit. Don't forget he witnessed you defying Lucivarsh. And he loves you."

Kim got to her feet again just as the doors swung open. She rushed over to Benji, but his tight-lipped grimace and cold eyes stopped her in her tracks. The look didn't suit him. She turned her attention to Carylinia and found her gazing right back at her. But just as she was about to speak, Carylinia addressed the Prof.

"You are the Wizard of Mount Laskala." It was a statement more than a question. "We met once, many centuries ago."

"I remember. You sought the wizards guidance to try to prevent the clan wars."

"Huh! Wizards, the 'wise ones,' you who are supposed to keep balance in Elysia – and failed." Long went to respond but she held up her hand and continued. "We have more immediate concerns. I understand you took Darsh to the dryads."

"Yes. She was in need of healing after her time in Arbani's dungeon."

"She is dark fae. The dryads are in mortal danger. You need to go now and transport her away before she regains her strength."

"No Carylinia, she is light fae. She has been working for me under cover."

"So my son tells me. But can you be absolutely certain? Go to Vaskra Forest, wizard, see for yourself. But then I suggest you bring her back here. We can treat any wounds she may have, and I will know immediately where her allegiances lie."

Long straightened his back and lifted his head. "You do not command me witch." He glanced at Carylinia. "However, I will do as you bid. I will be back by midnight." With that, Long swept away in a flurry of arms, cloak and spinning purple air. There was a brief chill on the empty spot, Long had vacated, that made Kim shudder.

She couldn't stay silent any longer. "Benji, I don't doubt your mum told you things about me. About who I used to be. But you must know by now that I developed feelings for you. I've even gone against my mother's wishes to keep you safe. I can't deny that when I came into your life it was at her behest, that my only interest was finding out if you were the one to restore us. I can't deny either, that I still want this from you. But I didn't expect to fall in love with you. You have to understand, I will not ask anything of you that you are unwilling to give, and I will not let any harm come to you."

Benji took a moment to answer. The air seemed suddenly heavy, and she could almost visualise the thought processes churning through his mind before he spoke. Finally, his expression frosty. "I don't know you at all. If you didn't have feelings for me, you would have happily thrown me to the wolves. I'd be in your mother's lab having goodness knows what done to me by now. You may love me, I don't know, but you are not benevolent by nature, that much is clear. You have manipulated my life for far too long. But no more. Nothing I've seen of the kelpies makes me feel I want to help you."

Kim saw the triumph in Carylinia's expression. Benji thought she was the one manipulating him, but what of his own mother? Well, he won't be open to the possibility that his precious mum had her own agenda, not at this stage. All she could do was to try to bring him back to her way of thinking. "Benji, I…"

"No Kim. Whatever it is you have to say, I don't want to hear it. I'm done with you." With that he and his mum walked away arm in arm, with Zebrella following behind.

Kim stood alone staring after them. Her eyes watered. She lifted a hand to wipe a solitary tear, looking at it on her fingertip in amazement. It had been centuries since she'd cried over a man. She looked back up to the closed door Benji had disappeared through as if she could picture him walking away from her on the other side, then she turned on her heel and went outside into the courtyard, her heart heavy. A short partially covered walkway and a set of steps led her to the ramparts where she decided to wait out the wizard's return with Darsh.

CHAPTER TWENTY-THREE – GAREMON

Kim waited half the night for the wizard to return, but there was no sign of him. The moon shone bright as she looked out across the plains in the general direction of Vaskra Forest.

Her thoughts had been in turmoil as she played out the last couple of hours over and over in her mind. She also thought back to the last few years with Benji. She had taken to him right away, even when he was just a spotty, gangly kid, and a bit of a klutz. Part of her knew straight away he would be the one to help her people, but she had to be sure. She also thought it best to avoid meeting his mum, the odds were high she would be at least part fae to have had a son with such potential, but she had no idea the woman would turn out to be the legendary Carylinia. Why would she? Everyone thought the witch had almost certainly perished in the wars. To have kept her identity hidden so well all these years was impressive to say the least. Her people, the kelpies, would have done everything to acquire her somehow had they known she lived. She is, after all, full light fae with strong magic. The fact she was alive should have let Benji off the hook, had he not been her son, but now, who knew what would happen? When her people found out Carylinia was alive, they would want Benji all the more – as leverage to force the witch's hand. It also begged the question, 'who is Benji's father?'

Right now, however, the wizard's absence was of more immediate concern. Was Darsh no longer with the dryads? If so why would he not have come right back? Perhaps she left and he went looking for her. 'She saved my life – she can't be dark fae! But if she is, what of the dryads?' Kim worried her bottom lip as she pondered all the possibilities. It was no use, she would have to go and talk to Zebrella and Carylinia.

*****

Benji's heart skipped a beat when Kim flung the dining hall doors open. It annoyed him after everything she'd done. The manipulation, the deceit, yet still, her very presence was intoxicating. Was it just her magic, or was there a real bond between them despite it all?

"Well Kimjora, it's hours since we dined, but I can have something brought."

"Thank you Zebrella, but I'm not hungry. The wizard has not returned, I am…concerned."

Carylinia answered. "We were just discussing it. It is only a day's ride to Vaskra Forest. We leave at first light, but you will not be accompanying us. I suggest you go home Kimjora."

Benji felt a bit panicky at the idea of travelling without Kim. She was such a big part of his life, he couldn't imagine his world without her close by. She directed her next words to him.

"Is this what you want Benji? I can protect you better than anyone if my people come after you."

"Herrr, Hummm. Well…"

"Benji!" His mum bore that familiar warning tone.

He caught her stern expression out of the corner of his eye. "I'll be travelling with Mum and Zebrella, and a whole load of other fae. It'll be fine…thanks."

At that Kim stormed from the room.

Benji cringed at her sorrowful face.

*****

Early the next morning Benji sat on a huge roan horse, much larger than any of the mounts he'd ridden before. It seemed a long way to the ground. He looked across at his mum. She seemed completely at home astride her black stallion and he wondered that he never before knew she could

115

ride. She smiled back at him and his tension eased. Looking around at the other riders, at least thirty of them, there was an intense air of excitement. They were all dressed in mid-green and brown riding tunics. Benji quickly revised his comment from before about this place looking like the set of Connecticut Yankee. It was more like Robin Hood.

The horses' breath steamed in the chill morning, and their hooves clattered on the flagstones. Horses whinnied as their riders swung up on their backs, then all of a sudden, a shout went up and they were off at a brisk canter down the wide track that led from the main gate.

After about an hour they slowed their pace to a walk, then after another hour or so they stopped by a fast-flowing stream to water and rest the horses.

Benji went and stood beside a large weeping willow tree, picking up a handful of small stones and throwing them randomly into the water one at a time.

"You're missing Kim."

Benji was startled out of his reverie. "Despite everything she's done, I can't just switch off my feelings for her Mum."

"I know Benji. I remember my first love, Kaylor. I was utterly besotted."

Benji was a little disturbed at the dreamy look on his mum's face. Then a sudden thought occurred to him. "Is he my father?"

"Good heavens no! He was killed a very long time ago. During the clan wars."

He could see the sorrow in her eyes. Is this how it would be for him? Would he spend the rest of his life hankering after Kim? That brought him to another point. "Mum, how long will I live, you know, what with being half fae and half human?"

She bit her lip as she looked at him then sighed. "It's obvious you've now recognised I am, shall we say, somewhat older than you will have previously thought. There are a few things I need to explain to you. Who your father is for instance…" There was a shout from the corral where the horses were tethered. Everyone was preparing to ride. "We will have a long talk Benji, but now is not the time. Come on."

116

Kim watched from the trees as Benji and the fae rode out from Rimor. The stables were right on the outer edge of the city walls, so they entered the woodland after only a short ride clattering down the stony track from the East Gate. Stealth was a skill she'd honed almost to an art form over hundreds of years. Even when they crossed the south-eastern edge of Plains of Garemon this noisy party of fae would never know she was behind them. It had been many a year since such a large group of fae undertook an expedition of this size. They would be disorganised, unprepared for danger, and complacent. Many of the grasses in Garemon were as tall as a horse, it would be an easy thing to track their passage through the trampled vegetation from a fair distance behind them. One thing was certain, she would not let Benji be taken. He was safer under her protection than he would be with the whole of this fae rabble.

*****

It was a hot day for mid-Autumn, so they stopped for lunch on the edge of the woods under the cooling trees before setting out across the south-eastern part of the Plains of Garemon. They had another six hours riding before they would reach the fringes of Vaskra Forest – the home of the dryads. Benji stayed close to his mum, and they rode directly behind Zebrella and the two fae that flanked her.

He was acutely aware of the riders behind them. He heard a few mutterings about the return of the witch Carylinia, and the strangeness of this hurried ride to the Forest. But when he overheard a conversation about Kim, how fickle the kelpies were in their dealings with humans, and how this boy – him – should have been sent back home once they'd got him away from the kelpie bitch, he'd had enough. It seemed not everyone was in the loop about him being Carylinia's son.

He slowed his horse allowing the offending fae to catch up. They had to part to avoid bumping in to him. This way he found himself riding directly between them. He looked to his right and then to his left, taking in the faces of the startled fae. "I'd appreciate it if you'd stop talking about me, as if I wasn't here. And leave Kim alone too."

117

"Well okay, but why are you travelling to Vaskra Forest with us? The dryads are wary of humans you know. They'll probably avoid us with you in the party. Anyway, all we were saying is that now we've got you away from that kelpie, you should be allowed to go home. Won't you mother be worrying about you?"

Benji was about to speak, but hadn't noticed his mum had broken formation, swung around and come up behind them. "His mother is right here."

The man's jaw dropped. "My lady! Humblest apologies. We meant no offence."

She looked the man up and down then dismissed him with a tiny turn of her head. "Come son, let us take our positions in the ranks again."

Benji was amused. She always knew how to make others seem small when she disapproved of them. Grinning he looked smugly at the two fae in turn, then trotted back into position alongside his amazing mum.

*****

Kim sat on a grassy hummock munching on an apple and wondering why the party she was following required yet another break when they were less than a half hour away from the Forest. She stopped, suddenly very still, as she heard riders approaching fast from the south. Getting her mount to lay down, she crouched low watching as grass seeds and dust were puffed into the air partially obscuring her view of the oncoming horses and their riders. She heard shouts from behind her then as the fae became alerted to the oncoming posse. It took another few minutes to make out her mother at the head of the galloping horses. Standing she urged her mount back to its feet then stepped up onto the hummock in clear view. The kelpies were closer than she thought and some had to swerve to avoid her. As they formed up behind her mother, she became aware of a row of fae riding into position behind her. Out of the corner of her eye she saw one of the flanking kelpies draw a sword. Her response was to shunt her knives from their arm-sheathes into her hands.

"Would you arm yourself against you own kind Kimjora?"

118

"Only in defence Mother." She pointed toward the armed kelpie guard with her chin.

Lucivarsh swung her head to the side. "You will not raise a weapon to my daughter Bromar." The man re-sheathed his sword, a little too reluctantly for Kim's liking. As she tucked her knives into place, her mother looked beyond her. "So Carylinia. The rumours are true. After all these years…"

Carylinia ignored her and addressed Kim instead. "Well Kimjora. Do you stand with Lucivarsh, or will you be true to your word and protect my son?"

Kim felt more helpless at that moment than at any time in her life. She looked at her mother, then turned to see Benji staring at her from his saddle, then switched to Carylinia, and back to her mother once more. She was shaking her head as if trying to rattle the answer out from her mind.

Her mother looked at her in amazement. "Kimjora, you surely wouldn't side with the fae against your own people. Against ME?"

"I don't want to side with anyone, but I have made a commitment to Benji. He is under my protection. I've told you before mother, he and he alone will decide if he wishes to help us. Why do you continue to pursue him? It will only serve to make the kelpies seem unworthy."

"Unworthy! I never thought to see my own daughter scorn our people so. But I have to tell you, that now we know Carylinia is alive, she will be the one that will give us back our shape-shifting abilities in the end. Bring the boy to us now Kimjora. He will not be harmed… so long as Carylinia does our bidding. The fae cannot stop us taking him by force. Better that he comes quietly. Better that you bring him now before lives are lost."

Kim was at a loss to know how to prevent her mother doing as she threatened. She hadn't envisioned this stand-off. Benji looked desperate. She knew that if he was ever going to forgive her, she had to make the right decision now. But many good people, kelpie and fae alike, would be harmed, some may even die if this moment came to blows. She had to do as her mother said. Lucivarsh smiled triumphantly as she read her daughter's decision clearly etched on her face. Kim

119

turned toward Benji, but was suddenly floored by a powerful downdraft of air.

*****

Benji, confused, looked first at Kim flat out on the grass, then at the source of the powerful wind and the rhythmic beating sound. His first thought was helicopter, but the winged man was no aircraft from his world. Fear rippled through his body as the strange apparition closed on their position.

Everyone was shouting, horses were panicking and whinnying. The beating sound of the huge wings briefly slowed. The flying man was heading straight for Benji. He kicked his horse with his heels trying to get it to run, but too late. Suddenly everyone was beneath him and the noises became distant. Far above the Plains of Garemon Benji turned his face from the tiny people on the ground and looked into the eyes of an angel.

CHAPTER TWENTY-FOUR– VASKRA

The near hysteria slowly waned around Kim as Benji became a dot in the sky to the north, and finally disappeared from view. She had failed. They had all failed.

She looked at her mother who sat dumfounded on her horse. Surveying around, kelpie and fae alike were recovering and calming their mounts. The great circle of flattened grasses put her in mind of the mysterious crop circles found randomly in the human world. Her mother's mount nuzzled at her hand. She looked down and was amazed to find she still had hold of the apple she was eating earlier. She flattened her palm and let the horse take his prize. Carylinia leant against her horse holding the rein. Are those tears? Kim found herself drawn to her. But to whom? The fae witch – a woman out of legend? Or just to Benji's mum?

Carylinia lifted her head as she approached and her face hardened. "We need the services of the wizards. We should continue our journey to Vaskra to check on the dryads and see if we can find the Wizard of Mount Laskala. If Darsh has harmed them or him in any way, I will hold you responsible."

Kim had no idea why any of this could be her doing, but she guessed it was a mother's worry talking. Maligning Darsh was another thing. "Darsh would never harm Long. She has worked for him for decades, and she saved my life. She is not dark, as you seem to think. Whatever fate has befallen the wizard may have come down on her too."

"Pfft! We will see." Carylinia tilted her head. "What will your kelpie brethren do now?"

"I'll ask my mother." With that she went back to the now tidy ranks of kelpies. "We are going to Vaskra to find the dryads, Darsh, and hopefully Long. What will you do Mother?"

"We will travel with you. We have come too far, and waited too long to let this opportunity slip through our fingers."

Kim nodded and reported back to Carylinia. A short time later a party of around fifty riders drove their mounts at a gallop out of the Plains of Garemon and into the shrubby region that flanked the vastness of Vaskra Forest. The fae in soft green and brown leather riding tunics and the kelpies dressed in all manner of blue, purple, and red flowing woollen cloaks. A sight not witnessed since the days of the clan wars, Kim mused.

*****

The horses puffed to a halt on the edge of the forest. The going would be harder and slower amongst the trees and the undergrowth. After the hard gallop they rested by the river Jinju, a substantial tributary of the great Dor River. The water ran brown with the tannins from the falling leaves, though the recent rains in the mountains to the north meant it was running high. They would have to track to the great north road in order to get across, taking them somewhat out of their way. This would mean finding a suitable place for an overnight camp once they were on the other side of the river as the dryads' arboreal villages were never close to the road.

That night Kim opted to be alone by her small fire watching from a distance as her mother and Carylinia sat on a fallen tree trunk quietly conversing away from the rest of the party. Under normal circumstances she'd be itching to listen in, but all she could think about was Benji, snatched away from right under their noses by… what? What manner of a creature came in the guise of a man, but bore vast wings? She conjured up an image of the strange being, or at least she tried. There was something indistinct about him, almost ethereal. She'd spent most of her life in this land. Could it be

122

there were still creatures in Elysia she didn't even know existed? She looked back across to Benji's mother. Carylinia would know what he was…and the wizards of course, yes, they would know too. She needed answers.

One of the fae, a quiet male approached. Kim peered sidelong at him. Mostly the fae and the kelpies remained in groups of their own kind these days, so she was curious when this one chose to warm his hands at her fire. The hubbub of people talking in their small groups seemed far away, and the sounds of the forest pervaded. An owl's call, the rustling of the drying autumn leaves that had yet to fall, the water passing over pebbles in the shallow edges of the river, and the gentle snorting of the horses as they settled down for the night. The man didn't speak at first, but nodded acknowledgement when she passed him her hip flask, taking a long draft of the spirit within. She went to warn him just to sip, but too late. He squinted as the strong drink burned down his throat.

Fae had no stomach for rosha, though she remembered Darsh had developed a taste for it. "Sorry it's not starmia, but it will warm you on a chill night."

Finally he spoke. "It's not so cold tonight, and I would have preferred a swig of starmia it's true, but I don't mind rosha…" He studied Kim intently. "My mother practically brought me up on it."

Her eyes widened as comprehension and wonder washed through her. "You're Darsh's son!"

"Rhio. My name's Rhio. I've been trying to find a way to speak with you alone. It's been no easy task. Carylinia, well actually most of my people believe Darsh is dark, and that she may have harmed the dryads." His eyes desperately appealed to Kim. "Tell me you don't believe this."

Kim put her hand gently on his arm. "She saved my life. She and I were partners throughout the clan wars. We shared so much together. We knew each other in a way only a fighting team can. Do I believe she could ever betray the light? Absolutely not. We will prove her innocence Rhio – together."

Rhio's relief was palpable. He nodded briefly, handed her back the flask and went back to one of the groups of fae.

As the night progressed, there was laughter, music and even voices raised in song. But Kim could only think of Benji and what he might be going through. There was nothing in the winged man's demeanour to suggest he meant any harm, but then what did she know of these strange creatures? She glanced back across at her mother and Carylinia. They were still deep in conversation. They wouldn't tolerate interruption. She decided to get away from the increasing noise of the camp.

From half a mile in the deeper woods, Kim could still hear them making merry, but it was a distant hum now. The wind had died down, and the river's tinkling was too far now to decipher the sound. She squatted with her back to a large oak and immersed herself in the gentle peace of the forest.

"Is that you Kimjora?" came the beautiful sound of a dryad voice.

Kim couldn't see anyone, but she recognised the speaker's rich tones. "Pel?"

Six dryads emerged from the treetops landing silently on the ground in front of her. "It's been a long time my friend." Pel waved an arm toward her companions. "You will remember Lom, Min and Kor, and these youngsters here are Zea and Wid."

Like the wood nymphs, dryads had green auras, and lived in the trees. The similarities, however, stopped there. Whereas nymphs were tiny, mischievous uncoordinated creatures, the dryads were human-sized, if petite, intelligent, benevolent beings with a complex social structure. They were also so beautiful they took even Kim's breath away when she saw them. "Yes it's been too long. I didn't expect to find you so far from your village."

Pel's brief smile at seeing her friend dropped. "Something awful has happened. I assumed you had knowledge of what has befallen us when I saw such a large group of riders entering Vaskra."

Alarm rippled through Kim as a whole range of possibilities jockeyed for position in her mind. The seeds of doubt about Darsh had already been sewn, though she constantly pushed such thoughts away. But she had to know. "Tell me."

124

The other five dryads took up positions in the branches of the big oak whilst Pel sat cross-legged beside her. "When the wizard brought the fae woman Darsh to us, her wounds, both of body and mind, were grave. We gave her torman root to knock her out while we treated her injuries. But then our healers were alarmed as her aura kept fluctuating while she was unconscious. One moment shining silver, the next dark, absorbing the light around her. Then gone completely for a while, then back to silver. We were perplexed by this and decided to keep her under until the wizard returned."

Kim too was ruffled by this tale, but still determined to prove Darsh's innocence. "She has been living among dark fae undercover for many years in the human world, working for the wizard Long, he who brought her to you. She has had to affect a dark aura during this time in order to pass as one of them. It's understandable that her body would emanate that which she has had to promote for so long."

"The wizard told us this same thing when he returned to us. But we decided to keep her asleep until she was healed. It seemed the safest option. Then we could waken her and the wizard could take her away."

"So Long did make it back to you. We wondered what happened when he didn't return."

"Indeed. It seems however, that Darsh's strange aura emanations acted like a beacon. One night the dark fae came." Pel's voice broke. "They killed nearly half the dryads in Vaskra Village, took Darsh, and put the wizard under some kind of spell. He's lying on a pallet in my house even now. Strange threads of purple light surround his body, and we are unable to wake him."

Kim's held her hand to her mouth as she tried to process the horror of Pel's story. Everything was going wrong. Benji was gone. The gentle dryads had suffered such terrible loss, Darsh was taken by the dark fae, and the wizard was out of commission. "My mother, Lucivarsh, and the fae leaders Zebrella and Carylinia are back at the camp. We should consult with them."

"Carylinia lives?"

"Yes she is mother to my…" She stifled her discomfiture as she struggled to find a word that described her position in

Benji's life. "Boyfriend. He has been taken by a strange winged man, the like of which I have not seen or heard of before."

Pel's eyebrow had gone up a notch at the word 'boyfriend' coming from Kim's lips. "These are strange times indeed. But we will not go to the camp with you. We will head back to the village. Somehow we need to get in touch with another wizard if we are to revive the one on my pallet. Meanwhile I have funerals to arrange. There is a clearing big enough about a mile from Vaskra Village for all the people in your party. Please ask them to send no more than six representatives to us once they have settled there."

"I will explain everything to them Pel. Then I will make a journey to the human world when I believe I can locate the Lomari River Wizard."

CHAPTER TWENTY-FIVE – JEANETTA

Kim phased back to the flat in Edinburgh. There was an unpleasant aroma. She knew she had to go and find the Wizard, known here in the human world as Jean, but as she looked around the little flat she's been sharing with Benji, she found she wanted to spend just a little time here, and wondered at her own lack of urgency. She set to emptying the fridge of all the perishables and bagging them up ready for bin day. Whenever that was. She'd lost all track of the days. She vacuumed, stripped and remade the bed, looked longingly at the place her cittern used to sit, and changed into clothes more suitable for being in Edinburgh. The normality of the mundane tasks acted as a balm for her frayed nerves, but she couldn't delay any longer. With a last look around and a sigh, she grabbed the car keys and went looking for the wizard Benji had found so intimidating.

There was a parking ticket and a police notice on the car. Well it had been rather unceremoniously abandoned. She was just grateful it hadn't been towed. Snatching the notices from the window and slinging them onto the back seat, she fired up the engine and was away. She had a rough idea where Jean lived. Somewhere near Long's cottage, so that would be the best place to start.

Kim heard Tina yapping as she got out of the car. She wondered, hoped, that Jean was the one given the task of taking care of the dog. Perhaps if she just hung out here, the

127

wizard would come to her. She broke in, fussed Tina, made some camomile tea, ate a couple of chocolate digestives and waited. It wasn't long before a car pulled up outside, setting Tina off on another round of yapping. The excited little creature spun around and around in anticipation.

Jean came in warily. "Jonas, is that you?"

Kim stepped into full view. "It's Kimjora, wizard. I have been waiting for you."

Jean came through the kitchen door and visibly relaxed as Tina ran around her legs. She opened the back door to let her out, then turned to Kim. "What the hell is going on? Where is Jonas? He just left a cryptic answerphone message asking me to take care of Tina, then upped and left without a word of explanation."

"You'll have to find someone else to care for the dog. I've come to fetch you back to Elysia."

Jean plonked down onto a stool. "Not likely! I haven't been back there in more than two hundred years. My life is here now."

"No one's asking you to remain there, but Longmarrino needs your help." Using Long's full name should have the desired effect.

Jean's expression turned to amazement as she let out a long breath. It took her a few moments to recover. "He would not have given you his name if he didn't have absolute trust in you. Tell me what the problem is, and what you need me to do."

Kim explained everything that had happened. When she got to the part about the dark fae's attack and their powerful spell that rendered Long immobile, Jean slumped back in her chair.

"This is not to be tolerated. The wizards are committed to remaining neutral when dealing with the light and dark clans. But to have attacked and indeed overcome a wizard of Long's formidable talents is unacceptable. In fact, I was unaware they had such power." She frowned, mulled over things for a few minutes then said, "I have a few things I need to attend to. Give me your address in Edinburgh. I will meet you there tonight, about nine-ish."

Kim parked the car in the garage. There was nothing she could do about the notices at the moment. She picked up a takeaway vegetable biryani from the Curry House a few doors down from the flat, then sat and waited for Jean to arrive. Nine pm came and went, then ten pm. 'What could she possibly be doing to take so long?' Just before eleven, the doorbell rang. 'At last!' Kim swung the door open.

The first person through was Osun, followed by Rola, Drima, then Jean… and finally Darsh. Kim stared at her erstwhile partner for a moment, then looked at Jean. "You! You are responsible? How could you of all people betray Elysia? What happened to wizard neutrality, and keeping the balance?"

Osun smirked. "The power of the dark clans is once more on the rise. Unlike you, we still believe in wizard rule. They deserve better than to have a life babysitting humankind. The dark fae will restore them to their rightful place. And now I have a new incentive."

Kim was incredulous. Much as she had her own personal issues with wizards, she couldn't believe any one of them would betray Elysia to any of the dark clans. Indeed the wizards always claimed neutrality. She hadn't taken her eyes from Jean whilst Osun was speaking. "You don't believe this shit, surely. They are dark fae Jean. They take power. They don't give it away. They're using you. Can't you see that? And what of the rest of the wizards?" She had no idea what Osun meant about his 'new incentive' and she didn't really care. She just wanted to make Jean understand the danger she was putting everyone in.

"Enough of this. I don't need to answer to a mere kelpie warrior. Osun, bind her, and don't underestimate her this time," said Jean.

Osun nodded to Darsh, who walked across and slapped Kim in a pair of restraints behind her back.

Kim didn't bother to struggle. It would have been a waste of her energy, and would achieve nothing. She half tuned her head, but couldn't see Darsh properly from that position. "I believed in you." She could hear the bitterness in her own voice. Darsh said nothing. Kim cursed herself for trusting this betrayer wizard, then she had an idea, could she use the power of a wizard's name against her? "Jeanetta. That is your full name right? Jeanetta?"

But Jean just laughed. "No kelpie. That's just my full human name, the one on my passport. You will never know my true name."

*****

Kim had no idea how long she'd been in Osun's cellar, but it must be at least three days. It was dark, so she couldn't properly gauge the passing of time. Even when she was first put in here it had a damp, musty smell, together with the distinct aroma of rodents. But now, added to that was her own contribution. There was no bathroom. A bucket in the corner had to suffice. It was also cold. The only thing she'd been able to locate in the dark to cover herself was an old sack. It had to suffice. When Rola brought her meals she tried talking to her, to get some information about their plans. But Rola remained silent. She'd taken off the restraints on the first day. That time, Drima was there too. They knew she could have easily overcome Rola, but Drima was a different matter, a big powerful fighter. Since then she'd tried everything to find a way out, but the cellar was solid, with only one way in or out.

Finally Darsh came.

CHAPTER TWENTY-SIX – ELEMENTAL

Benji gazed into the beautiful eyes of an angel. He must be dead. Why else would an angel be taking him to heaven? Well, he supposed, that answered that big question. He'd always been somewhat agnostic before. He looked down to the ground. All the people and horses, even the great Vaskra Forest itself, looked so tiny. The map Kim had shown him of this part of Elysia meant that he could get his bearings. The peak of Mount Laskala dominated the skyline. As he was dead now, it probably didn't matter that much. He should be cold but he wasn't. He supposed you didn't feel the cold when you were dead. They slowed as they approached the mountain range. That surprised Benji, surely they wouldn't be making a stop off – not on the way to heaven. But finally the angel started to descend.

Benji found his voice. "Is this the way to heaven?"

The angel smiled at him but said nothing. They touched down in a green valley nestled amidst an even set of four peaks, way beyond Mount Laskala. For Benji, amazement rode alongside confusion. At this altitude they should be freezing in the snow, but this place put him in mind of the stories about Shangri-La – warm, sunny, lush green, idyllic. Well, they couldn't be there. Surely they hadn't travelled for more than a few of hours.

The angel spoke at last. "Come. I'll show you to your room. You can rest a while then we'll talk. We have much to discuss."

Benji couldn't restrain himself any longer. "Am I dead? Is this heaven?"

The angel smiled again. "No. You are not dead. I will explain everything."

Benji couldn't help but remember when Kim had said exactly the same thing to him.

Benji's room was lovely. High ceilings, light, from no obvious source, white walls and green plants. Kim would love it. No, it was not as he imagined Shangri-La might look. The mosaic floors, statues and supporting columns seemed more Romano-Greek. He went into the bathroom. A big round tub filled with steaming, perfumed water dominated the room. He shrugged, got undressed and slid gratefully in, fully immersing himself for as long as he could until he needed to come up for air – definitely alive then. He stayed in the bath for at least an hour. The water remained at the same, 'just right' temperature throughout. When he finally got out and dried off, he went back into the bedroom to find his travel-worn clothes had been removed and there was a cream-coloured silken set of tunic and trews laid out for him. He lifted the tunic and sniffed. It smelled of fresh air and mild herbs. Perhaps this was heaven after all. He got dressed and left the room to go and find the angel.

"Ah! There you are," said the angel. "Please join us." Around twenty people occupied a large terraced room. There were no windows, it was open to the outside and overlooked the valley, with the snow-covered mountains in the distance beyond.

Benji sat down in the only unoccupied chair, next to the angel. He couldn't help but try to look at his back. The wings were gone. It was all very puzzling.

The angel chuckled. "It would be most uncomfortable to sit at dinner with our wings in place young Benjamin."

"Where did they go?"

"It's complicated. Suffice to say, they come when the need arises."

132

"What is this place? Why isn't it cold here? Who are you? Why have you brought me here? Are you angels?" Benji looked around at the people in the room. Some were looking at him in amusement, whilst others were engaged in their own, private conversations.

"Here have some food. You must be hungry."

Benji was hungry, and couldn't resist tucking into the scrumptious breads, fruits and cheeses laid out before him. A wooden goblet, with finely carved running deer in relief round the rim, contained a nectar that was even more delicious than starmia. It reminded him of apricots, only much, much better. But he still wanted answers. When he'd eaten his fill, he looked back at the angel. He was amazed to find him staring back at him with the same expression of wonder that he knew must be written all over his own face.

"Well Benjamin. What do you think of the eyrie city of Paradisa?"

Benji's shoulders slumped as he gazed into the angel's beautiful green eyes. "So this is heaven then!"

"No Benjamin. This is Paradisa."

Benji frowned, confused. Wasn't Heaven and Paradise the same thing? "Why did you bring me here?"

"I've been observing you all your life, and before in fact, as I watched over your mother as she carried you."

"Mum? Why? Huh! And why would she need anyone looking over her? She turned out to be some sort of witch or something."

The angel winced. "No Benjamin. She is not a witch. She is a benevolent soul and, believe me, she is so much more than just a fae with magic."

"I spent all my life thinking she was just my mum. A businesswoman with quite a lot of influence for sure, but just Mum. Now I find out she's a fae – a creature out of legend. What does that make me? A half fae, half human hybrid, but more human really as I'm just a regular guy."

A few of the other people turned to look at him, clearly shocked by his words. "There is nothing regular about you, and actually nothing human either."

"What?"

133

"You are my son Benjamin." He shook his head slowly. "I should have fetched you long ago and brought you here, but your mother was determined you should be brought up as human and allowed to lead a 'regular' life, as you would put it."

Benji stared long and hard, then glanced around at everyone else in the room before speaking. They had all stopped their own conversations to listen. "My mum is fae, and my father is an angel," he said, as if trying on the words to see how they fit – like putting on a coat – but it didn't fit, not to him.

"I am not an angel. This is not Heaven. I am an Elemental."

"Aren't Elementals meant to be transparent or something?"

"Mmm! Much of the time, but it is necessary to take solid form from time to time. I certainly could not have carried you here in my fully pellucid state. Indeed I could not have had relations with your mother, had I not been…solid."

Of course Benji knew what had to be done to make a child, but the thought of his mum and this elemental angel-man – doing it – ick!

"Carylinia took refuge here when she first discovered the dark fae were making moves in the human world. Oh, they'd been there a long time of course, but all the while they were content to run their business empires, make their money and make their lives comfortable, no one bothered about them, indeed most people hadn't even realised any of them stilled lived. Then something happened. One of the wizards betrayed Elysia, wanting power above all, and she spurred the dark fae into action. They have been quietly working towards domination over Elysia for some years now…"

Benji interrupted. "Jean! You're taking about Jean. I knew there was something off about her."

"Your instincts serve you well Benjamin."

"The others must be warned. Mum! We must warn her."

"Don't worry, she will come here now that I have brought you."

"What about the Prof?"

"Who?"

134

"Long. Oh um, The Wizard of Mount Laskala. He's got some kind of spell on him or something. It keeps him out for the count. That must have been her."

The angel leapt to his feet. "The Wizard Prime is out of action! How can that be? This is serious. That she would have enough magic to overpower him! I will send word to the wizard council at once."

"Wizard Prime?"

"Yes, he is the most powerful and most senior of the eighty three wizards that still live." He called one of the women from another table over to him and whispered something. Benji watched in astonishment as she became partially transparent, almost fluid. Her wings unfolded, apparently from nowhere, and she swiftly flew between the two wide pillars in front of them and was gone.

"Er. Sir. What do I call you?"

"One day I hope you will call me Father. But I understand if you are uncomfortable with that at the moment. For now you may call me Beluin."

"Beluin. Humph! Well, Beluin, I just want to point out that I think you may have the wrong guy. When I say I'm 'regular', well you know, I really am just ordinary. Surely the son of a powerful fae and an Elemental would, you know, be able to do stuff."

"There are talents hidden within you. Benjamin. Fae characteristics do not surface until puberty, and your kelpie girlfriend made certain those abilities have been supressed ever since then. This is a good thing. Such raw talent in the human world would have been undisciplined and, quite frankly, obvious to your enemies. Your kelpie has kept you alive, albeit for her own purposes."

"I didn't even have enemies until a few weeks ago," Benji said grumpily.

"Oh, but you did. You just didn't know about it, and fortunately neither did they. But you will not leave here until we have brought your talents to the surface, and trained you to use them. Your mother will be angry with me..." Benji couldn't help but notice that he said this with fondness, not with concern, "...but when she arrives, we will all work together to ensure you are safe. Now I need you to tell me

135

everything that has happened. We will ensure the right people get to know what they need to know. Your only task now is to learn."

CHAPTER TWENTY-SEVEN – DARSH

Kim sat on the floor with her arms wrapped around her knees. She ran her fingers through her oily hair. It clung to her face. She'd torn her clothes in her failed attempts to find a way out in the dark, having bumped up against various bits of broken furniture, large crates and broken bottles. Her hands stung and were caked in dried blood as she'd tried to fashion a weapon from pieces of timber and glass, but she hadn't been able to find any string or rope to act as binding. She'd been provided with food and water, but it wasn't nourishing or sustaining, and feeling her way around the blackness of the cellar had only served to weaken her as she cut herself and fell over barrels. She looked toward the door as it creaked open. Darsh's outline was just about visible as she slipped quietly into the cellar revealing a dim lamplight as the door shut behind her. Kim looked up at Darsh as she approached, shielding her eyes against the light. Even in its dimness it hurt her eyes after spending so long in complete darkness.

"You look terrible," said Darsh.

"Thanks."

"Can you walk?"

"Can you help me up?"

Darsh started toward her then stopped. "You know I'm not the enemy right?"

"That remains to be seen. Are you going to help me up or not?"

Darsh reached for her, still cautious, and hooked an arm under hers, gently pulling her to her feet. Kim managed to conjure up the last of her strength and pushed Darsh up against the wall, her forearm against Darsh's throat. "Explain, and make it good."

"I don't know what happened. The wizard took me to the dryads. They gave me a drink of some kind, next thing I woke up here. I've been waiting for the opportunity to come and get you out, but until now there's always been someone else around. Now will you ease up?"

"How did you explain my being alive, after you'd told them I was dead?"

"Didn't have to. Once Osun knew the wizard was involved, he just assumed he'd found you and healed you. He gave me an earache for not checking, to be sure, but I don't think he suspects anything."

It sounded reasonable, but Kim wasn't about to let her guard down again. "Can we get out of here?"

"That's what I'm here for." Darsh looked Kim up and down. "You're weak, my friend. I'll help you phase back to Elysia. I won't be safe here now either, not once I've let you escape a second time. Come on."

*****

Kim was totally wiped. Phasing between the worlds always weakened her, but in her current state, and without her hawbleberry juice, she'd be good for nothing for hours. She lay back on the grass. It was quite dry, like hay, and it prickled her skin, but she couldn't raise enough energy to move. Her eyes were closed, but the late afternoon sun penetrated her eyelids so all she could see was orange haze. She'd filled Darsh in on recent events. Long being out of action. The fae and kelpies working together again. Meeting Rhio. The loss of so many dryads and Benji being taken by the strange, semi-transparent, winged man. Darsh didn't react at all to the mention of her son. She seemed more interested in the winged man. She was quiet for a few moments, so Kim lifted her head and opened one eye, squinting and using a hand for shade. "What, does that ring a bell?"

"Mmm. There are rumours of such creatures. Elementals. I thought it was just a myth, I've certainly never

138

heard of anyone that's actually seen one. Zebrella might know more, or Carylinia. Certainly the wizards are sure to know about them if they are real."

"Well I'm certain my mother doesn't know anything about them. I don't think we should go to Prenya anyway. If Dom gets wind of me being anywhere near, he'll probably lock me up. I suggest we go to Rimor. If they haven't got back to the city by the time we get there, we could head toward Vaskra and intercept them."

Darsh's voice was hesitant. "Tell me. Did you doubt me? Really?"

Kim felt suddenly guilty. She finally managed to get to her feet, and took Darsh into an embrace. "Honestly, for a moment there I wondered. Pel told me how your aura was fluctuating from light to dark and back again. She believes it was when you went dark that Osun located where you were and came for you. I'm sorry Darsh, it's just that you were with them for so long. You didn't let me know you were alive for all those years. It just seemed…possible." She stepped back and looked deep into Darsh's eyes. Let's just see how it goes shall we?"

Darsh sighed.

*****

The sun was low in the sky by the time they got moving. Kim looked up. "We'll have less than an hour, then we'll have to stop for the night. If we can get to the Dor River we'll have some shelter at the wayfarer's hut."

"If we hurry we'll make it to Jewel Spring. I have my own hut there, it'll be more comfortable," said Darsh.

Kim struggled a bit, she was still quite weak, but the thought of a proper bed to sleep in spurred her on. It was completely dark by the time they got to Darsh's hut in the tiny village of Jewel Spring, so named from the coloured rock formations that shone brightly through the fast-running stream that rose from beneath the ground. The hut was quite large. The living section had enough space for two beds, a kitchen area and a fireplace. The privy was out back. Kim sank gratefully onto the narrow but deep mattress and was asleep in minutes.

By the time Kim awoke in the morning, Darsh had already been out and acquired eggs, butter and bread from one of the villagers. The smell of cooking made Kim's stomach grumble. "We still have a long way to go. We best make a start soon."

Darsh grinned smugly. "Oh! I've got a little something I brought across from the human world that'll get us where we want to go quickly."

"What?"

"Get yourself cleaned up, you look like you've been dragged through a hedge backward, and I wouldn't like to comment on the aroma. There are fresh clothes in the trunk under the bed. I'll get things ready."

"Get what ready? Darsh?" But she'd already gone out the door. Kim lifted her arm, sniffed, cringed and did her friend's bidding.

Clean now, and just pulling a comb through her long, wet hair she heard a most unlikely sound. She flung the door open and there was Darsh happily astride a Harley Davidson, patting the seat behind her. Kim grinned back and climbed on. Darsh revved, and shot down the road past the stunned villagers, whooping as she went. Both women laughed aloud as the wind caught their hair. In just over two hours they pulled up in the courtyard of the castle at Rimor to an amazed audience.

A fae official greeted them looking at the motorbike with disapproval. He ignored Kim and addressed Darsh. "My lady," he said with a slight bow of his head, "Rhio asked me to pass on a message to you. He asked that, should you come here, you should make your way to Vaskra where the lady Zebrella awaits the arrival of the wizards. She is currently protecting the remaining dryads and the Wizard of Mount Laskala until such a time as he can be revived." He looked again at the motorbike. "Can I provide you…" he directed an equally disapproving look toward Kim, "…and your companion with mounts?"

Darsh smiled wickedly at the man. "We're happy with the mount we have thank you."

Dryads and animals alike leapt out of the way of the growling monster that carried Darsh and Kimjora into the ground floor of the arboreal forest town of Vaskra. The two women quickly made their way up the rope ladder that had been hastily erected for the use of the unusual guests, to Pel's treehome. It was a large dwelling that spanned between and around two ancient oaks. As they approached they could hear an eerie, low humming that could only mean the wizards had arrived and were at their work.

Pel stopped them at the door. "They are not to be disturbed."

They sat with her on the deck, where she served them sweet berry wine in light ashwood cups. She looked warily at Darsh. "It is good to see you looking so much improved."

Kim remembered they had kept her friend unconscious while they were treating her injuries as they had their suspicions about her. "Darsh just saved my life for the second time in just a few weeks Pel."

"Mmm. Both the wizard and Kimjora claim you can be trusted... so be it."

Darsh's expression softened as she gazed into the eyes of the gentle dryad. "I want to thank your people for the healing Pel. I'm also aggrieved that it was my presence here that attracted the dark fae. I am so sorry for the loss of so many of your people. This travesty will not go unpunished."

"We do not blame you. The perpetrators are responsible, not you. I appreciate your resolve, but violence cannot be countered with more violence Darsh."

Kim couldn't understand Pel's attitude, and Darsh wouldn't get it either. But then dryads would be dryads. They were gentle in nature, and this incident would not change that. Her people had a saying, 'if you sit on a dryad, they'd ask you if you were comfortable'. "Pel, do you know where my mother is?"

"The kelpies are camped about a mile away, downriver," she answered, then turned back to Darsh. "The fae are about half a mile upriver. They chose not to camp together. You will no doubt wish to see your son." Darsh nodded. "Kimjora, the other thing I must tell you is that Carylinia is heading to the coastal town of Chimble Bay with a small group of fae warriors. She plans to travel by sea along the Island Straits and skirt around the Crusian Mountains. I understand an

Elemental took her son to their eyrie city. I have no idea why, but she has been on edge and distant since she arrived. We tried to get her to wait for counsel from the wizards, but we could not persuade her. It may be that you can catch her up on Darsh's motorbike."

Darsh looked surprised. "You know what a motorbike is?"

"Of course. Don't forget, dryads mate with humans. It's the only way for us. So we travel to the human world every five years."

"Yes. I've always been curious about that. How is it that dryads remain true when they can only take human partners?" asked Kim.

"It's simple. Something about our nature, your mother speaks of it terms of something called genetics. Well, I don't know much about that, but once impregnated, all girl children are pure dryad and all boy children are pure human. Fortunately for us, only about one in eight of our children are male. Now, if you are to catch up with Carylinia, I suggest you get a move on."

"I will remain here Kimjora," said Darsh. "You can take the bike and leave it in the stables at Chimble Bay, they know me there. If you don't come back that way, I'll pick it up another time. Good luck." They embraced and Kim headed out fast, kicking up dust as she went.

CHAPTER TWENTY-EIGHT – VOYAGE

The villagers of Chimble Bay stopped what they were doing and stared as Kim pulled up at the stables on the Harley Davidson. She explained to the stable girl how the bike needed to be stored and either she or Darsh would retrieve it later, then she headed down to the harbour.

After a brief word with the harbourmaster, she found out the ship carrying Carylinia and her party had left on the noon-tide for Bren Bay. She put her hand to her forehead to shade out the bright afternoon sun, and could just make out the white sails in the distance. So near yet so far.

The harbourmaster suggested three options. She could wait until lunchtime in three days for the next ship heading north, or she could take the evening trade scow across to the islands. The scow would stop at many of the islands in the chain, it would be slow, but there may be another boat heading north in one of the small island harbours. If not, she could still board the ship by getting a launch out to it as it passed. The other possibility, if she couldn't secure either of those, was that she went all the way to Bren Bay on the scow. It would take longer, but would put her about eighty miles south of Cape Las where the trail into the mountains began. From there she could travel along the coast road, or maybe pick up passage on yet another boat. Kim decided she had nothing to lose by leaving straight away rather than waiting around for the next ship. She headed into the town to get a new rucksack, stock up on supplies, and buy passage on the cargo scow.

Kim kept out of the way of the crew, standing by the starboard beam watching grain, vegetables, oil jars and barrels being loaded into its hold.

The crew were busy readying the boat for push-off, when another passenger arrived leading his horse on board. "Rhio?"

"I see you didn't make it in time. I thought that would be the case, Carylinia left Vaskra almost a whole day before you."

"What are you doing here?"

"I felt the urge for an adventure."

Kim couldn't help but smile at Rhio's easy manner and casual excuse for accompanying her. "Did Darsh send you?"

"Not at all. I just fancied a bit of sea air, and I've heard the Crusian Mountains are lovely this time of year," he said nonchalantly. "When we get to North Las Island, we'll need to get some suitable clothing. Carylinia told your mother the eyrie city is at very high altitude and then she, Lucivarsh that is, provided me with some herbs to help increase oxygenation of the blood. You know, altitude sickness?" He rattled the little herb pot to emphasise his readiness for the journey. "It's alright, there's enough for us both. Perhaps you should have made a point of having a chat with mother-dear before heading off."

"Huh! There was no time for that. Besides, I've been high up in the mountains before and not been affected."

"The Crusians?"

"No the Kaylen Mountains."

He appeared nonplussed at her ignorance. "The northern peaks in the Crusians are more than three times higher than any in the Kaylens. It's going to be a long hard trip Kimjora...sounds like fun to me." He was grinning ear to ear.

Kim was dumbfounded, she had no idea the Crusians were so different to the Kaylens. Well, she really hadn't given the whole subject any thought before. But actually it would be nice to have this young fae along, with his quick smile and his practical ways. Whether they caught up with Carylinia's party or not, she would find Benji and bring him

144

safely home, and a bit of help along the way wouldn't be such a bad thing.

*****

The scow docked in the tiny harbour on the biggest of the Verdan Isles. A cluster of three lushly forested islands inhabited mainly by humans, some of the male human offspring of the dryads and a few fae and water sprites.

Kim was already getting frustrated at the speed of their progress. "There are islands all the way up the straits, are they going to stop at every one? At this rate we'll be getting to the mountains just as the late autumn storms start to roll in."

"It's a trade scow. What did you expect? Anyway, I think they're only stopping on the largest of each island group. Come on, we'll be here for another three hours or so. Let's get something to eat at the Starfish Inn. I happen to know they make a wicked fish stew, and brew up a particularly fine beer."

"You've been here before?"

"I told you. I like an adventure. I'm my mother's son."

"Good. Just as well you're not your father's son!"

Rhio's face darkened momentarily. "Mmm. I'd like to meet him one day. Rumour has it his latest offspring has been born dark fae. So it looks like I have a little sister, lucky me. He's bumped off all his other children when they came out light. Until now, I'm the only one to have survived his murderous ways. I may just have to make him pay for doing away with all my other siblings."

Despite his smile and his casual way of speaking, Kim could see his anger and determination in the tilt of his head and the thinning of his lips. "Want some help with that?"

"One good turn deserves another. But let's get your boy back first shall we?"

Rhio was right, the fish stew in the Starfish Inn was excellent. She was vegetarian by choice, but understood the need to take what you could get when in the outer regions. Kim passed on the beer preferring the light, slightly effervescent wine imported from the Sorvian Region. "So do we eat this well on the other islands?"

145

"The Gem Isles are largely populated with transient miners, mostly human. They lead a hard life delving for precious stones for a few years, make their fortunes, and go home to live the life of luxury – or they waste their money gambling, then have to come back. The bars are rough, but the food is… wholesome and filling, shall we say. When we get to the north-most isles. Um well, they are populated with strange folk – people from some of the more obscure clans. It's best to steer clear of them. There's a trading centre on the wharf. We'll get supplies and warm clothes from there, plus I'll trade my horse for two snowbeasts to carry us into the mountains."

"You're kidding!"

"Oh no. They may be fearsome in the wild, but they can be tamed, you'll see. Anyway, what I'm saying is, we really don't want to venture off the wharf. The trade centre is guarded, and it's the only safe place on Great Mer Island – and there's a passable inn there."

They headed out from the Verdans on the next high tide. It was close to midnight. Captain Trant had given them a cramped cabin loaded with wool packs for trade on the northern islands. Kim turned her nose up at the raw lanolin smell, but the packs were comfortable enough. There was nothing else in the tiny space.

Rhio said, "By the time we wake up, we'll be docked on the largest of the Gem Isles, and actually we should be able to get a decent breakfast. Eggs, thick bacon, sausages, and fried potato. Sounds good don't you think?"

"I'm, vegetarian – remember, kelpie!"

"Oh. Well, you had fish tonight, that's meat."

"In my human form I occasionally eat fish, just not mammal flesh." Kim could see him raise his eyebrows, but she didn't have to justify her actions to him.

*****

It took more than a week, but finally they docked at the busy harbour of Great Mer Island. Kim and Rhio disembarked and headed for the trading centre where they found thick bearskin clothing and fur-lined boots. Kim abhorred the idea, but recognised she wouldn't survive the mountain climate without these things. Even here it was

146

bitterly cold, and the foothills of the Crusian Mountains were another eighty miles north yet.

While she purchased rations from one of the trade stalls, Rhio went off to see about their rides. Finally he came back looking perplexed. "No luck I'm afraid. There are no snowbeasts to be had anywhere. Captain Trant said he's not stopping at Bren Bay this trip, I've had to trade him my horse to get him to drop us off there."

Kim was mildly relieved that she wouldn't have to ride one of those terrifying creatures, but still, that left them with the problem of transport to Cape Las. They'd have to hope they could get passage on another boat. She thought that by now Carylinia will have probably reached Cape Las and will already have set off up the mountain trail. They'd never catch up at this rate.

Bren Bay was a much friendlier place. They took rooms at the Traveller's Rest Inn for two nights whilst they waited for passage to Cape Las with one Captain Corin. Corin was the biggest woman Kim had ever seen, well over six feet tall and built like one of those gladiators Benji liked to watch on tv. But she was a jolly character who spent a great deal of time in the inn swigging from her tankard. The night before they were due to leave, a group of traders came into the bar. Everyone in the room fell silent.

Kim whispered to Corin. "What's the deal?"

"Nasty pieces of work, the lot of 'em. They pose as traders, but in reality they're pirates. These are dangerous waters, and no mistake, but somehow when this lot are about, more ships get lost at sea than usual, if you take my meaning."

Kim looked more closely at them. They had very pale skin, skull ridges, and broad noses. Their hair was a kind of blue-black, and their upper bodies appeared disproportionate to the lower bodies. She didn't recognise their species. "What are they?"

"Who knows? They've got no auras light or dark, but still it's believed they're from the Dark Realm. I tried talking to their captain once. He just sat there and stared at me without saying a word. I gave up. The only time he speaks is to order food and drink for his crew. I've never heard any of

147

the others speak at all. We need to keep an eye on them. I don't want to be heading out at the same time as they do. I'd rather delay another day if necessary."

Kim didn't savour the idea of another delay, but neither did she want to encounter these creatures out at sea. "You're the captain. Whatever you say."

*****

It was two days later, in the end, before they left, having seen the crew of the strange trader ship leave the day before. There was a fair wind, and the atmosphere was positive.

Kim sat on a huge rope coil on the deck and watched as Rhio had a game of quoits with one of the crew. Corin joined her. "This is a strange time of year to be heading into the mountains. Do you mind if I ask why?"

Kim had taken to Corin immediately, and trusted her instinctively. She smiled. "My...boyfriend..." she was still uncomfortable with that term, "...was taken by a creature called an Elemental. Apparently they live in an eyrie city high in the mountains. This is a rescue mission."

Corin's left eyebrow shot up. "Elementals? I thought they were a myth. Anyway, I thought you and this one," she indicated Rhio, "were together. You seem so right for each other."

It was Kim's turn to be astounded. "Rhio? No. He's so young! He's the son of my partner from the days of the clan wars."

"Mmm. Thought you must be kelpie. Why do you hide your aura?"

"I don't particularly. The longer we go without changing to our natural form, the weaker our auras become. In some of my people it's almost completely gone."

"Hate to break it to you honey, but I think that applies to you too. Anyway, it's none of my business, but that boy really likes you, you know that right?"

Kim glanced over at Rhio, he grinned back at her, and for the first time in a very long while she felt the pangs of desire. But no. She was with Benji, even if he was pissed with her at the moment, she didn't need that kind of distraction. Corin read her face with knowing eyes, and she suddenly felt like some untried maiden at a coming-out ceremony. She frowned and Corin laughed.

Suddenly a shout went up. Corin was on her feet in a split second, Kim got up too. Everyone was running around, the crew were taking up weapons. Kim was a warrior and already had her knives down her sleeves and in her hands. The pirate ship, with the strange crew of so-called traders was bearing down on them. Before they knew it grapplers were pulling them in close, and the pirates were leaping nimbly over the gunwales. There were a lot more than those they'd seen at the inn, at least three times as many, and they were outnumbered more than two to one. Kim dropped two enemies within seconds, and got a brief nod of approval from Corin. She could see Rhio struggling as two men where on him, so she leapt on the back of one of the men, and pulled her knife across his throat. Rhio took the other out then. There were bodies everywhere and the deck was slippery with blood, but Kim could see they were losing this battle. Eventually Corin, Rhio and just three remaining crew stood with her in a small circle back to back holding their weapons – swords or knives, at the ready.

The pirate captain called a stop and approached Corin. "You loss," he was clearly struggling with the strange words. Kim vaguely wondered that there was anyone in Elysia that didn't speak the common tongue, "you swim or die."

Corin spat at him. "The water's freezing we'll die anyway. We'll fight."

The pirate shrugged. "Land just there," he pointed to the remote inlet his ship had been hiding in. "You swim now."

Corin was about lift her sword, but Kim put a hand on her arm. "He's right. There's been enough death, and we cannot survive if we continue to fight."

The pirate captain grinned as his men slowly drove them to the gunwale on the portside. They leapt over, and almost immediately both ships were heading away from them.

*****

The water temperature couldn't have been much above freezing. Kim was an excellent swimmer, she was, after all a kelpie, albeit Prenya and therefore of the plains, but she wasn't used to being so instantly and bitterly cold. It seemed

149

to solidify her muscles. She shivered for a while, then stopped shaking. That was a bad sign. She couldn't see the others. Tiredness crept in. Her heavy clothes, that had seemed such an asset before, were weighing her down. She was sinking. Kim knew this was it. She wouldn't survive, but she would not go down with her eyes closed, she would watch her death coming as a warrior. Her eyes flicked open… and before her was a beautiful, alien face…

CHAPTER TWENTY-NINE – EMERGENCE

"Aghhh! What's happening to me?" Benji's panic had risen to a crescendo. He'd woken that morning feeling comfortable and relaxed in his lovely big bed. He'd rolled over, then leaned up to plump his pillow... NO HANDS!

One of the female elementals, Raepha, came running in. "Benjamin, whatever's the matter?"

"Mmmmy Haaaands!" he was sobbing like a little kid. A tear dripped down his cheek and his breathing was hard and fast.

Raepha relaxed. "It looks like your kelpie's drugs are finally beginning to wear off. Calm yourself. It's fine. I'll wake your father." With that she swept back out of the room.

Benji had been in Paradisa for, by his reckoning, about two weeks. Beluin had explained a great many things to him. Details about the clan wars; about the many races of Elysia, some of whom even most Elysians had not heard of; about how he and Benji's mother had fallen in love against all odds. Many things. But he hadn't prepared him for this! Nervously he went into the bathroom and sneaked up on the mirror over the basin, not certain he wanted to see his reflection, but needing to anyway. He stood to one side of the mirror taking deep breaths like he was preparing to jump from a precipice. Finally he took a step to the right and faced the mirror. He could just see an outline. Tentatively he wiped the condensation from the glass caused by the steaming bath. His nose. He could definitely see his nose. And his left ear. He leaned in closer. An outline of his whole face. He twisted his mouth side to side and raised his eyebrows up high. He leaned back out again then jumped as he saw the reflection of someone right behind him.

Beluin was smiling. "Elementals rarely mate with other races. There's been no way of knowing what traits you would inherit from either your mother or indeed from me. It seems you have the gift of pellucity, at least partially."

"Pellucity?"

"The ability to become transparent, as you described it before, though it is much more than this. If you can become fully pellucid, you can travel great distances quickly, and you can put on a glamour allowing you to pass as any other creature, at least for short periods. This is a useful trait. We've been moving unseen among the clans for centuries." He laughed again. "The one the kelpies consider to be their leader is one of us."

"You mean Dom?" Benji was staggered as he began to weigh up the implications.

"They call him Domringa. He doesn't go out and about much, they think of him as reclusive, but in reality he can only hold his glamour for an hour or two at any one time." He laughed again.

Benji was both fascinated, but also a little disturbed. These Elementals seemed to be entertained by…well just about everything really. They dabbled in the lives of others then laughed about it from their mountain hideaway. And they loved to party, every mealtime was like a celebration. He wondered if they were somehow behind the stories he'd heard of the Etruscans. He was also put in mind of the nymphs, though a kind of intelligent version. Suddenly he felt cross. He rounded on Beluin. "Stop laughing for once will you, and tell me what I can do about this."

Beluin just found his tantrum all the more amusing. "Oooh! The puppy snaps. Don't worry my son. When your mother arrives, she and I will teach you everything you need to know. First we have to discover what abilities you have and to what degree." He tipped his head to one side and ran his glance up and down Benji. "I wonder…"

152

"What?"

"It'll probably take another couple of weeks for all the amnotin to clear your system completely. Then we'll be able to make a full assessment of what training you're going to need. Meanwhile, don't take too long staring into the mirror. At your request we had blueberry pancakes made for breakfast. We used to make them for your mother too." He turned to leave muttering, "I can hardly wait to see Carylinia. I've missed her so." Then he was gone.

Benji decided that speculating about invisibility could wait. There were pancakes to be eaten. Briefly he considered that a rather fickle thought, and wondered if being fickle was a trait he'd inherited from his father.

*****

All the Elementals seemed far too amused for Benji's liking as he went about the tiny mountain-valley city randomly shifting in and out of pellucity. Eating, however, was one of his favourite pastimes, and he found if he concentrated hard enough he could stay solid for long enough to enjoy a good meal. Bathing was interesting. One minute he'd be immersed in water, the next he'd almost be part of it, yet when he solidified again he wasn't full of it. It simply occupied the same space as he did for a while, then they went their separate ways again. Which was just as well he supposed. Then he wondered about his eyes. How was it he could still see when he was pellucid? He'd have to ask Beluin.

Since Beluin had told him his mum was coming, he'd regularly walked to the outer wall of the city where he could face south and see the trail that led from, what he came to think of, as the real world. Not this fantasy place. He was willing her up the trail. Raepha went with him sometimes. She told him that, though they could clearly see the trail from there, people that were on the trail couldn't see the city. He couldn't fathom how that could be, though he didn't doubt her words. Raepha was a young Elemental, not much older than him. She thought she was twenty-five, but she wasn't too sure. He was quite relieved about that. He had begun to assume that everyone he met was hundreds of years old. The two of them became firm friends and she loved hearing about

153

his world. At her age she hadn't been allowed to go to the human world yet, and she'd seen less of Elysia than even he had. But he found her fascinating. She had such a joyful way about her. Everything was wonderful to her, from the butterflies in the bushes to the tiniest plants growing in between the rocks on the freezing cold mountainside. They made a few trips outside the boundaries of the city where the temperature and the wild wind were just as one would expect high up in the mountains of the north. Wrapped up in thick skins from a small store by one of the smaller gates in the city walls, they ventured into the freezing Crusian Mountains. On one occasion Raepha showed Benji where the normally solitary snowbeasts met in the breeding season. "It's a wonderful sight Benji. Hundreds of them gather, and their dazzling mating rituals are like a wonderful dance. Oh and you should see their beautiful cubs, they're so sweet as they play together."

Benji studied Raepha with new eyes. She was so energising to be around, and so beautiful with her silvery blonde hair, her shining, blue eyes and her rosy lips. He imagined kissing those lips for a moment. Then he thought of Kim, and immediately felt guilty. "Perhaps we should be getting back now."

"There's one more thing I want to show you first. Come," she beckoned.

Twenty minutes or so later, they crept up to a large ice-coated rock that blocked what looked like a one-time trail, though it didn't seem to have been used in a long while. The rock had step-like protrusions all the way to the top. They climbed the slippery staircase carefully and peered over the edge. Benji couldn't see anything but the old trail, the mountain peaks and lots of snow. "What am I supposed to be looking at?"

"Shhh! Watch," she whispered.

He didn't have long to wait. Raepha pointed to a spot in the sky between two of the mountains. Benji gasped and nearly slipped back from his position. It was a long way off, and the visibility wasn't at its best that day, but there was no mistaking the dragon. It was an indistinct shade of greeny-brown, its wings dark and leathery looking. The head was

154

something between horse and crocodile, Benji thought. Then it was gone. They half slid and half climbed back down to the ground. Benji grinned gratefully at Raepha.

She grabbed his hand and gazed into his eyes. "Benji, will you show me your world one day?"

Before he knew what he was doing, Benji lifted his arm and gently stroked her cheek with the back of his hand. He realised he hadn't breathed for more than a few seconds, so he took a deep breath while he stared at her lovely face. "You're freezing. Let's go home." Briefly he wondered when he'd started thinking of Paradisa as home. They headed back to the warmth of the city hand in hand.

*****

It was on another of Benji's walks to the city wall that the unthinkable happened. An attack. There was shouting from some of the Elementals – a sound he'd never imagined could happen. Then another sound. A gunshot? Well the people of Elysia did have regular access to the human world. Why wouldn't some nefarious character bring guns here? He reached the wall to see a party of fae on the trail.

One, a female, was on the ground bleeding, and not moving. His mum was bent over her prone body. Had the woman been killed? The rest were making a rough circle around them armed with knives. Not much use against guns. Benji's eyes were wide. He was breathing hard. He had to do something. Someone had to do something. He scanned all around him to see if they were forming some kind of rescue party, but nothing was obvious. Someone was ringing a bell, must be an alarm call. The attackers were coming into view. Benji stared at the strange people. They had huge upper bodies, long blue-black hair and weird ugly faces. He thought they looked a bit like Klingons. They were bearing down on his mum's position, and still no sign of rescue. She'd be killed!

A shiver ran down his spine. More than a shiver – it felt like someone was pouring icy water down his back. There was a buzzing in his ears, and his forehead was clammy. He noticed his hand had become partially pellucid. Then suddenly the ground was several metres below him. He was in the air, his semi-transparent wings casting a hint of a

155

shadow below him. He should be filled with wonder, but his mum's predicament was foremost in his mind. After wobbling a bit from the sudden change in his centre of gravity, he pointed his nose toward him mum, and in just seconds she was in his arms and they were on their way back to the city wall. As he landed he could see Beluin and several other Elementals heading in formation to the rescue of the other fae, small, but lethal-looking bows and arrows in hand.

Carylinia gazed at her son in wonder. "Benji!"

PART FOUR

CHAPTER THIRTY – ISLAND

Kim came round to the sound of running water. The sunlight was weak, such that she could look straight at it if she squinted a bit. She was lying on a pallet with a fine silken cream-coloured wrap around her otherwise naked body, and forming a broad hood to cover her head. She sat up and pushed the hood back, the cloth slipping off her shoulders. As the freezing air hit her bare skin, Kim realised just how effective the material was. Quickly she pulled it back up to cover her body, but she left the hood down so it didn't impede her view. I wasn't until she stood up she noticed the warm boots too.

A nearby waterfall fell from at least thirty metres into a large steaming pool. Her muscles ached, and her head was throbbing as she walked over to see who the people were in the pool.

"Kim, you're awake at last."

"Rhio? Thanks goodness." As Kim looked from person to person she realised Corin and the three other surviving crew members, two men and another woman, were all relaxing naked in the thermal pool fed by several springs, the chill water from the waterfall keeping it at a comfortable temperature.

"Come and join us."

Kim was a warrior. Her concerns right now did not include bathing. There was no sign of her weapons. "Where

158

are we? Who brought us here?" Her eyes darted about taking in the scene. They were on a rocky, volcanic island. It was stark, though some low-growing plants and stunted trees grew close by the nearby hot springs and pool. Cliffs obscured the view of the sea on three sides. On the forth side waves gently lapped onto the beach. Through the sea mist she could just about make out the mainland to the west. Other than the six of them there appeared to be no one about.

Corin spoke. "Come on in lass, it's safe. Huh! In all my years at sea I've dreamed of seeing the merfolk. There's no bad in 'em. They rescued us from a sure watery grave, brung us here and tended our hurts. This pool, they say, helps with the healing, so get yer kit off and get in."

Kim took one more look round, dropped her garment and dove in. It was true. It felt amazing. She could feel the warmth seep right into her bones. "Where did they go?"

"Don't rightly know. Once they were done sorting you out, and laying you on that pallet there – goodness only knows where they got that from – they just seemed to get kinda absorbed back into the sea."

"Did they say if they were coming back?"

"Said nought at all. Not another word after tellin' us about the healing of the pool." Corin shrugged.

"Well how are we going to get off this island? What are we going to eat? Is the water in the fall drinkable?"

"Oh, it's a bit metallic tasting but you can drink it."

Rhio chimed in. "Relax. They wouldn't have rescued us just to let us starve to death. They'll be back."

Kim watched the others, worry niggling in the back of her mind. Rhio, Corin and her crew seemed way too laid back considering the circumstances – but yes it was nice in this pool. She floated on her back and could have easily dozed off, but something was still tugging at her memories – something about the merfolk. What was it? Her mind drifted. She started looking for patterns in the clouds. She spun around a few times in the water enjoying the sensation on her body. Feeling a little aroused Kim slowly eased her way with small movements of her hands over to Rhio. He really is quite sexy. What would Darsh think if she...the memory she'd been looking for resurfaced. That's it! The merfolk.

They lure other people into their realm, play with them for a while then drown them. Isn't that how the stories go? She remembered them helping in the final stages of the clan wars. They emerged from the sea and battled the dark clans with a few of the Mira kelpies. They didn't mix with anyone else, and then they just disappeared back to the sea. She'd only seen them from a distance. These short-lived humans would know nothing of them, and Rhio, though fae, was very young. She studied at the others again. They were writhing in pleasure, and not in the least bit concerned at their predicament. Ice ran down her spine at how close she had come to falling under their spell. Wading toward the water's edge she shouted at them. "Get out of the water. NOW."

Rhio's voice was dreamy. "Kim. Relax. We're here to heal. Can't you feel it?"

"We are healed enough. Get out now. These merfolk have their own plans for us."

Some sense of Kim's urgency filtered through to Corin. "Yes. There is somethin'." She frowned idly scratching her head. "Now what is it? Ok you lot. OUT." There were grumbles and protests, but the crew were used to doing what their captain said and slowly began emerging onto the black rocks. Everyone shivered until they put their covers back on.

Rhio was another matter. "Kim. You're worrying over nothing. I saw you coming to me. You want me. Come back in. I want to make mad passionate love to you." He was slurring, his legs had sunk low and just his head was above the water. His eyes were barely open now.

Everyone else was regaining their wits. Kim and Corin glanced at each other.

Corin said, "You'll have to go and get him lass."

Kim nodded, dropped her garment again and dove back in.

"That's my girl. I'm ready for you." Rhio leered.

The effect of the water started to impact Kim immediately. She smiled at Rhio. He moved slowly, almost drunkenly toward her. She kissed him full on the lips and wrapped herself around him.

Corin yelled from the water's edge. "Kim…
KIMJORA."

Kim snapped out of her haze once more. She disengaged her body from Rhio, reluctantly, and towed him to the rocks. The crewmen hauled him up and out of the water, and Kim climbed out behind him.

They sat on the rocks debating their situation.

"Captain Stoma will be along tomorrow. We'll just have to flag him down," said Corin.

"We should search the island. See if there is any shelter, food and a better water supply. I don't relish having to go back in the pool to retrieve the fall water, and it looks a difficult climb to the top," said Kim.

"There's a ledge part way up, I could get there and reach across, but we'd have to find something to put the water in first."

"Thank you Jorie," replied Corin, "but I think we should all start by searching the place. Let's split into pairs to cover more ground. I for one am hoping they've dumped our clothes somewhere on the island. The thought of wearing these things any longer..." she pinched at the cloth.

Kim and Rhio headed round to the south of the island.

Rhio kept glancing at Kim until she'd finally had enough. She sighed. "If you have something to say, then out with it."

"Well, er, um. About what happened in the pool..."

"We were all affected by whatever's in the water. It's just merfolk magic. Forget it."

"I can't. Kim, I didn't need any magical water to make me want you."

Kim stopped walking and laid a hand on Rhio's arm. "I know, and to be honest, my feelings of desire didn't start then either. But I have to give this some thought. You understand that I have a...boyfriend, right? She squinted, that word still didn't roll well off her tongue.

"Benji. The human boy."

"Half human," she said automatically. "Rhio, I do have feelings for you and I need to sort all this out in my head, but right now we are victims of merfolk magic, we are trapped on an island, that appears to provide no useful resources, and we are dressed in...hooded kaftans. Lets deal with our immediate situation first shall we?"

161

Rhio grinned. "Kaftans?"

"Never mind."

Their garments may have been warm but they weren't much good for clambering over smooth, slippery rocks, and the boots had no tread at all. Finally they worked their way around to the southernmost side of the island where the land opened up onto a bleak plain leading down to another black sand beach. Tough grass tussocks and low shrubs covered the ground where they stood. Way off in the distance the beach once again gave way to rocks, then to high cliffs. Kim and Rhio glanced at each other, shrugged and headed in that direction. Close to the water there was less plant life and the footing was slightly easier.

"The merfolk will be back. Let's hope we're off this hellish island before they come."

"Is that a cave? Look, there, between that twisty old tree, and that jutting cliff," said Rhio.

"Lets take a look."

As they made their way to the cave they could see Corin and Jorie edging round the rocks the other side of the cliff edge. They'd taken their boots off to wade around the section that jutted out into the water. Kim waved, and after ten minutes or so they met outside the cave entrance.

"The tide is out, this cave will flood later, but it might be worth checking it out in case the merfolk have dumped our stuff in there." Corin's fingers were white as she pulled her boots back on. "Damn it my hands and feet feel like blocks of ice."

"I was surprised to see you, were you not heading out to the eastern coast?"

"We tried, but it's just sheer cliffs, so we climbed up, headed over the top – pretty damn windy up there I can tell you – and came back down a small pathway."

"Pathway?"

Corin shrugged. "Probably a natural formation. Anyway, there was nothing much to see and definitely nothing to eat. There seems to be a spring though, must be what feeds the falls, but damn strange how a fresh water spring emerges in such a place, and high up like that too. Don't seem natural to me. Jorie, stay here and keep an eye out for merfolk, we don't want them coming at us inside the cave. Whistle if you see anything."

He nodded.

Kim, Rhio and Corin went inside.

CHAPTER THIRTY-ONE – TRAINING

Benji and Carylinia stood arm in arm watching events unfolding down the trail. There were Elementals in the air with their tiny bows firing arrows at the attacking party. One of the attackers had a handgun. Something he could only have picked up from the human world, or at least from someone trading wares from the human world. He was firing at the Elementals, but they were all in a semi-pellucid state, and the bullets passed harmlessly through them. One by one the enemy fell until none remained standing. Some of the Elementals scooped them up and flew off with them, to where Benji had no idea. The rest carried Carylinia's fae escort up to the city.

Carylinia sighed. "Beluin will not be pleased that I led these dark folk up here."

"They look like Klingons. What are they?"

"Half-goblins. Nasty creatures. They are dark, sort of, but have no clan structure, and generally no auras to speak of. Full goblins are so dark they couldn't cross the Boundary into Elysia during the clan wars, but the half-goblins have enough human, or sometimes fae blood, to pass into our world. In a way they don't belong in either Elysia or the Dark Realm, and of course they certainly don't belong in the human world. Some of them are actually ok, but most of the few that remained and interbred after the clan wars are pirates.

164

Always wanting to take from others, never wanting to lead a productive life and integrate."

"You feel sorry for them," Benji accused.

"There's nothing sadder than someone that has no place in the world Benji."

"But you said they won't integrate. So that's up to them isn't it?"

"Indeed. But that doesn't stop me feeling sad. Compassion is one of the things that define the light clans. I want you to think about that before you make harsh judgements."

"Where have the Elementals taken them?"

"To The Boundary."

"What's that?"

"It's where the dark and light clans can sometimes pass to and from Elysia and the Dark Realm. They will be left inside the gateway – a kind of nomansland. Their goblin parents will come for them – or they won't."

"Aren't they dead already?"

"Good heavens no. Elementals don't kill unless they absolutely have to. Those arrows are not lethal. They simply put them to sleep so they could carry them to The Boundary. Come on, let's go and see how my people are and on the way you can tell me all about your time here."

*****

"I had no idea they were behind us, surely you understand that?"

"You should be more careful Carylinia. This is not like you. In your haste you lost your objectivity and your caution. You must have known Benjamin would come to no harm here. Do you think I would let anything happen to my son?"

"Well, I wouldn't have thought so, but where were you when he went headlong into battle and rescued me? And why did you not wait for me before you started teaching him his skills, we always agreed that we would do this together if and when the time came?"

"Oh, I didn't teach this to him. It was your predicament that made him spring his wings instinctively."

"What! but…"

Benji moved his ear from the door.

165

"Were you eavesdropping?

"Oh. Hi Raepha."

"What's up?"

"The first time I've ever seen my parents together in the same room, and they're having a fight."

"They're always like that. Don't worry, they'll be kissing and making up soon."

Benji knew it was irrational given the circumstances, but it peeved him that Raepha could casually discuss his parents' behaviour to him. "It's me they're arguing about," he snapped.

Raepha just smiled. "Come on, let's go for a walk. The early camellias will be coming out in the south garden."

Benji frowned. "I'm not sure I've been there."

Raepha leaned in close. She smelled delightfully of spring flowers and sweet spice. It was intoxicating. She took his hand and led him through the door. "It's by the gate in the south wall, and awkward to scramble down to, so no one goes there much. There's a summerhouse that's always warm too."

Benji had a pretty good idea what she was implying and little waves of pleasure sent fire around his body. His face and ears felt hot so he knew he must be blushing. A moment of guilt flashed through his mind as he thought of Kim. But then it was gone. After all Kim had betrayed him, lied to him and drugged him. Raepha on the other hand was kind and sweet, and he knew now she was also his species, at least in part. Why not?

*****

"Where have you been? I've been looking all over for you."

"Sorry Mum, I just...well...we were..."

Beluin, grinning widely, had taken in the scene immediately when Benji and Raepha came into the room hand in hand, a little flushed. "I see you two have been getting better acquainted. Whatever will your kelpie say?"

"Benjamin?"

"Mum, I'm a grown man now."

His mum sighed, seeming more worried than annoyed. "What?"

166

Carylinia glanced at Beluin, and then turned back to Benji. "Relationships with Elementals are…well, let's just say they have their drawbacks. But never mind that now. Your father and I want to start your training. Much as I appreciate what you did for me, we can't have you sprouting wings every time you get worried or emotional, now can we. We also need to ascertain what else you may have inherited from us."

"Leave us please Raepha."

"Yes Uncle."

"Uncle! We're cousins?" Raepha shrugged and left.

"I didn't know."

"Don't worry about it son, we have more pressing concerns for now. We will start by finding out if you can become fully pellucid."

*****

"I'm done with this. It's pretty obvious I've got no magic in me, or pellucity, or whatever."

It had been more than two weeks since Benji's parents had started trying to get him to do all this weird stuff. It wasn't working.

"Benjamin, we know you can do it. You called your wings when you mother was in danger, and we know you must have become at least partially pellucid to have reached her instantaneously as you did. You have to understand that we teach our children from the time they can sit up on their own as babies. You can't expect a lifetime of learning to happen overnight."

"We also have to get past your mental block," said Carylinia.

"What are you on about?"

"The decision you've made that you 'can't' do this. When you finally decide that you 'can' do this, we'll be on the right track I think."

"Well maybe I should have been learning this stuff since I was a baby too. Why did you wait? Why didn't you tell me any of this Mum? And you," he waved his arm at Beluin, "Why now? Why have you kept away from me all these years?"

Beluin and Carylinia glanced at one another. His mum answered. "It was my decision. Your father wanted you to come and live here right from the start."

Beluin butted in. "We did meet once Benjamin. I came to the human world and handed you a book the wizard had written. Do you not remember?"

Benji's mind flashed back to the day in Waterstones, and the mysterious, disappearing, Dick Tracey man. "That was you?"

Beluin nodded.

His mum frowned at Beluin's interruption then continued her explanation. "I believed you could lead a normal life as a human. Elementals normally manifest their talents at a very early age. When you showed no signs, I…we, believed you have no Elemental traits. Then when you reached puberty, which is when fae characteristics normally come to light, there were no signs there either. Of course we didn't know at the time that your little girlfriend was a kelpie, she hid it so well, but then that's quite easy to do in the human world." She shook her head. "I should have realised your faeness was being suppressed. Anyway, your father and I then agreed, that as you had neither Elemental nor fae traits, the kindest thing was for you to live as a human. We weren't to know that in the end you would demonstrate the traits of both our species."

"That you could call your wings, and then fly on that first calling indicates that your abilities are quite strong. Now, we need you to commit to this training Benjamin. Can you do that for us?" asked Beluin.

A range of emotions and denials passed through Benji's mind, but finally he nodded his agreement.

CHAPTER THIRTY-TWO - MERFOLK

The inside of the cave was wondrous. The first chamber had a wet floor from the previous tide, and water dripped down the dark walls, echoing eerily. But from somewhere there was light. They had nothing from which to make torches, and hadn't expected to be able to see anything beyond the cave entrance, yet they could see other chambers beyond. Some were elevated and could be accessed via wide lava tubes.

"Where is the light comin' from?" Asked Corin.

"I don't know," answered Kim. "Did you see any holes in the ground as you came over the cliffs? Perhaps the light is coming through natural fissures in the rock."

"Didn't see nothing like that, but then we weren't lookin' with that sorta thing in mind."

They clambered up one of the lava tubes to, what appeared to be, the largest and brightest of the chambers. There were no windows, natural or otherwise. The light came from luminescence in the walls of the chamber itself, and was then reflected by gemstones, also embedded in the walls, boulders and floor of the chamber, adding to the colourful brightness. Kim was put in mind of Mary Stewart's novel 'The Crystal Cave'.

"This must be one of the Gem Islands, but I thought we were too far north for that," said Rhio.

"We don't know where we are," said Kim, "but I'd hazard a guess this is not one of the known Gem Islands. There are clearly no mining operations here, and I don't think the merfolk would make use of an island occupied by other people."

"Yes, and this is just a tiny island. Even given the difficult footing, you could circumnavigate it in an afternoon. I just think it's one of the little unnamed isles close by Great Mer Island. Borth and Shola can probably see Great Mer from the north coast I'd wager," Corin put in.

'Damn it, yes," Kim hissed, "that means we're going backwards now."

Rhio had been exploring as they talked. "Hey you two, I've found our clothes and things."

Kim only found one of her knives, though both the arm sheaths were there. They gathered up their belongings amidst the tattered remains of clothing and personal items that must have once belonged to other travellers unfortunate enough to fall victim to the merfolk. It was a grim sight.

Once changed, and carrying the clothes and belongings of the others in their party, they half slid, half scrambled back down the lava tube and back to the entrance of the cave, now starting to fill with water from the incoming tide.

"Jorie? Jorie, where have you got to? Damn the man."

Kim put her hand on Corin's shoulder and pointed with her chin. Off to the left stood Jorie, a knife to his throat, Kim's knife. The merman holding it had Jorie pinned to a large boulder. Another merman and two mermaids lounged on nearby rocks.

One of the mermaids still wore her tail as the tide lapped over her lower body. Her voice sounded inhuman, slow, echoey, hissy, like the sound of the sea when you put a shell to your ear. "You escaped our pool. How? Who are you? Are you fae?"

Kim answered, addressing her formally. Legends and indeed protocol, from their Mira Kelpie cousins resounded in her mind. "This man is fae, though he is young and as yet untried. These two are human. I am Prenya Kelpie."

"Aghhh," she sighed, "You saved these others from the pool. Is it true the Prenya Kelpies cannot take their natural form?"

"It is so. We are currently on a mission to rescue one that may be able restore us."

"A noble mission. You and the fae can go. We will keep the humans."

"No. They are my companions and under my protection."

The mermaid looked across to Jorie. "Your protection would appear ineffective."

"My people are diminished by our confinement in this human form. I would ask a boon of you, to let the others go so that I can complete my mission. I have need of them for this task."

The mermaid tipped her head to one side as she considered Kim's words. Then she nodded to the merman holding Jorie. He loosened his hold. "I will grant your boon as you have shown proper respect. But it comes at a price. You will be indebted to me, and one day I will call in that debt. However, it may already be too late for the other two." She nodded to the other mermaid who slid gracefully into the water. "She will save them if she can." With that the remaining merfolk were gone.

"Lucky I suppose, so long as Borth and Shola are still ok of course."

"No Corin, not so lucky. I now owe the merfolk, and that can't be a good thing."

"Well, just steer clear of them. What can they do?"

"They are a vengeful people I think." Kim's heart was heavy with an unknown burden.

They got back to the beach by the pool to find Borth and Shola lying unconscious. There were bite marks on their faces and arms, and probably elsewhere too under their garments. There was no sign of any merfolk.

"Let's get them dressed and wait for rescue," said Corin.

CHAPTER THIRTY-THREE - PASSAGE

"What the devil are you doing stuck out here? I almost missed you," said Captain Stoma. "Where's the Starfish?" He scanned around as he heaved to on the bleak little isle.

"Tell me about it! I thought you were going to sail right passed us. Anyway, it's a long story. I'll be happy to tell you all about it over a hot meal and a keg of ale. We've not eaten in two days, and these two…" she waved toward the semi-conscious sailors, "…have a tale even we have yet to hear," said Corin.

"Cook'll have the food ready shortly." He squinted one eye and lifted his chin as he watched Rhio clambering over the gunwale half dragging Borth with him. "Is that a fae?"

A prickle ran down Kim's spine and she diverted her attention more closely to the conversation between the two captains.

"Pull yer neck in Stoma, he's alright. But get this, that other one, she's a kelpie."

Stoma pulled a knife and went to move, Kim automatically took up a defensive stance, but Corin grabbed his arm. "Hey! Do you think I'd be asking passage for one of them? She's Prenya Kelpie." Stoma sheathed his knife again, though his eyes remained wary. Kim relaxed, but only a little.

Over dinner that evening Corin told Stoma about their attack by the pirates and their little adventure with the merfolk, with Rhio occasionally butting in with a detail she'd missed.

"Mmm. Some good folk have been lost to those pirates. We're just going to have to form up yer know and do away with them, that's what I think."

Corin nodded at Stoma's wisdom.

"So if you two are up to it now," Stoma said to Borth and Shola, "I wanna know what them merfolk did to yer. 'ow you ended up with bites all over yer, and then left wrapped up in them funny clothes. Out for the count, as yer were."

All eyes turned to the two crewmen. Borth spoke first. "Well, we went round to the north of the island like the cap'n said, but there was nought there, just an empty beach, and a load of cliffs. The only useful information we got was that we could see Great Mer Island from where we was standin'. Funny, we musta sailed past the merfolk's isle a hundred times, an' just not noticed it before."

"Probably enchanted," Kim said.

Corin nodded sagely. "That's why we had to make such a hullabaloo to get your attention."

"Mmm," muttered Stoma as he waved at Borth to continue.

"Well anyway, we thought we might as well go back to the pool and wait for the others. We only just got there, and we was looking out across the sea, 'cos we could see the mainland like, and then, humph, well it was odd…"

Shola took up the story, her voice strained. "It was like a freak wave come up the beach, but then it wasn't water anymore it was a bunch of them merfolk. Their tails jus' disappeared and they 'ad legs of a sudden. They jus' walked up to us. Their faces was so scary, like fish only pretty, with big eyes what yer could'n stop lookin' at, an' they jus' kinda drove us into the pool."

Borth chimed back in. "We did'n wanna, we could'n 'elp it."

Shola continued. "Them cloths we 'ad on, jus' floated away and we were naked as babies, but the closer that merman got to me… well it's embarassin' yer see… they 'ad us, right there in the water, an' we couldn't resist, we didn't wanna resist. It was…"

173

Shola was struggling.

Borth came to the rescue. "We'll it was a mermaid for me, at least... well you know... anyhow, once they 'ad their way with us, they attacked us. They bit us. We couldn't stop 'em. We'd gone all sleepy like before. We couldn't breathe, we was drownin'. Then I can jus' remember seeing another mermaid – I wondered if she was gonna jump my bones too, but next thing we knew we was waking up ready to board this ship. What do yer think that bitin' was all about?"

Kim grinned. "Tenderising."

Borth appeared so shocked, she couldn't help but laugh.

Corin had other concerns. "So I take it there've been no reports of where my ship might have gone? No sightings?"

"Not as I've heard. We can ask around when we get to Cape Las, but don't 'old yer breath mate, I don't reckon there's much 'ope you'll get her back."

*****

The Sea Quest tied up alongside the pier in Cape Las three days later. There were no other ships in the little harbour, but that, Captain Stoma assured Kim, was not unusual at this time of year. Trade in goods from the year's harvest was pretty much complete. The Sea Quest was on her last run north before the winter started. She was carrying oil and preserves, and would be taking back woollen goods made throughout the summer and autumn from the fleeces of the tough little sheep that lived in the foothills of the Crusians. There would also be meat from the excess stock culled for trade, and possibly some of the prized snowbeast skins. These fetched a good price at market.

The dark, wintery sky reflected Kim's mood as the party, plus the captain and crew of the Sea Quest disembarked and headed for the only Inn in Cape Las. It was a crude hostelry, but had a cheerful fire burning in the big square hearth in the centre of the main bar area, giving it its name – The Square Hearth Inn.

They were much further north than Kim had ever been, and they were not done yet. Their options were limited. Get passage from another ship, find the Starfish and retake it, though that seemed unlikely, or go on foot. Kim didn't relish the latter of these options. They were headed for the northernmost foothills of the mountain range. It was a long way. They were weeks behind Carylinia by now, and winter was already pressing down on them. If only she'd waited a few days for the ship from Chimble Bay! She cursed her own impatience. It was bitterly cold, there would probably be snow blizzards, and already the days were short. She also heard that wayfarers' huts were few and far between in the northern reaches. It seemed a grim prospect.

"Higgs, have you seen any of them ugly looking pirates lately?" Corin asked the man serving the drinks.

"Oh aye! They were in here a week or two ago, unsavoury lot they are."

"Did they come in on my ship?"

"Nope."

"Any idea what they were carrying?"

"Nope. You know what they're like. Don't speak unless they have to, but their ship seemed low in the water, they must have been carrying quite a bit I'd say."

"Damn it. They must have unloaded all my trade goods into their own ship. I wonder what they did with the Starfish."

Stoma came up behind her to get another ale. "Took everything off and sunk her I expect. Get rid of the evidence so to speak."

Kim listened to the conversation with growing dread. Stoma had already said he'd be heading back as soon as possible after he'd dealt with the local traders who came down to the market hall. He'd offered to take them all back to Bren Bay. But she couldn't turn back, not now that she'd come so far. She knew Rhio would stay with her. But what about Corin and her three crew?

"What will you do now Corin?" she asked.

"Maybe go home. Build a new ship. Start afresh. What about you?"

"I will continue."

"It's a bad time of the year to be headin' up into the mountains. There is a bay, Eternity Bay it's called, that'll bring you right to the bottom of the trail that leads into the northern peaks," she paused her eyes distant for a moment, then she said, "them pirates were headin' north. It may be

175

they stopped there. It may even be they got the Starfish there. No one really knows where they go, an' if it's true them lost ships are from them lot o' pirates doin' the dirty, may jus' be they take the ships there before headin' off into the unknown territories. I think I might come along an' see if the Starfish is there, an' perhaps I can help keep you two outa trouble at the same time."

Kim grinned, a tiny light amidst the grey pervading her mind, and thinking Corin's presence hadn't exactly saved them from trouble before. But she'd be a good travel companion, and if they were lucky enough to pick up a ship to this Eternity Bay, she'll probably know the captain and crew. "Good to have you along my friend."

The next day the local traders come to the market hall next to the inn, Captain Stoma made his deals, then he, his crew and Corin's crew sailed on the afternoon tide leaving Kim, Rhio and Corin seeing them off from the pier. A lump of lead formed in the pit of Kim's stomach as the ship disappeared around the headland to the south.

There was very little to do in Cape Las, so they hung around in the Square Hearth Inn playing knucklebones, cards and something called 'chucks' that Kim told her companions roughly equated to the human game of darts.

As the days dragged on, Kim was getting more and more frustrated with their slow progress, or right now, no progress at all. She knew she was getting snappy, but just couldn't seem to help herself. One evening the three travellers sat in the bar drinking ale having dined on fish stew and flatbread for the third day in a row.

"This is ridiculous. It's only the start of the winter, surely they have other food in their stores."

"Give it a rest Kim. We're the only folk staying here, if they make a pot of stew it needs eating up before they make anything else, they can't throw it away just because you're bored with the food," said Corin.

"It's alright for you, I don't even like bloody fish, not really, I'm vegetarian by choice."

Corin gazed at her in exasperation, was on the verge of saying something, but then sighed, and headed back to her room.

176

Rhio waved a finger at Kim. "I have to say. That was most ungracious of you. You do realise, I assume, that she doesn't expect to get her ship back. She stayed to help us. You."

"Huh! Well she needn't have bothered. It looks like we're going nowhere fast."

"Mmm. What a strange turn of phrase. But really Kim, she doesn't deserve the sharp end of your tongue. This situation is not of her creating."

"Oh, I know, I know. I'll apologise to her at breakfast. What about you though, does nothing dampen your spirits?"

Rhio smiled broadly. "What have I got to complain about? I'm on and adventure, actually quite an exciting adventure, and I'm with a beautiful kelpie woman who's bound to realise sometime soon how much she wants me. I can kick my heels until that moment sparks in those stunning eyes."

Kim stared at Rhio in amazement coupled with a little tingle of excitement. "I thought we'd decided it was the merfolk magic influencing our...thing...thing that we...well you know."

"On the contrary, I thought we recognised there was an attraction even before that...interesting event. You said you would have to think about it and sort it out in your head. Don't you remember saying that?"

Kim fidgeted and cast her eyes around the bar, not looking at anything in particular, and half wishing one of the dark corners would swallow her up. She shook her head then. What ever was the matter with her? She'd never behaved like a giddy girl before, and let's face it, Benji hadn't exactly left her thinking there was much chance for their continued relationship. She had, after all, lied to him and betrayed his confidence. Her mission had been to secure a human specimen with fae blood that may potentially have fae magic too. Now that Benji knew that, there seemed little hope for them. She turned her gaze back to Rhio. Biting her lip she weighed up his qualities. He was charming, funny and sexy. He wanted her, and if she was honest with herself, she felt those tell-tale stirrings of desire every time she saw him.

Besides – anything to alleviate the boredom. What did she have to lose? Pointing to the staircase, she just said, "bed."

*****

A few days later a ship called in to the pier. Kim, Rhio and Corin practically ran down to the water's edge, Corin taking the first mooring rope as a crewman threw it toward her. Suddenly there was more activity in Cape Las then they'd seen in nearly two weeks.

Whilst securing the rope to one of the big cleats on the pier, Corin called across to the captain. "Ho! Tebbin. Am I pleased to see you!"

"Hellooo there."

"What brings you to the outer reaches at this time of year?"

"Ran into Stoma at Bren Bay, he said you were looking to gain passage to Eternity Bay. I dropped a party of fae up their a few weeks back…"

That made Kim's ears prick up.

"…they paid well and asked me to come back for them before the winter set in. I wasn't going up there for another week or so, but when Stoma and that crewman of yours, Borth, told me what you were up to, it just seemed a good idea to bring my plans forward. Just as well anyway, if the snows start to drive down early, as it seems they might, I could easily miss the window."

Kim breathed a sigh of relief. At last they could get moving again.

CHAPTER THIRTY-FOUR - LONG

Benji's days were full. He spent a large proportion of his day with his parents, either together or separately, learning about both Elemental and fae magic, or practising his emerging skills. He also spent a lot of time with Raepha. He found her enchanting, always laughing, and full of mischief.

As the last of the amnotin in his blood and tissues dispersed from his body, he changed. His face became more like his Mum's, a striking face that he'd not realised until then was distinctly fae. He looked in the mirror one morning and studied his face and upper body. He saw eyes that were almost cat-like, skin that seemed to glow, and his hair became more lustrous and lighter in colour. His cheekbones were a little higher making him look older, and he thought, more muscular, more handsome. He couldn't help but smile at his own reflection.

"Hey you, stop admiring yourself. Come back to bed and admire me instead." Raepha pushed the covers off. Her naked body shone in the sunlight coming through the window.

Benji did just that. He lay down, propping up on his elbow. He ran a finger down her neck, across her erect nipple and continued down her belly. She giggled in pleasure and they made love once again.

Afterwards, as they splashed each other in the huge bath, Raepha asked, "So how's the training going?"

Benji shrugged. "Actually ok! I can call my wings in now, and I can become both partially and fully pellucid at will. I'm still working on going solid again without crashing into things, but Beluin thinks I'll get the hang of it with practice. I seem to have a bit of fae magic too. Mum reckons it won't be much though, and I'll only ever be able to do small things. I seem to have heat. I can light a fire, or warm up a cup of wine. She's concerned that until I've practiced a bit more I could accidently set fire to things if I get pissed off or something."

"Cool!"

As Benji and Raepha lay happily chatting, there was a disturbance out in the main hall. They glanced at each other in mild alarm, jumped up, quickly dressed and went to investigate.

Benji was shocked at how emaciated Long appeared. Last time he'd seen him, he been kind of rounded and jolly. Today his face was gaunt, he was unshaven, and his eyes darted nervously about as he breathed heavily. There were a number of strangers with him. He counted three men and two women, all dressed in purple robes – wizards. "What's going on?"

"Benjamin, there you are. Thank goodness. Come and join us," said Long.

Benji eyed the gathering. Six wizards, Mum, Beluin and four other Elementals – Playa, Jania, Dorbin and Tremin. Beluin had told him there was no hierarchy amongst the Elementals, but he couldn't help but notice these four, plus Beluin, always seemed to be in the thick of it when decisions needed to be made. Jania had been the Elemental chosen to take the information about Long's predicament to the wizard council. She'd returned ages ago. He wondered why it had taken so long for them to get here. He and Raepha went and sat at the long table where food and drink had already been laid out.

Long told his story. "I headed back to Vaskra Forest at Carylinia's bidding," he nodded across to Benji's mum, "at first everything seemed fine. Pel told me Min had kept Darsh unconscious the whole time just to be on the safe side. You see they'd watched in alarm as her aura fluctuated between

180

light and dark, or no aura at all at times. They weren't at all comfortable with having her there, but they will always do the bidding of a wizard. I can't tell you how much I wish I'd taken her direct to Rimor instead, but I had no idea of Jean's treachery…"

Beluin interrupted. "Jean?"

"Jeanetta, The Wizard of Lomari River. "Long shook his head slowly. "That a wizard could sink so low as to collude with the dark fae and betray their own kind."

Carylinia spoke softly. "Please keep to the story. There is much to discuss."

"Apologies, it's just that it is such a shock and utterly unprecedented. I went to take a look at Darsh, and indeed found her continually changing aura most disturbing. However, I've been working with Darsh for many years. I know her character. Yes, she is a bit volatile, but she's good person. She has had to emanate a dark aura for so long while she's been in place with Osun and his cronies, that it's become a part of her, but I know for certain her heart is light. I told this to Min and Pel. I think they were inclined to believe me, but still they kept Darsh under."

Benji could see his mum was getting a little frustrated by Long's verbosity, but she kept her voice gentle. "The point?"

"Well, actually that is the point. Because she was unconscious, she had no control over her aura. When it was dark, it acted as a beacon to the dark fae – and to Jean is seems."

Benji could hear the Prof's voice break.

All eyes were on him as he spoke. "They came in the night. When I awoke I couldn't move. Jean was leaning over me. Her face showed no remorse, no regret. She was already most of the way through the binding spell. Had I been awake when she started, I could have resisted, but I was completely immobilised. She knew exactly when to work her evil. I could hear the screaming. The dryads were dying…" Long's sobs as he spoke were heart breaking, "…there was nothing I could do for them. I tried to speak, but even that was beyond me. I felt the tears welling, but Jean just stared at me, expressionless. Just before I lost consciousness she spoke. She said that I was the betrayer, and the rest of the wizards

181

too for allowing the clans and even the humans to dictate how we lived, when we should be the ones who were in control. She had been my friend. My sister. Her eyes were cold even amidst the sound of the dryads perishing. I knew nothing else after that until I awoke with my brothers and sisters here around me breaking the spell she'd cast."

Benji, like everyone else in the room, sat and stared at Long in horror. During the rest of the evening everyone had their two-penneth worth to say, adding to the chain of events and filling in the gaps that had led them all here.

*****

By the end of the evening it was concluded there needed to be a conference to decide what steps needed taking about the dark fae and about the rebel wizard. But this affected all the clans, so would need to include Lucivarsh, Zebrella, Arbani, and if possible at least some of the leaders of the smaller clans. It was agreed the wizards would transport to each leading house and pass on the invites. There were a number of suggestions as to the venue. Carylinia suggested Rimor, but Long thought perhaps they should gather at Prenya. "Now that we are aware of Domringa's true identity, it seems likely Lucivarsh will become the Prenya kelpie leader. We can take the opportunity to officially acknowledge this, then we can get right down to business there and then. It seems the most logical approach. I will go on ahead and discuss the situation with her, and at the same time warn her to keep her own agenda regarding Benjamin, and indeed Carylinia, in check for the duration of the conference."

Thus it was agreed to schedule the meeting for 10 days time in Prenya.

CHAPTER THIRTY-FIVE - SHIPWRECK

Captain Tebbin was keen to get going as soon as possible. His crew readied the Porpoise and they left just as the sun crept above the horizon, it's journey spreading yellowy-orange and red streaks across the morning sky, that were quickly masked by the gathering clouds. The weather had deteriorated over the last few days, with high winds and a significant drop in temperature, so the voyage began amidst choppy water and almost horizontal sleet. Kim thought she'd never been quite as cold as she was at that moment. Rhio, she couldn't help but notice, was just as cheery as ever. It made her scowl as, pink-cheeked, he chatted happily to the woman crewman on the tiller. She admonished herself as a brief moment of jealousy betrayed the indifferent image she liked to portray. Kim had been sitting on a box on the deck, but got up and went inside, deciding the queasiness she felt below decks was preferable to the bone-chilling cold she suffered topside, at least for the time being. She didn't last long. She was back up on deck breathing deep of the fresh sea air within the hour, her mood as grey as the clouds, but at least they were moving again.

The squally sea and northerly blow meant the crew were run ragged keeping the reduced sails trimmed efficiently so they maintained forward motion. So long as they kept the mainland in sight on the portside, they were making headway in the right direction. The dark outlines of rocky islets could just about be seen to starboard. Once or twice Kim thought she saw merfolk breaking the surface, but it may have just been the shape of the waves.

A few days later, conditions hadn't improved much, but the captain told them they were close to Eternity Bay, and should reach a sheltered mooring there before nightfall.

Kim had too much time on her hands. She was feeling reflective as she gave some thought to the men in her life. On the one hand there was Benji. At first he was just another project, one of many over the centuries. Later she'd come to love him, but still she'd drugged and groomed him, just as she had so many other lads before him, and one or two lasses too. This whole quest was about Benji. She wanted to save him, needed to, to make up for her betrayal, as he saw it. Maybe she now viewed it that way too. That he turned out to be half fae may account for her change of perspective about him. On the other hand there was Rhio. Full fae and the son of one of her oldest friends – her partner in the clan wars. He had a vibrancy and a personality she found irresistible. He was also remarkably pleasing in bed. These were the things she'd always required from her lovers. So why did she feel so guilty when she made love to Rhio? Why was she risking her life for a 'gangly youth', as her mother called Benji?

"You seem deep in thought lover."

"Don't call me that."

"Why not? It's true."

Kim turned her face away from Rhio. "So why are you helping rescue Benji?" She expected a quick, witty response, yet Rhio gave her question serious thought before answering.

"I'm very motivated to spend time with you Kim. You make me feel…alive. I also have to make a bit of a confession."

That sparked a bit of suspicion. Kim narrowed her eyes as she braced herself for Rhio's real reason for coming.

"When I heard about the winged man that took Benji away, I just had to find out…"

"Kim asked, "Find out what?"

"I've heard stories about an enchanted city in the northern peaks – an eyrie city occupied by Elementals. It's a story that has captured my imagination since I was a nipper. I just have to know."

"Elementals in an enchanted city! You're kidding."

"Do you have a better explanation?"

Kim gazed at Rhio in amazement, then burst out laughing. At first he seemed put out by her response, then he began laughing too. The two of them laughed so hard, they were tearing up.

Their hilarity was cut short as Captain Tebbin yelled across the deck. "You two get below," he directed his instructions elsewhere then, "Drosa get some more sail up and tack to port, quickly now."

Kim and Rhio looked at each other in alarm. Kim said, "What going on Captain?"

He answered impatiently. "Whirlpool. Now get out of the way of the crew."

Kim was close to the back of the ship. Momentarily she caught a glimpse over the stern of the eddying great maw of the whirlpool. Her eyes widened in terror and the ship lurched. A shiver that had nothing to do with the cold ran down Kim's spine. Rhio took her roughly by the arm and pulled her toward the hatch. She didn't resist. She could hear shouting from the captain and crew even over the roar of wind and water. They were thrown against the bulkhead as the ship suddenly spun a hundred and eighty degrees. In the next moment they were on the floor – no not the floor, the bulkhead! The ship was on its side. Kim's head spun with the erratic movement of the vessel. She may throw up any moment. Then she was wet. She shook as freezing seawater rushed into the cabin area. Grabbing for Rhio they both tried to stand up, but they were knocked down before they could gain their feet. More water poured in…

*****

Kim awoke on a small, rocky beach. Weak morning sunlight shone on the wet sand around her. She tried to move but was stiff from the cold, and a pain shot all the way from her head, down her side and into her leg. She rolled over and managed to force her protesting body up into a kneeling position. Taking a breather from the effort she scanned around. There was a long plank beside her. A flash of memory popped into her head of being in the water hanging onto that piece of wreckage for dear life. She remembered the salt had stung her eyes with every wave that had washed over her, and now she became aware again of the salt, now dried, encrusting the corner of her eyes. Trying to rub it away with the heel of her hands just made her hurt more, and only served to blur her vision.

There was no one else on the beach, just a few other small bits of wreckage. Mercifully the icy winds had abated, and a warmer, southerly breeze had taken over. Kim wondered then if she would have survived the night had the penetrating cold of the north winds continued.

Slowly she got to her feet. Dried blood soaked her tunic on her left side. All her warrior instincts came to the fore. Her injury can't be too serious if the bleeding had stopped, and the salt water and cold should have precluded the likelihood of infection. She needed fresh water as a priority, then food and shelter. Eternity Bay could not be much further along the coast and Captain Tebbin had told her there was a large wayfarers hut there. This had to be her goal. If anyone else from the ship had survived they would head there too.

Kim limped slowly to the northern end of the beach. Though the air wasn't as cold now, she was still chilled to the bone, her clothes were drenched, and the weight of them dragged on her, slowing her progress further. Against all odds she spotted a strip of lush green growth extending down from the hills to the edge of the beach. That could only mean fresh water. Quickening her pace as much as she could she found a small trickling stream of clear, sweet water. After swallowing her fill, she rinsed the dried salt from her face, neck and hands. She had no container to take any of the water with her, and reluctantly left the stream behind to clamber awkwardly across the big boulders that separated that beach from the next.

It took half the day and almost all of Kim's remaining energy to work her way along the coastline until she finally came to a wide bay. She'd seen bits of wreckage along the way, had tried unsuccessfully to retrieve a barrel, that may have contain food, from the surf, but as she rounded a corner and found the next bay, there was the main hull of the

186

Porpoise washed up on the beach. She half ran and half stumbled toward it, finally tripping on a protruding rock in the sand. She fell, her head spinning with exhaustion. She couldn't move. So near and yet so far. Darkness took her.

*****

Voices filtered through the fog in Kim's mind. She was warm. It seemed odd, like she'd been cold forever and was meant to be that way. Finally she opened her eyes to find Rhio smiling down at her from a chair beside her bed.

"Hello sleepy-head."

"How long?"

"Almost two days."

Alarm washed through Kim. She went to get up.

"Lie still. You had a concussion, and you lost quite a bit of blood from a wound in your side…" Rhio stopped smiling, his voice cracking, "…I thought I'd lost you."

Kim tried unsuccessfully to sound casual, but her voice was ragged. "It takes more than a bit of a swim to take me down." She paused then asked, "how many made it?"

"Just you, me, Corin and Drosa."

Kim's heart sank and she felt a tear rolling down the side of her face into her ear. How many more people would be lost in these dark times?

CHAPTER THIRTY-SIX – RAEPHA

Raepha wasn't pleased about being left behind when Benji left with four of her own people, the wizards and the fae. Now that she had bound herself to him her place was at his side. But Beluin disagreed. He said he wanted her to stay in Paradisa and 'hold the fort', whatever that meant. She thought it more likely he was trying to keep her and Benji apart, that he had other plans for his son. She screwed her face up. She couldn't for the life of her imagine what that might be.

Raepha walked down to the place by the city wall that overlooked the trail. It was Benji's favourite spot, and they'd spent many hours there talking about their very different upbringings – and about what their futures may hold. It was also the place where they sneaked out of Paradisa without permission and explored the cold mountains. She sighed. They'd only been gone for three days and she already missed Benji so much. It wasn't the way of her people to become so attached, but he was just so unlike anyone she'd ever met before. Also he could be her way out of this place. A thrill went through her as she thought of all the wonderful places they could go together.

As Raepha mulled over such thoughts she glimpsed people coming up the trail. She shrugged, it happened from time to time, but the enchantment surrounding Paradisa meant they were hidden to travellers. Still, it was unusual for people to venture up into the mountains so late in the year. She watched with mild curiosity. There were four of them, three women, human by the look of them, and one male fae. A strange mix of people. It piqued her interest a bit more when they stopped at the spot where the half-goblins had attacked Benji's mother and her party. One of the women was pointing at some debris left behind when the attackers had been whisked away to the Boundary.

Calling in her wings, Raepha became fully pellucid and swirled down to hover above the travellers and listen in, invisibly, to their conversation.

"It's definitely a piece of a human style knife sheath. Some of those damn pirates must have been here." It was the biggest of the three women speaking.

The petite one responded. "Why would they have come up here Corin? Pirates steal goods and sell them on. What would possess them to leave their ship behind and head up the trail? It makes no sense."

"Honestly Kim, I couldn't say…"

Now Raepha was fully alert. Kim was the name of Benji's ex-partner. She studied her more closely. Yes, you could be a kelpie.

"…but maybe they followed that Carylinia woman you told me about, your boy's mum, up here."

Huh! Not your boy any more Kimjora! He's mine now. She sighed again. Under the circumstances, she supposed she'd better rescue them from the cold. Besides, she'd like to get a better look at this woman. Mmm! Would she get into trouble for taking humans to Paradisa? It had never happened before. If they ventured into the Crusians, they normally left them to whatever fate the mountains doled out to them.

She partially materialised and gently stepped to the ground in front of them. They almost jumped out of their skins. Raepha got a little rush of pleasure at the effect she had on them. It gave her an edge. So she lifted her chin and put a slightly superior voice on. "A fae, a kelpie and two humans. You are an unusual collection. Are you here to seek the wisdom of the Elementals?"

The fae was the first to speak. "I knew it. I just knew it. We are most honoured you have deigned to appear before us."

The one called Kim appeared a little exasperated at the formal discourse. "One of your people kidnapped my friend. We are here to rescue him."

Raepha was genuinely startled, both at Kim's impertinence, and her total lack of understanding of the situation. Well, they could talk about it later. "You people will freeze to death out here, and honestly you look like you've already been through significant adversity. Follow me." She didn't wait for a response. Still partially pellucid so she didn't feel the cold herself, she floated slowly up the trail. Her wards gasped when the city walls manifested out of nowhere right in front of them.

The two humans and the fae chatted expansively as the warm air took the chill from their bones while they walked up the hill to the main part of the city. Kim, she noticed, was silent.

As they arrived in the hall, food and drink was being laid out for them. Raepha addressed Kim as the kelpie scanned suspiciously around her whilst the other three tucked into bread, fruit, cheeses and wine. "You may safely eat Kimjora of the Prenya Kelpies."

"You know who I am. How?"

"I listened to a little of your conversation on the trail before I revealed myself to you. And Benji told me about you."

"Benji? Is he here? Is he alright? I need to talk to him."

Raepha scanned at her rival in love up and down – and found her wanting. A rangy creature, not pretty, though she could be attractive, she conceded, after a bath and when her injuries were treated. She smiled. "Huh! For a rescue, you've come rather late to the party. Just as well he was never in any danger."

"Please, I need to talk to him."

"Sorry, you're too late. He headed out to Prenya three days ago to a gathering of the clans and wizards."

Kim stiffened and shook her head. "That's not possible. We would have seen him on the trail surely."

"Everyone that went either flew or went with the wizards." She studied Kim more closely and changed the subject. "You are in need of healing. I will arrange for rooms for you and these others, and I'll send a healer over when you've bathed and rested."

"Thank you, but no. We need to get to Prenya too."

"In your current state you won't make it."

The one called Corin came over. "She's right Kim. That wound in your side only stopped bleeding because of the salt and the cold, but it's far from healed. You should eat something too, get your strength back."

Raepha nodded in acknowledgement of the human's wise words.

CHAPTER THIRTY-SEVEN – PRENYA

Benji was more than a little nervous at being in Prenya. Kim's mum and her people had been trying to bring him here since even before they left Edinburgh, and now he'd come here voluntarily. Was that such a good idea? What if they take advantage of the situation? After all, their party was few in number compared to a city full of kelpies. Still, he had to trust in the Prof to secure his safety.

He'd been allocated accommodation with his mum and Beluin. Huh! He thought, happy families – not. The guest rooms were in the oldest buildings in Prenya, and he was bemused to see the city was made up of about ninety per cent stable-like buildings with converted upper floors. He tried and failed to imagine what this place would be like if all these people where in their natural horsey form.

Lucivarsh, Kim's mum, came to find him. "Well young Benjamin, at last you've arrived at Prenya. I thought you might like to see our laboratory." Benji could feel the tell-tale prickling in his skin that went with nerves, and this woman made him very nervous. He saw from her satisfied smile she could sense his discomfort.

"Oh, don't worry, I've had to bow to the wizard's wishes. You will not be harmed. It's just an invitation to see the work we've been doing. I understand you are still cogitating about whether to help us or not. So please, let me have the opportunity to make our case."

Benji could feel his temper rising, but pushed the feeling down. "Perhaps if you'd invited me before, instead of trying to kidnap me, things would have gone a little smoother." He smiled too feeling that he'd now taken the upper hand.

"You must understand Benjamin, to us you were just one of many potential candidates for our programme over the years. We had no idea of your…unusual heritage, indeed we believed Carylinia had been killed in the clan wars, and we did not know the Elementals were anything more than a myth." She changed the subject briefly. "Tell me, do you know where my daughter is?"

Benji had been about to ask her about Kim's whereabouts. He sighed. "Sorry no."

They'd been walking as they talked, and had arrived at a large single storeyed building at the centre of the city, close to the shops. Benji looked around before they went in, it seemed a little like a human city centre, with stores selling clothes, shoes, kitchenware, groceries and so on. There were also busy cafes and restaurants, and people chatting on street corners. It was nothing like Rimor at all, or any of the other places he'd been in Elysia, all of which had seemed like scenes from a historical film set.

As if Lucivarsh could hear his thoughts she responded whilst unlocking the main door and walking in. "The Prenya kelpies believe in embracing the best of the old and blending them with the new. Our genetics laboratory is equipped with the latest technological equipment. Our medical facility, also at this site, is the same, and our people have trained in the sciences in the human world." As she spoke she pointed through various doors into rooms where staff worked dressed in white lab coats.

Benji frowned. "It seems to me that you've made your lives so good, so much that you can be proud of, I wonder why you are so keen to become…well, you know…what you were."

Lucivarsh appeared genuinely astonished. "We are kelpies. Our human form is useful to us in many ways, and we have adapted to live like this. In fact I would say we've evolved alongside humans much more readily than any of the other clans. But Benjamin, if you could only see us as we

193

truly are, you would understand our need to be able to revert to our natural state whenever we wish. To run across the plains with the wind in our beautiful manes and our auras shining bright – oh the joy!"

Benji didn't know what to say. This woman had seemed so harsh and dangerous to him before, and now here she was caught up in emotional reverie. He gazed at her face. She seemed lost, so desperate, he was forced to make an instant reassessment of her.

They stopped then, and Lucivarsh led him through a door into a well-appointed lab. It was all white and sterile with shiny steel surgical tools and mostly unfamiliar machinery, though he did recognise a few things, like the autoclave, racks of test tubes, flasks, pipettes and so on.

"As you see our labs are not draconian. This is a hospital too, and we look after our patients well. The gene analysis is not an invasive procedure. Once we have found a fae with genes that indicate magic in one of our…projects…" Benji wondered what word she was going to use, "…we have developed a therapy regime which, in theory, should stimulate those dormant genes. It's as simple as that."

"But that would make your 'subject' something different, something they were never meant to be. Anyway, the Prof is concerned that if you regain your shape-shifting abilities, you will stage a final war with the dark fae, wiping them out and upsetting the balance. I can't say I understand what he means by this, but he's given me reason to trust him, whereas you…" Benji shrugged.

Lucivarsh scowled, but made a concerted effort to remain polite. "Let's get a coffee, and I'll fill in some of the obvious gaps in your understanding of our histories." She led him through to a cafeteria that reminded Benji of Starbucks, where she poured two coffees and went to sit on a stool at a tall round table. Benji joined her, and she began to make her case. "Firstly, the dark clans normally live in the Dark Realm. Like all warlike folk they always crave more territory. As we understand it, the demons that dominate in the Dark Realm have become more numerous. They sent the dark clans to Elysia as they cannot come themselves. At least for the moment."

194

"Why not?"

"Elysia repels demons. However, their minions, these are the dark elves, half-goblins – you've seen some of those – boobries, harpies, and a few other smaller clans, are not fully dark, so they are able to spend time in Elysia. The belief is that the more of the dark clan folk that come to Elysia, the more the land here will change and become more tolerant of them. It's thought that if this continues for long enough, then eventually the demons, goblins and dark fairies will be able to come, and that this land will eventually become dark enough to accommodate them. During the clan wars, we favoured driving the enemy back to the Dark Realm over actually killing them. Sadly they had other ideas, and were determined to fight to the death rather than have to admit failure to their demon lords."

"In all fairness it must be horrible to live in a perpetually dark place."

Lucivarsh's eyes widened, her frustration at his ignorance clear on her face. "It's not dark, as in lacking daylight, in the Dark Realm. It's dark more by way of evilness… if there is such a thing."

Benji frowned in confusion. He'd need to give it more thought. By then he had drunk his coffee and was running a finger round and round the rim of his cup as he processed all the new information. "So why do you think the wizards are so against you regaining your natural form?"

"They are concerned we'll take our fight to the human world. They are committed to preventing that. It is true that we wish to kill the dark fae. You see, dark fae don't really belong anywhere. All fae were light until after the clan wars. The change that occurred in some of them to make them dark should never have happened. It's not natural. None of the dark fae in the human world have ever actually been to the Dark Realm, and they don't answer to the wizards, or even to the demons. They are, how is it you people express it? They are 'wild cards'. They have no proper governance, and Osun rules supreme. Though there are some vague rumours of a dark witch pressing her influence in the background. We have no idea how many hybrid offspring the dark fae have spawned, we didn't even know they lived in the human world until recently – but it has to stop. As far as we are concerned they play no part in maintaining the balance. For true balance, the light clans live in Elysia and the dark clans live in the Dark Realm. There are dark-light hybrids that have always lived among us, and maybe some in the Dark Realm too. This also helps to keep the balance. What the wizards should be doing is working towards getting everyone back where they are meant to be. The Prenya kelpies can see they have done little to achieve this, and we are willing to take on that role in their stead. It seems now there are battles to be fought on two fronts. Here in Elysia, and yes, in the human world too."

"Well, you've given me a lot to think about. But one thing that's bothered me all along. If it was a dark fae that removed your ability to change, surely they are the ones that can change you back. Yet you are looking for an answer in modern technology instead of the magic that started all of this."

"What you say is true, but as I said, we thought all the original dark fae were dead, so we searched for their magic in their hybrid descendants. This is what we thought you were. We now know your heritage, and of course we also now know your mother lives. It's possible that she can help us, but you almost certainly can with your Elemental background too. I would ask that you attend the gatherings over the next few days, listen to all the arguments and make up your mind about helping us – sooner rather than later."

Despite the fact Lucivarsh had stalked him in Edinburgh and half way across Elysia, Benji thought her arguments were sound enough. He needed to be sure though. "I will be there, but first I need to talk to Mum."

PART FIVE

CHAPTER THIRTY-EIGHT – OSUN

Osun had never doubted his right to draw power to him, and use it to eventually gain dominion over Elysia for the dark fae. Living all these years in the human world was the perfect cover to build his power base and form links with like-minded folk of the light clans in Elysia, with the light-dark hybrids living in Elysia, and indeed with the dark clans in the Dark Realm. He even had sympathisers amongst the kelpies. As soon as that bitch Lucivarsh found a way to stimulate the fae genes in the dark fae hybrid descendants in the human world, he would take that technology and use it to rally them to his side. The beauty of it was that the technology would never work to restore the kelpies ability to revert to their natural form. Lucivarsh had no idea all she was really doing was working for him. He knew the time was coming soon. The boy Kimjora had been working on, the one everyone believed had the genes for fae magic, had already arrived in Elysia a few weeks earlier. It was only a matter of time before Lucivarsh had what she needed from him. He'd let her perfect the gene stimulation process, then he'd just get one of his people to take it from her and 'awaken' his descendants to their birthright. It was so perfectly simple. He smiled at his own brilliance.

He also had spies in position in Rimor and even in Arbani's court in the Kaylen Mountains – that idiot sprite Atloni.

That Darsh had turned traitor was a disappointing loss, but nothing could dampen his ardour now that he had finally bred a dark fae child. Olia had given birth to his beautiful daughter Opina. Power surrounded her, was drawn to her, right from the moment of her birth. He knew now that he would not be the one to ultimately rule Elysia, but he would prepare the way for his daughter and be her regent. Opina's birth came at an auspicious time. It was clear she was the one whose coming was foretold. Poor Olia, her daughter was sucking the very life out of her with every feeding. Olia's own limited power had already been transferred to Opina, and she was now weak and emaciated. He would be sorry to lose Olia, but her sacrifice would not be in vain.

It had taken all the dark fae's power to boost his pet wizard's sorcery enough to overcome the Wizard Prime. Whether the other wizards were strong enough to break the spell didn't matter now. The message had been sent that even the wizards were no match for him and his fae princess daughter – because that was surely what she was – and she would be a formidable queen.

*****

"Osun, we've had word from that sprite. Arbani left the Kaylen Mountains a few days ago. He's headed for Prenya with his personal guard and thirty warriors to attend a meeting of the clans called by the wizards. Apparently the Wizard of Mount Laskala has been revived and he's on the warpath."

A moment's irritation snapped through Osun, but he pushed it away. His path was set, and he would not be thwarted by some jumped-up magician. "Thank you Rola. It seems we need to step up our plans. Mmm. It may be more difficult to secure Lucivarsh's gene treatment if Prenya's crawling with light clan folk. I need to go to The Boundary and mobilise the dark-light hybrids, and then bring our allies from the other side across." Osun was rubbing his chin and talking more to himself than to Rola, but he turned to her then. "Can you go and fetch…I mean request the presence of the wizard Jeanetta please?" Rola nodded and left silently.

*****

199

"It's a bad idea Osun. It could mean all-out clan war – again. The plan has always been to restore the wizards to their rightful place, and to put the dark fae in a position of power. These are good aims. Bringing these forces across the barrier before we've secured our position in Elysia will not have the results we desire. It will simply pave the way for more and more of the dark clans to occupy the territory, and inevitably the demons will finally break through. Believe me when I tell you, the demons will not share power. They will take it. Elysia will become no different to the Dark Realm. We've discussed this before, I thought you understood the implications."

"I can do this without you if I have to. Can't you see it Jeanetta? Opina is the true and rightful heir. Her birth is a sign the dark fae are destined to rule. The demons will bow to her, or they will be destroyed."

The way Jean looked at him then, he knew he'd lost her allegiance. Stupid woman had cold feet, after all their planning and scheming. Well, no matter. One less wizard in the world was no bad thing. Her startled expression didn't even change as she fell to the floor with his knife protruding from her chest. He called out. "Rola. Get someone to clear this mess up."

Fear rippled across Rola's face as she stopped short and stared at the dead wizard. Osun just smiled. Rola was a weakling, but she was loyal and would do whatever he told her to.

Walking over to the crib, he gazed at his daughter's lovely face. She was still such a tiny baby, yet her dark aura already surrounded her, a deep, rich violet. Her bright blue eyes stared back at him. "I will be back soon my beauty." With that Osun quietened his own dark aura and phased to the backwater gateway on the edge of the Crusian Mountains of Elysia.

CHAPTER THIRTY-NINE – GATHERING

Benji watched from the upstairs window of the apartment he and his parents had been assigned as the endless stream of people poured into Prenya. Many camped in the fields surrounding the city, whilst the delegates continued into the main complex below him. Most had arrived on horseback and numerous young stable hands rushed about helping people down from their saddles and leading their mounts away to be tended. He could see his mum in the crowd greeting Zebrella and some of the other fae. Part of him regretted leaving Raepha behind, though at the same time he couldn't help but search the throng for Kim's arrival. Surely she would come.

Around noon Darsh came and found Benji. "I'm going down to the food hall. You hungry?"

"Sure."

They served themselves with a plateful each of lunch, buffet-style, and took seats on one end of a long table. Darsh was eager for news. "Have you heard anything about Kimjora?"

"No nothing. I've been looking out for her." He shrugged, trying to appear nonchalant. "You know Kim, she can look out for herself."

"You do know she went looking for you?"

"So I've heard. But when she doesn't find me, and hears about this gathering, she'll show up here sooner or later."

"Aha, you can bet on it. What you may not have heard is that my son Rhio went along to join her search. They couldn't have been more than a day or two behind your mother's party, yet no one's heard from either of them in weeks."

A mix of both worry and jealousy rippled down Benji's spine. He cursed himself. Why should he be jealous? He had no reason to think Kim would be interested in Darsh's son, and anyway, he'd dumped her for lying to him and drugging him. And he was perfectly happy with his sweet Raepha – wasn't he? He poked at his food, pushing some kind of sticky savoury patty thing around the plate. "Perhaps with all these people arriving in the city, someone will bring news." Lucivarsh will be asking the new arrivals I'm sure."

Darsh hissed, her whole body suddenly tense. "Arbani."

Benji swung round on his seat to face the door. Arbani was just inside, flanked by two of his personal guard. His eyes were sweeping the room, apparently looking for someone. That someone wasn't likely to be Darsh, but he caught sight of her anyway, briefly held her gaze, smirked, then continued looking around the room. Finally he headed for a table where Dailabi was already sitting talking to a group of other sprites.

Benji glanced back at Darsh. She was a coiled spring. Just like a wild cat at that moment when they stop stalking and pounce. "Darsh," he said urgently, "don't."

Darsh stared at him then slowly eased back. "I will make him pay for what he did to me."

"What he did will be nothing compared to the consequences of taking out a head of state here, in public, at a peace gathering."

She paid a little more attention to him then, studying his face like she was seeing him for the first time. "When did you get to be so wise?"

"Let's get back to Kim and Rhio. What kind of folk live along the east coast and the north? Who might be coming to the gathering that might have seen their movements?"

Darsh frowned and bit her lip as she thought about it. "Mmm. Mostly humans and a few fae. Of course there are also the Mira kelpies and the merfolk. I doubt they'll be along. I've also heard rumours about strange looking pirates in the northern waters."

"Yeah. Seen them!" He had a sudden inspiration then. "Hey. Why not ask the wizard? He can flash around from place to place in an instant, I guess the other wizards are the same and there are at least a dozen of them here from what I've seen."

Benji left and went in search of Long.

"It's not as simple as that Benjamin. We can only transport to somewhere within a line of sight. We have to focus our thoughts on a spot and…send ourselves there – agh! It's a bit hard to describe. We can't just float around randomly." He rubbed his chin. "Oh, but one of the Elementals could head home and see if there's been any sign of Kim and Rhio. Why don't you go and talk to your father?"

"Alright Alright." Beluin had finally been worn down by Benji's insistence. "I'll ask Playa to go back to Paradisa briefly and get Raepha and Tremin to organise a search." Benji heart skipped a beat at the thought of Raepha and Kim meeting. 'What would they talk about?' But the main thing was to make sure Kim was safe.

*****

The first meeting of the gathering was underway. Benji wasn't really listening to the proceedings. He was more interested in studying all the different types of people. Mostly fae, kelpies, sprites, and humans – or at least they appeared human. But there was a smattering of other Elysians that he couldn't name. The Elementals, he noticed, listened hard, but said little. The other clan delegates kept breaking out into arguments about whether there was or wasn't a threat. It all seemed rather pointless discourse to him. Curiosity aside, all he really cared about was news from Playa, but she hadn't yet returned.

The afternoon dragged on. The Prof had a lot to say for himself. Not surprising really after what he'd been through. His mum was speaking now so Benji tuned in for a while to hear her telling the gathering about her long exile, and how the dark fae had finally revealed themselves. Benji was surprised to hear Dailabi speaking up then, claiming it was all conjecture and that there was no reason to assume the dark fae were on the move. They had good lives in the human world, why would they compromise that? Benji had noticed previously that Dailabi was a gentle soul, always wanting to see the best in people. Arbani was a different matter – aggressive, self-serving and opinionated. He took over from his wife, patting her hand condescendingly as she sat back down. He, however, called for a reckoning. "We should bring Osun here and question him. It would save a lot of time." Despite Benji's dislike of the nasty little sprite, he couldn't help but agree with the idea.

Suddenly a shout went up. The doors flew open with a loud bang and Playa staggered into the hall. She looked terrible. Her left wing was damaged, and her arm hung limply at her side. Her hair was in disarray, and her face was swollen and bruised. Beluin was beside her in a moment. He helped her to a chair and they talked quietly as the gathering watched in stunned silence, some standing to get a better look.

Finally Beluin stood and turned toward the people in the hall. "Osun has called the dark forces across the Boundary. Brave Playa stayed a while to observe their numbers and movements, but was spotted when she took solid form to warn a party of humans and direct them to safety. She barely escaped with her life. Thousands of half-goblins, elves and even a few harpies have crossed into Elysia and are even now heading south. They have boobrie lookouts flying overhead too." With that Beluin led Playa out of the hall.

For a few moments there was complete silence, then all hell broke loose as everyone had an opinion on what to do next. Finally Long's voice projected from the head of the table. Not loud, just penetrating. "Silence." Everyone stopped talking instantly, such was Long's power. "It is clear this gathering is too little and too late. Call your forces people and be quick about it. In one week we will assemble in The Triangle. We march to war."

CHAPTER FORTY – EYRIE

It had been several days since Kim, Rhio, Corin and Drosa came to the eyrie city of Paradisa. Kim had to admit she may not have survived the journey home to Prenya had these strange Elementals not treated her wounds. The baths she had each day accelerated the healing process, and despite a persistent twinge in her side she felt ready to travel. Her companions, however, didn't seem in any hurry to leave, seduced as they were by the luxurious lifestyle the eyrie had to offer, but Corin at least had some sense. She sought her out.

"It's time we were leaving."

"Huh! Which of your boys are you most worried about? The one at Prenya getting mixed up in clan politics or the one that likes to take long hot baths with Jania."

Kim was taken aback. It occurred to her then she'd not seen much of Rhio since they arrived. She'd spent most of her time either undergoing treatments in the healing baths, or pacing around the city walls getting more and more frustrated that she wasn't where she was meant to be – in the thick of things. Right on cue Rhio and Jania came down the passageway arm in arm heading for the food hall. Kim had mixed feelings about that. Her relationship with Rhio was never going anywhere, it was just a bit of fun, and she taken some comfort in having this charming young man warm her bed for her. At the same time, he'd taken up with some

205

Elemental female she hadn't even noticed before, and a tingle of jealousy assaulted her. She forced it down when she saw that Rhio did at least have to decency to look embarrassed.

"We'll be leaving in the morning. Will you be joining us?" Kim asked him.

"Of course. I've joined you on your quest. I will see it through."

Jania just smiled, unconcerned, and wandered off. Kim found these Elementals rather fickle. They were a gentle people, but they lacked passion or very much interest in the world outside their hidden eyrie city. As for Raepha, well she seemed to constantly wear a kind of supercilious expression, like she knew something important that Kim didn't, but wasn't letting on. She found her tiresome company.

Kim turned to Corin. "Where's Drosa?"

"I don't know. She's taken to walking outside the city wall. For some reason she seems to like the cold mountains." Corin shrugged. "Beats me!"

"Well, when she gets back can you let her know we're leaving?"

"Sure."

*****

Kim was packing a rucksack with supplies ready for the journey. Raepha had agreed to get four of her people to transport them as far as Bren Bay. This would get them past the Crusian Mountains, and save several days journey. They just had to hope they'd be able to get a ship from there. Kim had asked the Elementals to take them further, but Raepha explained it was only the ongoing presence of the Elemental people in the city that kept the shield active. With so many of their people already away in Prenya, they couldn't afford to have too many of them leave the city for more than a few hours at any one time.

"Where the hell is Drosa?" Kim repeated.

"I don't know Kim. It's not like her to be gone so long," answered Corin. "Perhaps we need to send out a search party. She may have slipped on the ice and injured herself."

"I'll talk to Raepha."

Dorbin and Tremin accompanied them in their search outside the city walls. They went partially pellucid so were able to search from the air and cover more ground, yet still be just about visible to Kim and her companions.

After about an hour, Dorbin stepped gently down in front of them carrying Drosa. "We need to get back to the city as quickly as possible."

Corin asked, "Is she ok?"

"She is badly injured, but we can heal her. Right now there are more important matters. I need to report what I've seen to the others. I will take Drosa back, but you must come as quickly as possible. Tremin will see you heading back up the trail. He will know to come back too. Do not delay." Kim and Corin passed a worried look between them, and headed quickly along the path, urged on by Dorbin's unusually urgent demeanour.

Kim and the others dropped their heavy cloaks on the floor of the hut just inside the city wall where the main gateway to the outside world stood. They rushed up the hill and into the hall. Raepha was talking to Dorbin and Tremin, who'd flown in ahead of them. Raepha explained. "There has been activity in the area where The Boundary lies."

"The Boundary?"

"It's the main weak point that separates Elysia from the Dark Realm. Some even consider it a portal as there's a kind of nomansland between the two realms. Going by the signs of footfall there, it would appear many folk from the Dark Realm have crossed into Elysia."

A rush of adrenalin pumped through Kim's body. Her warrior instincts were immediately in play. "Many? How Many?"

Raepha hesitated only a moment. "At least hundreds, possibly thousands. It seems Drosa may have seen them, tried to get to safety, and fallen into a crevice."

Corin asked, "How is she?"

"The healers say she will recover, but it will take time. She will not be travelling back with you."

"Raepha, it is imperative that we get word to my mother, the fae and the wizards. Is it at all possible that you can find some way to take us a little further?"

207

"I'm sorry Kim. This invasion only means it is all the more important to keep the eyrie hidden. However, Dorbin saw Playa, one of our people that had gone with Beluin. She was hurt, but still able to fly. She had been coming here, but flew straight back to Prenya instead. The warning has been delivered by now."

Kim addressed Dorbin. "Did you tell this Playa to let them know we were here?"

"I did not."

Kim rolled her eyes. She found the vagaries of behaviour in these Elementals all too frustrating. "Rhio, Corin, we need to get moving straight away. If we get to Bren Bay now, we should be ahead of them, assuming they all came through to Elysia together that is."

"But we can't assume that can we. They may have been passing into our world for days for all we know," said Rhio.

"Well, if any of their force has passed through Bren Bay already, we'll know it as soon as we get there, won't we?"

CHAPTER FORTY-ONE – DECISION

"What's The Triangle?" Benji asked as they sat at dinner.

Carylinia explained. "It's a broad grassland and arable farming area south of the Jamion Hills, but also flanked on the east by the Aberne Marshes, and Vaskra Forest to the west. The Lomari River flows along nearly half of its outer edge. It will be a good vantage point to rally our forces. It's also fairly close to the coast. I know Long is hoping to entice the Merfolk and the Mira kelpies to join the battle."

Beluin was watching him closely. "You will not be going Benji."

"What do you mean, of course I'll be going."

"This will be a vicious battle, and you are not a fighter. I had hoped this renewal of hostilities would never happen, but alas..." Beluin was shaking his head sadly.

Benji was incensed. "What do you know of battles? From all the accounts I've heard, the Elementals didn't get involved, in fact no one seemed to even know you existed."

Beluin briefly glanced at Carylinia. "Some knew – those with magic – that could see us. When we are fully pellucid, we are invisible to most people. We were able to fly above the enemy and drop them with our arrows."

"But I thought your arrows didn't kill."

"It was a dark time in our history. At first we just dropped them, rendering them unconscious. But in doing so we left them helpless against the Elysian forces. We may as well have been killing them ourselves for all the difference it made. So toward the latter part of the clan wars, we learned about poisons from those fae that knew of our existence," he glanced at Carylinia again, "and we dipped our arrows. It was a cleaner death for the enemy."

His fathers' furtive looks were not lost on Benji. He stared at his mum, incredulous. "You? You taught the Elementals how to kill?"

"Such is the nature of war son. Kill or be killed." Her look was cold, or maybe even a little proud. Benji couldn't read her. She was like a stranger to him these days. What happened to the mum who would kick a ball about in the back garden with him? Where was the mum who took him snorkelling in Trinidad and sailing in the Med? Somehow she'd melted away to be replaced by an ancient, magical, killer fae. Suddenly Benji found himself yearning for the simpler days of his childhood when it was just the two of them.

Long came in and joined them, helping himself to a bowlful of stew. "Sorry I'm late. Mmm! Looks delicious."

"My...father, "Benji was still uncomfortable calling Beluin that, "wants me to stay here."

"I agree with him..." Benji was about to protest, but Long raised his hand to stop him, "...but for more than one reason. Yes, I want to keep you safe, you have no idea what a battlefield is like, you need to keep it that way."

"And the other reason?"

"I've just spent the last hour or more getting earache from Lucivarsh. It would appear, under the circumstances, that...well...maybe the wizard council was...you know... a little mistaken in our conviction that the kelpies shouldn't regain their shape-shifting abilities."

Carylinia's eyes widened. "After all this time? You're kidding."

"All the while the dark fae kept themselves to themselves in the human world – and all the while the light-dark hybrids in Elysia just went about their lives without interfering with anyone, the balance was tentatively maintained. Now, however, Osun, it seems, has taken it upon

210

himself to incite a second round of clan wars and is bent on conquering Elysia. He's not only somehow managed to corrupt one of my wizard sisters, but has rallied forces from the Dark Realm to aid him in his ambitions. We will be hard pressed to overcome them. This is unexpected and we are not prepared for all out war, not in the least. The kelpies, it seems are the only clan that has kept it's warriors trained up. We need them, and we need them at full power."

"What are you saying?" asked Carylinia

"Your magic, my dear, has passed to your son. Oh he has no knowledge how to use it of course, but since Kimjora's drug ministrations have worn off, I've been able to sense an ever-increasing power emanating from him."

Benji was utterly startled. "I don't have much fae magic at all. I'd know it if I did." He scoffed.

"How exactly?"

"Well, I'd be able to…do things. Magic things. Things that are more than just lighting a fire without a match… oh I don't know!"

"You are only minimally trained and totally undisciplined. But power resides within you. However there's no time to deal with that now. Your mother should have dealt with that long before this."

Carylinia was getting exasperated. "I repeat. What are you saying?"

"You will use your magic to restore the kelpies – and you will draw power from Benjamin to help you achieve that."

"I WILL NOT."

"Carylinia, I'm sorry, but this is not a request. You are still subject to the rule of the wizards. We require that you do this. Elysia will be lost to the dark clans, Osun will rule, and maybe even the demons will cross The Boundary. All this will happen if you do not comply."

Carylinia stormed out of the room. Benji just stared after her as the door swung shut.

*****

Later that day Benji went to find Darsh. Their friendship had grown over the months they'd known each other, albeit from a dodgy beginning.

"I can't believe they would deny you the right to join the battle Benji. You have as much of a stake in the outcome as anyone else. If your mother can restore the kelpies, all well and good, but you should be with us."

"I knew you'd understand. This is my decision, I'm a grown man now, but what am I to do?"

Darsh thought about it for a moment. "We are leaving for The Triangle at first light. Join us. We'll be well on our way before they even realise you're missing."

The next morning Benji quietly got up, dressed, and headed for the stables where the fae forces were gathering. Darsh nodded in acknowledgement and indicated his mount with her chin. Within minutes forty or so fae were on the road heading out to join the rest of their people at The Triangle, with Benji secreted amongst them.

CHAPTER FORTY-TWO – ARMY

Three of the Elementals from Paradisa took Kim, Rhio and Corin to Bren Bay. They had to remain partially pellucid and partially solid in order to carry their burdens. This slowed their journey time, but only by a little.

They were high up in the sky during the journey, but still they could see the enemy's army heading south on the rarely used coast road. Their line stretched for miles, and Kim thought there must be between twelve and fifteen thousand of them. They put her in mind of a line of marching ants – a dark scourge on the land now dusted in winter snow. There were a few ships heading south too but they were too far away to make them out. Were they enemies too, or would at least one of them be a friendly ship to carry them further south? Finally the vanguard of the enemy line came into view in the distance, about half way across the Jamion Hills. She cursed under her breath – the bulk of their forces were even now passing through Bren Bay. They would be dropped off slap-bang in the midst of the advancing army.

The Elementals set them down discreetly at the back of the Travellers Rest Inn and, after brief farewells, they vanished into their fully pellucid state and were gone. The three travellers entered the inn through the back door. The place had been ransacked. Beer barrels overturned, bottles broken and the furniture smashed to pieces. Corin turned her nose up at the smell of stale beer and rancid food. Rhio ran up the stairs to see if the innkeeper or staff, or indeed anyone, had hidden in one of the rooms, but there was no one to be found.

Kim crossed to the window and took a sharp intake of breath. Dark clan soldiers were everywhere. Mostly elves, but also many of the ugly brutes that had taken Corin's ship were milling about too. She now knew they were half-goblins, and shuddered at the thought of how they came to be. No human would willingly mate with a goblin. "They're heading this way, we need to get out of here NOW."

Corin said, "We need to get eyes on those ships. If one of them can carry us, that's where we need to be. Otherwise we need to find horses in order to outflank them."

Kim shook her head as they sneaked back outside. "I remember during the clan wars before, these creatures don't carry much in the way of supplies. They eat everything they come across. There'll be no horses left anywhere they've been."

Corin shuddered. "Let's hope for a ship then, but they'll see what going on and steer clear of the harbour. Once…or rather if…we've identified a suitable vessel, we'll need to take a tender and row out to it. The timing needs to be right. We'll have to go under cover of darkness, but still be able to intercept the ship."

"We should be able to skirt around them. If we can get to the lookout without being seen, will you be able to see who's about out there?"

"Sure. I know everyone in the trade fleet in these parts."

Kim and Corin hunched together on their bellies up at the lookout. "Yes! It's the Sturgeon. Captain Grawd is a friend of mine."

Kim wriggled back from the hilltop, stood upright, stretched and shivered from the damp that had seeped through her clothes. "It's almost dark, we'll have to chance going now otherwise that ship will be beyond our reach."

They joined Rhio in the little boathouse. He'd readied a tender that was only just big enough for the three of them. They untied the painter from the stanchion on the side of the wooden floating pier and eased the boat quietly out into open water.

214

"Careful not to splash, and keep low."

"Aye Cap'n."

They were well out in the channel when a call went up from the shore. They'd been spotted. Suddenly there were enemies lining the harbour wall holding torches and shouting.

"No help for it now, they've seen us, might as well stop creeping along and get those oars moving harder."

They all sat up straight. Before long Kim's arms were all but spasming from the cold and exertion, but she kept rowing. There was a whooshing sound, then a hiss as a flaming arrow extinguished in the water not ten feet from their position, then another and another, getting closer until finally one hit. Rhio grabbed the bailer and put the flames out straight away. They all sighed, but their relief was premature. Corin screamed as the next arrow thudded into her arm. Her sleeve caught fire and she dropped her oar in the water. Rhio doused the flames as she sobbed in agony. The little boat wasn't moving toward the ship any more. It spun around and was lurching sideways as Rhio stood to reach Corin. Kim frantically tried to turn back round again, but the boat was listing badly. One of the arrows had penetrated the hull and the freezing water was pooling around their feet. The Sturgeon was still a long way from their position, but the crew had spotted them and they had changed course.

Corin's voice was husky from the pain. "They won't get to us in time. We're going down."

Then there was a new voice, a hissing, watery voice. "It seems Kimjora of the Prenya kelpies, that you are in need of assistance once more."

Kim gazed at the mermaid with mixed feelings. Yes they needed help, but what would be the price? She already owed this creature. But there was no other way. "Can you get us to that ship?" Kim pointed at the Sturgeon.

A moment later the tender boat was moving toward the ship so unnaturally fast it was creating a wake and within minutes the Sturgeon's crew helped Corin and Rhio on board.

Reluctantly Kim stayed put, dreading what would come next, and frustrated she couldn't head back into the thick of the action with her comrades. She gazed up at Rhio, now leaning over the taffrail.

"Kim? What are you doing? Climb up," he said.

She studied his face sadly and shook her head. "I will see you on the battlefield."

"Kim, Kim, come back!" Rhio's voice faded as Kim, in her leaky boat moved swiftly away, carried by the merfolk.

CHAPTER FORTY-THREE – BATTLE

More than three thousand fae were camped in The Triangle when Benji rode up alongside Darsh.

"What have you got there Darsh? Is that a human?"

"No, not really. He is, however, the man who saved my life. You will show him some respect. Now, what's going on?"

The soldier at least had the decency to look a little contrite as he gazed at Benji more closely before he spoke again. Then he was all business. "Our scouts got back an hour ago. The enemy vanguard is already half way across the Jamion Hills. Their lines are anything up to six abreast, and they go back as far as the eye can see. They just keep coming. There must be tens of thousands of them. They are not slowed up by the burden of a supply chain. They just eat everything… and everyone they come across. And Darsh – Osun is at the head of the army."

Benji went weak at the knees. It was one thing to get involved in a battle, he'd seen hundreds of them on tv, but to be eaten by the enemy!

Darsh scowled at the mention of Osun. "Who else is here?"

"Aside from us, around two thousand kelpies, about a thousand humans, a couple of hundred sprites – more to come they say, a few fairies and dryads, oh and there's even a couple of visiting gamayuns. No good in a fight, but they can

217

scout from above, which will give us a tactical advantage. There are some other humans, merchants I think, due to arrive any time with supplies, useful, but again not soldiers. In fact there's not nearly enough fighters if our numbers don't swell soon. There are four wizards over there in the command tent making plans."

Darsh nodded dismissing the fae warrior. "You'd better stick with me for now Benji. Come on lets see what the wizards are conjuring up."

"Ukrit, it is good to see you."

"Darsh? It is agreeable to see you too. This is Rana, Wizard of the Great Desert, Marinara, Wizard of the Eastern Ocean and Panuk, Wizard of the Kraynor Tundra."

Darsh nodded to the other three wizards. "So, what's the plan?"

The six of them stood around a crude map on a central table. Benji got a little tingle of pleasure to be in the thick of things, it made him feel important. Ukrit explained their thoughts so far. "Assuming there are a lot more of our forces arriving promptly, we thought to flank the invading army to the west and drive them into the Aberne Marshes."

Darsh waited a few moments for the rest of the plan, looking expectantly at the wizards from one to the other and back again. But they said no more. "That's it? That's all you've come up with?"

"Well we only got here yesterday, and we thought to wait for the clan leaders before deciding on a strategy. But this seemed like a good start, and we can start moving troops into position straight away," said Ukrit.

"You mean spread our troops thinly so that they can be picked off a few at a time. I know it's been a long time since the clan wars Ukrit, but you were a formidable strategist in your time." Darsh shook her head and sighed in resignation. "We will keep everyone together here for now. The rest of the kelpies, fae and sprites should be here in the next few days. Lets just hope that's soon enough. I'm amazed at the distance the enemy has covered already. We could be engaged within a week at this rate. Do you know where I can find the gamayuns?"

"Panuk sent them out this morning, they should be back soon."

"Good. When they get back, please send for me. Come on Benji."

Benji was beginning to wish he'd stayed behind after all. What did he know about battles? He'd never lifted a weapon in his life, well apart from having a go at archery at the Kent County Show when he was about twelve, but he guessed that wouldn't do him much good.

"This battle will be a proving ground for you Benjamin. Tell me, what weapons can you wield?"

'Ugh oh!' But he didn't want Darsh to think him useless. "Just a bow. I had little use for weapons in my…in the human world."

"That's good. We can always use more archers. I will hand you over to Captain Sima tomorrow. He will equip you with what you need and assign you to a one of the archery battalions."

Benji didn't want to be separated from Darsh. He felt safe with her. "Where will you be?"

"On the front line. Look, I know you don't know anyone else here, but the front line of a battlefield is no place for an untried warrior. You would only get yourself killed, and I've no mind to explain what happened to Kim – or to Carylinia for that matter."

Benji nodded. He really really wished he'd stayed behind now.

Over the next few days more and more troops arrived in The Triangle. They were mostly fae, kelpies and sprites, but with a sprinkling of folk from other clans too, some of whom Benji couldn't identify. He wondered how his parents and the Prof reacted when they realised he'd disappeared. He didn't have to wait long to find out.

"Of all the selfish, irresponsible, stupid things to do Benjamin. Do you know how frantic your mother has been?" said Long.

"This war affects me too you know."

"Well of course it does. That's why you should be doing everything in your power to help. That means letting your mother draw power from you to use her magic and restore the

219

kelpies. It doesn't mean putting yourself in danger, not to mention putting all those around you in danger. Word has gone out, you know, about who you are. All these people around you here will put their own lives in danger to protect you, because goodness only knows, you can't take care of yourself. You couldn't even do that as a mediocre student in the middle of Edinburgh. Have you any idea what this battle will be like?"

"Um well…"

"That was a rhetorical question. So I'll tell you. These people around you, they'll be killed, maimed. The ground will be slippery with their blood. People will scream and cry. The smell will be nauseating – blood, vomit, urine, faeces. The enemy will have no mercy. They'll be no Geneva Convention here. These will be killing grounds. If the enemy prevail, they will leave no one alive, and they will take pleasure in torturing and killing us. Even if we prevail, it will not feel much like victory when so many lie dead. This isn't a computer game Benjamin. This is real."

Benji's heart was racing as Long's words conjured up graphic images of what was to come. He didn't know what to say, but it was too late to say anything. Everyone was shouting, bugles and bells were sounding. Long rushed outside the makeshift shelter just as an arrow buried itself in the ground right by his feet. He jumped back away from the arrow and turned back to Benji. "Come with me."

Benji ran low following the Prof dodging the flaming arrows as they whistled by setting flames to canvas tents, carts, and even people. Already there were cries as clothing caught fire and people were being doused with water bucketed out of the Lomari. Some ran screaming to jump into the fast flowing river, too desperate to avoid the jutting rocks. Long led him to one of the tents where the wizards were trying to put up a magical shield against the sudden assault. Benji waited outside but could hear the Prof barking orders.

"Rana, I need you to transport this boy out of harms way."

"What boy?"

Meanwhile, Captain Sima had come. "Boy, get to the lines, now."

Before Long could stop him Benji was following Sima. And now Long had other matters to attend to as the whole tent went up in flames.

Benji found himself lined up with thirty fae, his bow pulled back. He let his arrow fly. At first he was gratified that he'd hit home on the first shot, but as his quarry groaned in agony on the floor, he saw a tear escaping the creature's eye, and his natural compassion kicked in. Suddenly he wanted to save the… well he didn't know what it was… but he wanted to save it anyway. It was a living thing and he'd caused it to suffer. He started to move forward. The fae next to him grabbed his arm to stop him, and got his own arm half shot off for his trouble. Hot blood splattered Benji's face and neck, the man rolled down the bank behind the line cradling his arm, what was left of it. Benji couldn't breathe. He wiped his face and sticky blood came away on his hand. What was he doing here? He felt suddenly hot and dizzy, though the air was only a few degrees above freezing. He dropped his bow, and just caught a glimpse of more of the strange creatures, like the one he'd shot, scrambling up the hill toward their lines. Then all went black.

*****

"Benjamin. BENJAMIN. Wake up." Slowly the words filtered through. He was lying on something soft and comfortable. Beluin came into focus.

"Father?"

"So, you've finally acknowledged who you are."

"Where are we?"

"At Prenya. I found you on the killing fields and brought you back here. I thought you'd been killed when I saw you lying there covered in blood and surrounded by dead fae. What you did was extremely misguided, but brave. Son, I'm proud of you. Your mother however doesn't quite see it the same way." He cringed a bit.

Benji recognised the expression as one of his own. It was the first time he'd seen Beluin anything but completely confident. Apparently his mum had the same effect on his father as she did on… well, pretty much everyone. "Where is she?"

221

"She's been trying to create the magic that will restore the kelpies on her own, but I'm afraid it isn't working. She will need your help."

"I don't know how to do magic."

"You won't need to," said Carylinia as she entered the room, "I just need to draw on your innate, magical strength to bolster my own power."

"Mum…"

"We'll discuss it later. Right now I need you to drink this Hawbleberry juice restorative. I'll come back for you in an hour. We have work to do."

CHAPTER FORTY-FOUR – DEBT

The merfolk were not a people to mess with. They weren't dark, not at all, they were just passionate about honour and debt. Yes they killed people sometimes, mostly humans, though they did this painlessly and actually blissfully from what Kim understood, but this was just their way. You wouldn't condemn a lion that killed to eat, or a bear that killed to protect it's young. Merfolk were creatures of Elysia and they had their own place in the world. Mostly they didn't affect anyone, in fact few even believed they existed at all, such was their desire for isolation.

Kim was back in the cave on the tiny island they'd been on when they encountered the merfolk before. A collection of merfolk had half carried, half floated the leaky boat with her in it to the island.

The mermaid she'd conversed with before came to her then. "So, Kimjora of the Prenya kelpies. You are now doubly indebted to us. Tell me, did you find the one you were looking for?"

The mermaid's slow, hissy voice was as disturbing as the fishy aroma. She hadn't noticed that before. She supposed it was because she'd been under the influence of merfolk magic. "I did not. Now tell me, what is it you want from me? I fail to see how anything I can do will benefit folk such as you."

"This is where you are wrong, Kimjora. We have a task for you."

Kim cringed inwardly, but maintained her confident demeanour on the surface. She would not show fear, or indeed the panic she was feeling. It would only serve to give the mermaid a further advantage over her. "Well?"

"Do you know he wizard Marinara?"

"Not personally. Though I've heard of her. Why?"

"She took something from us. We want it back."

"You can't be serious. You want me to steal something from a wizard?"

"She is the thief."

Kim pursed her lips. "What is it?"

"A pearl. The biggest ever found, it would barely fit in your hand, Kimjora, and it is most unusual. It is all colours. We call it The Rainbow Pearl. It is very old, magical, and it is sacred to us."

"Can't you just ask her for it back?"

"We tried. She believes that as the Wizard of the Eastern Sea, it belongs to her. A most strange turn of events. She had always admired its beauty and power, but had not shown any desire to possess it until a few years ago. It was our most sacred possession from a time even before she came into existence. We require its return. This is our price. You will do this for us."

"You know the dark clans have invaded Elysia? These are the ones you rescued us from. Right now the world is going to war, and you want me to do some breaking and entering? – now?"

"We are aware of what is happening. We too will fight the dark forces. Half-goblins drown easily, and elves are even more readily seduced than humans – they will come to our pool. But we will do nothing until you return The Rainbow Pearl to us."

Kim remembered the pool almost longingly. She remembered its powerful pull on her senses. Her mind wandered. She ran her hands over her own breasts and down her undulating body. She was breathing heavily, then she caught sight of the mermaid's amused smile, and snapped out of it, frowning at how easily she could be rendered helpless in this place.

"I see even you are not immune to our allure. It seems the Prenya are weaker than the Mira. Perhaps when this is all over you can come back and join with us in the pool. You are kelpie, so we won't kill you. The Mira join with us often."

"I'll bear it in mind. As for the elves, most will already be beyond this point by the time I can return the pearl to you. But what of the Mira kelpies, will they fight?"

"Some will join us when the time comes, as they did before."

"Ok so what do you know of this wizard? Where will I find her?"

"She has gone to war. She will have the Rainbow Pearl with her as she draws on it when she uses her magic. She will not give it up readily."

"The front line is a long way from here."

"Your boat is on the shore on the other side of the island. It has been repaired. We will take you in this boat as we did before down the coast to the Lomari River Delta. Then we will take you some of the way up the river, but river water reacts badly with our skin. We cannot take you all the way to The Triangle. You will have to make your own way for the last forty-five miles or so. Your journey with us will be fast. You may even get there before your travelling companions on the ship do. My people will then wait near the delta for you to deliver The Rainbow Pearl."

*****

Kim scrambled up the riverbank. She was right on the edge of the Aberne Marshes. They could be treacherous, she couldn't risk travelling at night, but she found a wayfarers hut an hour along the rough track that led by the riverside. The hut was in poor repair. Half the roof had fallen in, and the fireplace had collapsed. She made a fire on the floor from some of the roof timbers and was mildly surprised to find a tin of baked beans in the food cupboard. Someone had been here that had also been to the human world at some point. She smiled at that. Benji loved beans, he'd be jealous she got to have some. She lay back on the soggy mattress that night mulling over how Benji might be faring, but also how to affect her heist. Try as she might, she couldn't come up with a viable plan. She'd just have to wing it.

The next morning Kim got up as soon as it was light and set out at a steady run, following the barely-visible riverside track. It was overgrown, though much of the foliage had died back for the winter – a small advantage. In distance she could just about make out the hazy edge of the Vaskra Forest, but she would need to turn slightly back northwards before she reached the treeline in order to get to The Triangle. This surely was where the light clans would gather ready to engage the enemy. Even the mermaid believed this, though Kim had no idea where or how she got her information.

It was wintertime. The dark drew in all too early, and Kim was thinking about another overnight stop. She'd just cleared the marshes when she heard voices, but couldn't make out who they were or what they were saying. Keeping low she slid quietly behind a slight rise in the land. She breathed a sigh of relief, had it been a mile back along the path there would have been no opportunity for cover at all. The voices got closer. They weren't speaking English. It was a language she'd not heard for centuries. Elves! The enemy had advanced far more than she'd expected, how could they have already outflanked the light clan's camp? There was only one possible answer. Somehow they started arriving and setting up outposts long before Osun brought the bulk of the army across The Boundary. It was the only explanation. But how did they come without being detected? Their dark auras should have sent ripples through The Ein. They must have had help. Who would have such power? Only a wizard. Jeanetta. It had to be. She must get past them and warn the others. Her foot slipped on some loose stones. They rattled down the slope. The talking stopped. Kim's heart thumped in her chest, her palms were sweaty despite the cold. The urge to bolt had to be resisted. She kept quiet and low...
footsteps... getting louder, heading her way... they stopped. She bit her lip. The creature was so close she could hear it breathing and smell its musky aroma. She held her breath. A quiet moment that lasted a lifetime. Then the elf spoke in its bizarre guttural language and the footsteps resumed, but now they were moving away. Kim let her breath out. She waited,

just to be sure, then crawled on her belly slowly, quietly along the back of the rise until she was sure she was clear. She'd have to travel in the dark after all, but it was ok, the footing was firmer, the marshland left behind. She began to run, tripping on roots of low shrubs that now dominated the landscape, but continuing to keep the silver strip of the moonlit river in sight to her right.

Finally the dark blur of the Vaskra forest was visible ahead, the weak moonlight that had guided her along the river's edge also served to distinguish it from the rest of the night's landscape to the west. Now she had to make her turn back to the north. Kim was relieved to see the route was well trampled. The troops had passed this way. She was on the right track. She walked for a while as the hours of running, interspersed with recovering from trips and bumps along the way, had exhausted her.

Early morning light crept over the horizon as Kim cautiously found her way toward The Triangle where the sounds of battle put her on alert. She was utterly wiped out and knew this was when a warrior could make mistakes. She needed to be extra careful. Her knives slid smoothly into her hands as she saw a half-goblin about to strike a final blow to a fae warrior down on the ground. In moments she was on the enemy's back. Slinging her arm around its neck she slashed her knife across its throat, then rolled neatly away as it dropped. A quick scan round showed this to be an isolated attack. She reached out her hand to the fae warrior who took it and got up, nodding her thanks.

"Take me to the command centre, quickly." The fae nodded again and led Kim just a couple of hundred yards to a ruined stone building hidden amidst some evergreen shrubs.

"Kimjora! Where have you been? We thought you were dead."

"Hello Long. I'll explain later. First you need to know there are elves camped along the Lomari on the edge of the Aberne Marshes, and there are tens of thousands of enemy troops heading toward this position, closer than we could have anticipated."

"Sit down, you look exhausted. Someone get this warrior some food and water. We are aware of the troop movements, though we didn't know the elves were so close. Thank you for bringing this to us. Kim, you need some rest, you look fit to drop. There's a bunk out the back there. We'll debrief later."

Kim downed a cup of water and a hawbleberry biscuit, and went for a lie down. She didn't expect to sleep, she was so hyped up, but the next thing she knew a wizard was shaking her awake.

"Kimjora, I am Marinara, the Wizard of the Eastern Sea. Long asked me to wake you and bring you to the front."

Kim could hardly believe her luck. Marinara was right here right now, and what's more there was a distinct round bulge in her pocket. All she had to do was extract the Rainbow Pearl, get it back to the coast – that would go a lot quicker on horseback – and then their forces would be swelled by the merfolk and Mira kelpies. "Of course," she said.

They headed across to the front. The light clans had set up a line and already there was fighting on the other side. A few bodies strew the ground this side too. Some of the enemy had got through, like the one she'd encountered when she arrived. She lifted her head to the sky, but it was too overcast to make out the sun's position. "How long have I been asleep?"

"About three hours."

"Ah Kim, there you are," said Long, "We need to catch up on each others info, but quickly. I've dispatched a group of kelpies to take out the elves you told us about. I'm hoping you have at least some better news for us?"

Kim thought for a moment, then made up her mind to go for the straightforward approach. She pierced Marinara with her best glare. "I have been with the merfolk. They say you stole an artefact from them. They say it's sacred to them." She could see Marinara's eyes flickering about as she fingered the bulge. Definitely it's what she has in her pocket then.

Before Marinara responded, Long spoke impatiently. "That's fascinating, but hardly relevant to our current situation."

"On the contrary. The merfolk and the Mira Prenya will join the fight if the Rainbow Pearl is returned to them."

Kim and Long stared at Marinara. "I did not steal it. It is mine by right. I use it to enhance my magic. I am no use here without the power it gives me. It is tuned to me. This is how I know it is mine."

"How is it you've never mentioned this before?" asked Long.

Marinara was stumbling over her words. "I don't see what difference that makes. I need the pearl to make me an effective wizard."

"Wizards don't need such trinkets to use their power." Long was staring her down now. Kim glanced from one to the other and back again, fascinated by the exchange. "Hand it over. We are losing this war, Carylinia and Benjamin are clearly not having any luck with their fae magic, and the merfolk and Mira could literally change the tide of this war."

Marinara was backing away, her eyes wide. "I will not."

"Hand it over or I'll take it from you."

She turned ready to bolt, but Kim had already anticipated that, and stood in her way, one of her knives in clear view. Marinara turned around looking for another escape route, but there was none. Kim grabbed her trying to get to her pocket, but she was slippery for an old woman, and Kim couldn't reach the prize.

Long raised a hand. "Enough of this." He'd exerted a small amount of magic, amidst an amethyst smoky swirl, and Marinara briefly froze where she stood. Long frowned. "Mmm. I'm surprised that actually worked. Kim get the pearl quickly before it wears off."

Kim reached into Marinara's pocket and drew the pearl out. It shone from within, all the colours of the rainbow emanating light. I was beautiful, and it almost distracted Kim and Long from seeing the change in Marinara, or at least in the woman that had been known as Marinara. She shook so hard she seemed to blur. Then she started to change. They watched, fascinated as her body stretched, retracted and stretched again, then completely transformed. Finally there stood a dark fae. Light was being drawn into her from all around.

229

Long gave a sharp intake of breath and took an involuntary step back. "Orma!"

Orma laughed, changed form again into a dark grey cloud of smoke, and shot up into the sky. She was gone.

Long was beside himself. "All these years I have called her sister, and all that time she's been plotting against us."

"You don't know how long it's been since she took the wizard's form. The mermaid told me she took the pearl just a few years ago. Maybe that's when..."

"You are wise Kimjora." He pulled himself together. "Right now, we have to get that pearl to the merfolk. I will ask Playa to take you. She can have you there and back in a couple of hours." He motioned to a fae guard.

"Long. You mentioned Benji."

Long smiled. "He is safe back at Prenya, working with his mother to restore your people's shape-shifting abilities. Alas, they don't seem to be having much success, but we are still hopeful."

"If you hadn't blocked this for so long, we might have had a solution long ago. We could have nipped this war in the bud by taking out Osun."

"Don't remind me. Anyway, if Orma is in the picture, it's more likely she is the one who brought the vanguard of dark forces across The Boundary, when all this time Osun was deluded into thinking he was calling the shots. Orma will have her own agenda, you can be sure of that."

"Can it really be her?"

"Oh, it's her alright. Like Carylinia, she has been in hiding all this time. She is the one who cast the original spell on the Prenya kelpies. Did you know that?"

Kim's face darkened. "I did not. I would have killed her where she stood had I known."

"Don't be so hasty. If Carylinia and Benjamin do not succeed, she may be the only one that can reverse the magic."

"I can't see her agreeing to that."

"She caught me by surprise today, but the wizards are still stronger than any fae queen with magic, even Orma. She can be coerced."

With that, Playa arrived, stepping lightly to the ground.

CHAPTER FORTY-FIVE – KELPIES

Prenya had almost emptied out as its people had gone to war. A small force had remained behind in case the city came under attack, though it seemed unlikely, it was a small fortress. There were also those too young to fight, and older folk who looked after the city, or were too infirm to contribute any more. Other than that a few of the kelpie scientists, and the medical staff that hadn't accompanied the troops to The Triangle to set up a field hospital, remained behind.

Benji felt redundant. His mum had been working around the clock, though he couldn't for the life of him work out what she was doing. She gathered herbs, well that all seemed like a bit of a cliché to him! She'd been meditating a lot and consuming high protein and restorative food and drink – and making him do the same. He was buzzing from the energy, and couldn't stop pacing and fretting. His friends had gone to war – were they friends? He wasn't sure. Certainly Darsh had become a friend. He'd failed miserably as a soldier, having shot one enemy, got an ally badly injured then promptly passed out. Once again he had to be rescued. How many times had that happened over the last couple of months? Huh! Had it really been such a short time? So much had happened. Now here he was, an instrument of his mum's magic, but once again useless, unable to do anything constructive.

Perhaps he should go down to the kitchens and do the dishes. At least that would be useful.

Finally Carylinia sent for him. He headed to the lab where she'd concocted something very pungent, though not entirely unpleasant, kind of sweet and acrid at the same time. Perhaps she's cooking up a Chinese, he thought flippantly. The thought of a box of ribs and prawn balls from Ken Wong's made his mouth water.

"Good, there you are. Something's happened. I'm not sure what, but it's like my magic's been freed somehow. I thought it was just all the centuries not practicing that was blocking my abilities, but no. There was some kind of restraint that's now been relieved. I'm ready to do this now. Are you ready?"

"Ready for what? I still don't understand."

"You don't need to. All I need you to do is lie back on the couch and relax. A very powerful dark fae witch cast this magic. I believe I can undo it, but I need to draw some of your magical strength. Don't worry it won't hurt, but it may knock you out. Once this is done – assuming I can do it – and that's still not certain, you will be weak, and will need a few days to recover. This is why I've been getting you to build yourself up. Now, take you shoes off, lie down and get comfortable. This may take a while."

"What about you? Will you be alright?"

She smiled at him and gently laid her hand on his cheek. "I'll be fine. With you to bolster my strength we'll get this done. I'll need to rest afterwards too of course, so if it doesn't work, it'll be days before I can try again and by then it may be too late." She spoke to one of the kelpies in the lab. "I'm going to begin now. Please can you assist me to the other couch when I'm done, then go and ask Beluin to come and watch over us?" The technician nodded his assent.

Benji watch from his couch as his mum sat on the floor in front of the powerful brew she'd concocted. She began muttering. The steam coming from the pot took on a life of its own, swirling around her head. She breathed deeply, drawing in the vapour. The muttering was more rapid now, more urgent. His mum was swaying. He wasn't sure how long it lasted as the intoxicating brew was affecting him too. His

232

head was spinning. He could feel his energy sapping out of him. It was like a tangible thing that travelled from him to her. Just when he thought he could no longer sustain such a loss, it was over and he slid into darkness.

*****

Kim delivered the Rainbow Pearl to the merfolk waiting at the Lomari River Delta. She knew they could travel through the water at incredible speed, but was staggered at just how quickly they swam. At first she could see the wake they created in the shallows, but as the water deepened they disappeared. It was then she spotted the Sturgeon at anchor far out in the bay. By now all the harbours would be occupied by enemy troops, they'll be reluctant to come in. She smiled. It won't be long before the merfolk deal with those creatures. "Playa, two of my friends are on that ship, is there any way…"

"Consider it done."

In minutes Rhio and Corin stood beside her.

"I wasn't sure if we'd see you again. What was the disappearing act all about?" asked Rhio.

"It's good to see you too. I was meeting my obligation to the merfolk. Enough said for now. Lets get back to The Triangle, we can talk later."

Playa took Kim back, then returned with Jania to collect the other two. When they reached the camp they were taken directly to the ruin that served as the command centre.

"Hello Mother."

"Rhio!" said Darsh as she gathered him up in a bear hug.

Suddenly Kim wondered how she was going to tell Darsh about her relationship with Rhio, but that was for another time.

Once again the wizards, now with the clan leaders, were standing around the table with the map. They had small counters, like tiny draughts pieces, representing troop movements, white for them, black for the enemy. There were many more black pieces.

"Your mission Kimjora?"

"Successful. I believe you can soon eliminate all those black counters you have there lining the coast road."

"That's good, but we are still heavily outnumbered here in The Triangle, and in the Jamion Hills. Further bad news, some of Arbani's sprites have gone to the other side, led it seems, by Dailabi."

"Dailabi? You're kidding."

"Strange as it seems, she has turned dark, along with about a quarter of the sprite troops. It's the balance Kim, I've been saying it all along. The last clan wars left us with dark fae, and this one has left us with dark sprites." He was shaking his head. "I've also heard news that Jeanetta is dead. Killed by Osun. I don't know quite what misguided campaign she was on, but she could not have gone all bad if she ended up opposing him. She was my sister, and I'll miss her."

"I'm sorry."

"Do you know what happened to Tina when you were back in Scotland by the way?"

"She's fine. Jeanetta took her to your neighbour before all of this took off."

"Mmm. Not all bad." Long repeated, more to himself.

Lucivarsh and Zebrella had come in while they were talking. Lucivarsh took in the scene. "Quite the family reunion I see."

Kim hardly knew her mother these days, so she chose to ignore her sarcastic, imperious tones.

"Half-goblins and elves hold the eastern front, but we've made some headway in the west. The dryads are standing firm at the fringes of Vaskra. Kimjora, did you secure the merfolk?"

"Yes Mother. I fulfilled their requirements, and they will join the fight along with a contingent of the Mira."

"Good, that just leaves…" Lucivarsh doubled over.

"Mother?" Kim went to reach for Lucivarsh, but then she too keeled over.

Corin went to her. "Kim? What's the matter?"

Kim stood back up then, as did Lucivarsh. Right now they emanated strength and power.

"What's happened?" asked Rhio.

Darsh was smiling at Kim as she answered in her stead. "A miracle."

Kim and Lucivarsh headed outside where they had more room. All around the kelpies were visibly increasing in size. They blurred for a moment, then as one, they began to transform. Some of them were crying out in fear, they were younger, born after the clan wars, and had never shape-shifted. Their older compatriots went to them and gave comfort. Within less than ten minutes an army of kelpies in their full, natural form filled the camp.

Corin stood with her mouth open, then turned to Long. "Where did all that extra…body come from? These creatures are at least three times the size they were just minutes ago."

"Actually 3.14 times. Like pi. Don't ask me how, or what the significance is, after all they're clearly not round, but that's the factor."

"Weird!"

"Indeed."

Then the fae were swiftly all around too. Old partnerships from the previous clan wars renewed, and new partnerships amongst the younger kelpies and fae forged instinctively. Darsh gleefully leapt up on Kim's back, then they were all off, heading toward the enemy to the east.

The galloping of the kelpies was like thunder, and the enemy fell before them, or ran screaming. More thunder came from the northeast as the Mira, mounted by merfolk joined the fray.

Rhio and his mount, a first-timer, pulled up beside Kim and Darsh just as they spotted someone in the crowd of elves and dark fae. Osun. Both pairings made a beeline for his position. Darsh gathered up her spear and threw hard. It struck the ground inches away from him. He laughed, but not for long. In moments she recovered her weapon and buried it in his chest before he had time to react. Darsh slid from Kim's back and closed in on him with Rhio at her side. Osun was pinned to the ground as the spear had gone through and through, yet somehow he still lived. She would remedy that. Drawing her knife, she bent close, ensuring he could see just who was to be his nemesis. But Rhio reached for the weapon, and with a flash of understanding, Darsh handed it to him. Osun's lips were moving, they bent closer to hear his words. But all he said was "Opina." Rhio stared coldly at his father's

235

face. "This is for all my dead baby brothers and sisters." With that he slashed the knife across Osun's throat. Osun's head fell sideways, his dead eyes staring at Kim, who nodded once at Rhio as she finally witnessed his revenge.

By nightfall the killing fields were all but silent, just the sobs of the wounded and bereaved, low talking and the wind interrupted the quiet evening. Back at the camp, however, nothing was going to prevent the kelpies from celebrating. Despite their losses, there was singing and dancing, eating and drinking. Even Long, saddened as he was by all the loss, found himself capering about a bit to the jolly music. Kim had transformed back to her human form and joined him, Darsh, Rhio, Corin and Playa.

Corin scanned Kim up and down, one eyebrow lifted high, with something akin to awe. "So, where does it all go? I mean, an hour ago you had hooves, and a lot more hair."

Kim laughed. She was invigorated. She'd forgotten just how empowering it was to change. She felt so strong. "Kelpie and human forms are all we do. We don't shift to any other shape. We call the shift to and from our human form as 'going full circle.' The features we have in any one form that we don't have in the other are held in a transitional dimension. Rather like the wings of an Elemental I guess."

"Does it hurt, you know, when you change?"

"Not really. At least not normally. This time was the first in centuries, and it happened unexpectedly, so it was somewhat uncomfortable. Carylinia and Benji were successful. I can't tell you how joyful and powerful it makes our people."

"You are magnificent, no argument there."

"We will head to Prenya tomorrow. I'm keen to see Benji."

Rhio bit his lip as he peered sadly at Kim. Darsh caught the look, glanced at Kim and back to Rhio again. "Well my son, it seems you've been playing around with my partner."

Rhio and Kim glanced at each other, then at Darsh. The moment had come. "Darsh, I know he's young and well…"

Darsh held up her hands. "It's alright. Just so long as he understands it was a fleeting thing, and there's really only one man for you."

"I think he gets it, especially when Jania's about," said Playa.

Rhio appeared like a rabbit caught in the headlights. He started fidgeting.

Kim put his mind at rest. "It's alright. You are young, and should enjoy playing the field. We had some fun that was all. My future lies with Benji."

It was Playa's turn to look uncomfortable. "Well, actually, Benji might not see it that way." Kim stared at her. Playa quickly retracted, holding up her hands. "Oh no, not me. But well, Benji and Raepha..."

"Raepha? She didn't say a word when we were up in the eyrie city, I knew she was keeping something from me, little minx!"

"That sounds like Raepha. Happy to be in the know, when others aren't. I mean, I'm not saying he'll want to go back to her... although... he did say he would." Her discomfort was only matched by Kim's outrage.

"That two-timing..."

"Kim," said Darsh, "he only did the same as you."

Kim scowled.

The next morning the kelpies transformed and prepared to head for Prenya.

CHAPTER FORTY-SIX – EDINBURGH

"You knew this could happen Carylinia."

"But all the things he's been through Beluin. He's grown so much."

"Maybe it's for the best."

"You were always the one that wanted him to come to Elysia and learn our ways."

"Yes and you were the one that wanted him to live as a human. It seems you will have your way. We'd best get Kim and the wizard in here. We have some planning to do."

Kim gazed at Benji unconscious on the bed. "Is he going to be alright?"

Carylinia answered. "He'll be fine. But all his magic is drained. He will no longer be able to fly, turn pellucid or do the small fae magics he was learning."

"He could do all that?"

"Of course, you never saw him. He was amazing Kim. The first time he called his wings in, he saved my life."

"Benji?"

Long spoke then. "Here's the plan. We keep him under for the time being. Dose him up with a full shot of amnotin then put him in a hospital bed." He pointed to Kim and Carylinia, "you two will be sat beside him when he wakes up. We have a doctor and two nurses in place that will go along with things. You will tell him he fell and bumped his head, and that he's been in a coma for ten weeks. We'll all go back to the lives we had, and he'll be none the wiser."

"And how will you explain your absence Professor Long?"

"I'm an old man," he chuckled, "older than anyone at the university can even begin to imagine in fact. I've been on long-term sick a number of times before. I'll probably semi-retire now, on the basis of ill health you understand. I'll just teach on Benjamin's classes. Then I can keep an eye on him. The two of you will need to monitor him as well. Are you Kimjora ready to be just Kim again? And are you Carylinia ready to be Mrs Cary Jarrett again? Are you prepared to go back to your human lives?"

*****

Edinburgh – December 18th

"Oh my head!"

"Benji, you're awake. Kim, call the doctor."

Kim went and retrieved the doctor Long had arranged especially for that moment.

"Hello Benjamin. I'm Doctor Milliner. How are you feeling?"

"Did somebody sit on my head?"

"You've been unwell, but you'll be fine now. We'll keep you for another night and monitor your recovery then I can discharge you. I expect you'll be glad to be home for Christmas."

"Christmas. What are you talking about? It's October."

Kim spoke. "No hun. You've been in a coma. It's been weeks. We were beginning to wonder if you'd ever wake up. How are you feeling?"

"Fuzzy-headed. I've been having the weirdest dreams," he frowned, "but they're slipping away now...I can't quite remember..."

"Don't worry about it hun. They're just dreams. Now you need to focus on getting better."

Benji nodded then cast his eyes to either side of his bed. Kim on one side and Mum on the other. "I see you two have finally met."

"In the face of adversity it seems." Cary said. She and Kim glanced at each other. "I've invited Kim for Christmas. I thought it would be nice." I've spoken to your tutors at the university. They understand the situation and will give you some catch up work next term."

*****

The air fizzed and suddenly Raepha was there.

Benji's eyes widened. "Who are you? Where did you come from?"

Kim was on her feet in an instant hustling Raepha out the door just as Cary explained to Benji that is was just the medication making him see things, and that it was probably just someone who got the wrong room.

Once in the corridor Kim spoke. "What are you doing here?"

Raepha was looking a bit shocked. Feeling herself with her hands, and turning her head to take in the scene. "Huh?"

"First time phasing into the human world I take it."

Raepha nodded then seemed to gather her wits. "I'm here to see Benji. He and I were…together…in all senses you know, in Paradisa."

"Not any more."

"He has the right to choose, and back home he chose me."

Kim thought she sounded like a pouting, stupid girl. But she had some sympathy for her. "I'm sorry Raepha, he remembers nothing of our world. The working that restored the kelpies drained him of his magic, both Elemental and fae. He's had a full shot of amnotin, and all the memories of our world have gone now. It seemed the kindest thing to let him take up his human life again."

"NO! I don't believe he can't remember our time together." Raepha slipped passed Kim while her guard was down and went back into Benji's hospital room. "Benji? You know who I am don't you?"

Benji frowned as her gazed at her, then smiled knowingly. "Yes. You're the girl from my dream. You're not real. I'm hallucinating." He glanced at Kim as she came back in. "Can we go home now?"

Raepha ran back out the door sobbing. This time Cary went after her. Kim had no idea what she said to her, but by the time Cary came back in, she just nodded and sat back

240

down beside the bed. "We'll bring some clothes for you tomorrow, and then you can come home."

*****

It was January. Benji and Kim sat next to each other in the back of the lecture theatre for the first psychology session of the term. Benji was fidgeting.

"Benji, sit still, "Kim hissed.

"Can't help it, it's so boring. When's he going to get on to the mythology bit?"

"This is a whole module. You've already missed most of a term, you need to buckle down and get some work done. I'm in much the same boat you know. I spent hours sat by your bed waiting for you to wake up. I did a lot of reading, but I'm behind too. We'll have to work on it together."

"You? You're behind? Well wonder's never cease."

A voice floated up from the podium. "Mr Jarrett," said the Prof. "Did you have something you wanted to add?"

Benji stared at Professor Long. Why did this man always seem to be putting him on the spot? "Er, no sir. Please carry on." Kim cringed.

"Well thank you Mr Jarrett I'll do that."

Everyone in class laughed – except Benji and Kim.

THE END